DATE DUE			
MAR 7 79	SEP 4 1980	MAY 2 1 1993	
MAR 19 79	SEP 2 2 1982	MAY 10 1994	
APR 3 79	JAN 3 1 1983		
APR 18 79	JUL 2 8 1983		
APR 24 79	JAN 1 1 1984		
MAY 14 79	SEP 1 8 1984		
MAY 30 79	DEC 7 1984		
JUN 13 79	AUG 1 0 1985		
JUL 3 79	MAR 7 1990		
AUG 1 79	NOV 1 6 1992		
AUG 8 79			

BY ROSELLEN BROWN

Some Deaths in the Delta and Other Poems

Street Games

The Autobiography of My Mother

Cora Fry

TENDER MERCIES

TENDER MERCIES

Rosellen Brown

ALFRED A. KNOPF   NEW YORK   1978

ℨℨ0ℰℨ

THIS IS A BORZOI BOOK

PUBLISHED BY ALFRED A. KNOPF, INC.

Copyright © 1978 by Rosellen Brown

All rights reserved under International
and Pan-American Copyright Conventions.
Published in the United States
by Alfred A. Knopf, Inc., New York,
and simultaneously in Canada
by Random House of Canada Limited, Toronto.
Distributed by Random House, Inc., New York.

Library of Congress Cataloging in Publication Data

Brown, Rosellen [date]

Tender mercies.

I. Title.

PZ4.B87992Bo   [PS3552.R7]   813'.5'4   7720352

ISBN 0-394-42741-6

*All characters and events in this book are fictional,
drawn solely from the imagination, and any resemblance
to real persons, events, or institutions is unintentional.*

Manufactured in the United States of America

First Edition

again, for Marv

For helping me into this book and out again
I am immensely grateful to the John Simon Guggenheim
Memorial Foundation for their support;
to Denise, Willie and Doris Pelletier, Rhea Taylor,
Dan Steinberg; and especially to Judy Gilliom,
for her immense generosity of time and spirit.

Body my house
my horse my hound
what will I do
when you are fallen
—MAY SWENSON,
"Question"

All the being and the doing,
expansive, glittering, vocal, evaporated;
and one shrunk, with a sense of solemnity,
to being oneself, a wedge-shaped core of darkness,
something invisible to others . . . and this self having
shed its attachments was free for the strangest adventures.
When life sank down for a moment, the range
of experience seemed limitless. . . .
—VIRGINIA WOOLF,
To the Lighthouse

TENDER MERCIES

Town lies in a wide valley between two hills. You can come off the highway and coast down into it and halfway up the other side without so much as a tap on the gas pedal. Dan Courser drives with his foot poised between accelerator and brake and allows himself to be overwhelmed by Main Street. It is Hyland's unreal time of day, when the sun seems to be setting inside the Unitarian Church, its windows, the whole brick building eaten by discreet flames. There is no one on the street except an elderly woman in a flowered house dress who is walking a small fluffy dog along the curb, genteelly grazing, as though they are in some city. Empty as it is, everybody home for dinner, Hyland is uncomplicatedly beautiful: clean and familiar, small and close as the palm of his hand (which opens, then, into long fingers of roads out into the woods, the meadows, up those hills impossible in winter).

Hallie and Jon call out at every landmark they remember, as though they've expected it all to have vanished since summer: the bank, the town hall with its green screen door, summer and winter, the little pillared library with a fresh sign listing its hours; these are silent as murals or backless movie sets, the whole length of Main Street swept by some giant machinery. The sky is just darkening at the flute end. Dan feels as if they are stealing back home.

He turns up the hill towards their house. The trees are not quite in bud, the best of spring still coiled, waiting, and they will have it. Mill Road winds through that barrenness that lies between New England seasons, in which only a primitive trust leads from day to day into a lusher season. All the houses need paint; there is one half-built colonial garage abandoned for the winter, lawns barely beginning to push up green out of their pallor; the blacktop is wavy as surf with frost heaves. But the car makes its way as automatically as any horse that smells home. "Lorelei," he says, turning his head an instant, "almost."

"Fedders got a goat!" Jon cries as they come up the final turn. "Look what's eating out there." The neighbors do have a small grey goat who stands with his delicate head down facing their house from across the road, half on lawn, half on pasture. He does not look up as they slow.

"One bump, hon," Dan calls out cheerfully in warning. "Driveway's never going to grow back, is it?" Which was once a joke about the scourged surface of the little incline whose broken tar and stones, gravel and grass could make one seasick. Laura grunts in the back of the car at what is no longer funny: when it comes to healing she is no example. But Dan thinks it either appealing or therapeutic not to indulge such delicacy. He does not believe that she ought to be hurt by remarks. "Hurt is hurt enough, I'd think." And then says what he pleases.

The car stops in the gravel with a lurch of finality. He opens the door for the kids and they scamper out, fly up like birds and are gone around behind the house: they have their hundred secret places to check out. He squats down at the doorway to the back seat and smiles. "Okay."

She makes no sound or movement where she sits propped between pillows like a Russian princess in a carriage; absence is one of her only remaining defenses. He understands it, has no right to an opinion of it, deplores it, mocks it, and is angry. "Alone" was one of the first words that had come back to her. Whichever it was, complaint or plea, it left him out. Now when she might smile—restored to her front door, her children darting like barn swallows all around their house, yipping giddily, reporting, too far away to be understood, on the state of the rabbit warren and the chicken coop, the fallen clematis vine and the hole in the tree that's full up with starling babies—she stares straight ahead and gives no evidence of knowing or caring where she is.

"I'm going in," he tells her, more sharply than he'd intended. "Do you want to stay here while I have a look around?"

She has the capacity not to blink. Sometimes it is clear to him that it is easier for her not to give a sign of life than to give any at all. That giving anything is what she resolutely will not do. Her small head with its raggedy boy's haircut— nurses' convenience, one more retribution—stays inclined precisely where it is.

"Well, all right," he says to her, and stands. "Let me see what kind of shape they've left us in." He goes down the walk briskly, half for spite, half excited by the feel of the blue-grey-pink flagstones and the little rise of the doorstep. He wants to shout like the children, one huge whoop of greeting. For Laura he is quiet.

Then how peculiar and painful, to walk across the threshold of his own house and to reclaim it from the anonymous care of strangers. The kitchen has a faintly unfamiliar feel to it—not a feel, a smell, an odd tinge of apples and fresh paint that lodges far back in his nose, bitter and flat with an overlay of sweetness. And light. Laura's white curtains are tied back to let in what dim late afternoon brightness can penetrate the lilac bush, even out of bloom. The floor's not buffed, there is a great expanse of dulled tile linoleum lying under a scum of grey soapiness. It's *all right*, though: not abused, he can see at the door that the couple who lived there, surrogate, through fall and winter, did their best, and a decent best, to keep things in shape. He'd have to write and thank them, back in Maryland or wherever it is they come from. But they were not Dan and Laura, Jon and Hallie Lavender, who had spent the worst year of anybody's life, just now, in New York City, and so the house looks distant, untouchable, separate from him. He remembers all of it, knows every corner, but still it floats just out of reach, like a friend who has been changed by a year of unshared experience.

The long wooden living room must always have been this dark. The fireplace is so empty of ashes he winces. Nobody cleans a fireplace like that—maybe they lived in a "garden apartment" (he'd discovered the genre just this year) or the kind with an elevator. Had they done all the good things on the hearth that made it so valuable? Bingo with the kids, and dominoes; stew in a big pot on the crane? Love, one side of you tanning against the fire, after the kids were in bed; then love again, spectacular comfort in the warm hollow of light with the room chilly outside it, because there was that extra excitement, waiting to get caught by Jon or Hallie tiptoeing down, and you two naked on the wide granite gravestone. Hearthstone. Jesus.

Every other word is crooked these days, as if he were Laura whose prepositions were blasted to hell the first few months. (Who could believe they lived in a place in your brain—at, to, in, out—like pollen in flowers, ants on sugar; could be scooped, tweezed, scratched, *stolen*? And then grow back? They had met a man, in the hospital, who had lost the number 6.)

He had brought her flowers yesterday when he came to tell her they were going home. On the card he had meant to write Bon Voyage but it was twisted too:

YOU ARE BEING KIDNAPPED.
BONE VOYAGE, MY BEAUTY.

His brain in sympathy with hers. But she had laughed for the first time in a long time at that.

Upstairs the bedrooms are so clean, the effort that has gone into leaving the house in good condition is so palpable it hangs in the air in place of the banished dust. They are very young, if he recalls right (friends of friends of his sister), and they are free of children, of responsibilities, of endless obligation—why did they feel bound to be so meticulous? Pity, probably, pity the great universal, the best and worst that strangers have to offer. Look, let's make it as decent as possible so those poor people won't have to come back and begin cleaning up. The kind care taken: he could see the girl, she'd be standing in the doorway with a broom, slender in her dungarees, and when she'd bend down to sweep the dust into the pan her boyfriend (or was he her husband?) would smile a little and take a peek down the front of her shirt;

he'd say "Come on, leave all that" and she'd poke the broom
into his hands and say "You finish it, I've got to pack." Dan
would have gone on spinning out the scene, he is dizzy with
lust, with need, with broken energy, but he makes himself
quit; Laura is captive in the car and it is getting dark. On his
way out, through the kitchen, he sees they've left a note, one
corner held under the vase of paper flowers on the table. It
is a welter of small details and apology, the kinked washing
machine hose and the cracked upstairs window; it ends: Good
luck, our prayers are with you and we know it will all work
out. The Lallys.

They are married then; still he won't revise his imaginings,
what wouldn't he give, twelve years married, to peer down
the neck of Laura's blouse right now? (That is considered
undignified, one of her nurses had told him, shocked, when
she overheard him whispering lewd daydreams in Laura's
ear. Undignified or impossible? he asked her, furious. Does it
make any difference? she answered, fixing him with a narrow
satisfied smile. And still he doesn't know.)

As for the prayers part of the Lallys' message. . . . His
own friends, too, will congratulate him (for returning? sur-
viving?) and be wary, both, and they will come as fast as
they can to see Laura for themselves; their eyes will hurt her,
however kind. The more kind the more humiliating. No win,
no win.

How, Dan thinks, eager to sit down—he feels the way
he does in the eighth inning of a double-header on a steamy
August Sunday—how would it be if you'd just come back
from the war slightly wounded but decorated nonetheless,
wearing the Purple Heart: dishonor, would you call it? Honor
by accident? Relief, a hint of distant bravery with a flaw in it
somewhere, survival as the best you could make of bad news?
He is a man who has very nearly killed his wife, though that

may not have been the story his friends had heard. He is a young, dark-haired, good-looking man who had taken the tiller of a boat he couldn't manage, far from home, and had cut his wife in two. Somehow, somewhere. She was swimming over the starboard side. Shreds, one could say, absolute bloody *spaghetti*, his brother John had told them with a mean angry eye. Though his brother didn't like him, that old Courser clinch of love-hate, and they knew it. Still . . .

The men will ask a lot of questions about the how and where of the winter and he'll tell them about his job, they'll laugh about taxi-driving in the jungle, how he'd never even heard of Staten Island when he started. He'll feed them bits and pieces of horror turned slightly comic, by time and their accomplished return, about the kids' year in school, P.S. 197, imagine 196 others just like it, not to mention four other boroughs' worth which were like separate cities ten times the size of Manchester. And he'd wonder what they are thinking, which would be just what everyone up to now had thought: Danny, Danny, good she was in a top-notch hospital, dedicated doctors, good, good, but who do you fuck? How do you stand it? And does she blame you, pretty Laura with her long brown hair and her dancer's arches? Not a single moving finger, can it be? Cat-got-her-tongue-Laura, will she live, back in Hyland with her bedsores and her hospital fat, or will she die? Or will she neither? And then what?

He walks out through the clean, caretaken rooms, through late-afternoon light that makes tan squares on the kitchen floor like foursquare boxes to bounce a ball in. There are tissue-thin copies of oil bills, bills for propane and for the snow plow, bills for a life not lived, held together in a clothespin and suspended near the door: the heart of the house has gone on beating steadily without them, thriving on any life that came in off the flagstone path and claimed it. It measures its vitality by comings and goings, by feet crossing thresholds, water faucets turned on and off, left running nights, a charm against freezing; by calls up the stairwells and out the upstairs windows over the apple trees. It doesn't care whose voices they are, only life matters, human movement, warmth. This house is going to recoil from Laura's presence now like some animal that can tell who intends to feed it, because she will never be able to touch it, to use and replenish it. The house is going to shrink around her.

He opens the car door, pushes the front seat forward and discovers his wife in her very special state of tears; she hunches there silent, a photograph of herself as a small boy, poised apparently forever, unmoving.

Billy Bickford and Louise have come to say welcome home. Louise, rolls of her, is a rose of a woman, she appears to have bloomed, opening outward, all her busy petals flopping around a lovely surprisingly small face, the flower's pink heart. She is wearing a blue Peter Pan blouse and brown Bermuda shorts and apparently does not intend to stop smiling. Her husband has his new summer crewcut. He never smiles, it would violate his hidden flamboyance and theatricality to do anything so ordinary and undramatic. Louise is carrying a pot of forced daffodils of an unreal uniformity, fussing at the ruffle of gold foil paper in which they sit. Billy is bringing a six-pack, just in case Dan hasn't had a chance to do the shopping yet. Louise talks a solid five minutes in the first minute, Billy says nothing but looks gravely around the room like a detective on duty.

The Shurrocks are there; they are Laura's parents. The incomparable car sits out front with two wheels on the lawn. The Bickfords, seeing it, would have been relieved to have gone home, but when cars drive up to the Coursers' they are always heard, grinding on gravel. The dog barks. Dan knows everyone who goes past, his peculiar concentration allows him to see through walls out to the road. So, exchanging fatalistic looks, they have come in, trying to look eager.

Eva Shurrock is seated at the table. Louise knows, from having "run into her" often, that Mrs. Shurrock tends to lag half a season behind in her dress, as if the effort it takes to be stylish exhausts her until well after it's time to change again. It is a mild spring day—doesn't Billy have his summer haircut already?—but she is wearing boots, elaborately laced, and she is chain smoking. She is one of those anxious total smokers who infects the entire area around herself with smoke and spilled tobacco and half-crushed butts with lipstick on them: very old-fashioned, Billy says. Probably her mother never let her smoke. Her knees pucker above the boot tops like wizened old ladies' faces.

Louise and Billy huddle in the doorway, watching the smoke from Eva Shurrock's cigarette, which does not come and go but hangs there like fog in the riverbed on a warm morning. DeWitt Shurrock sits next to her, stealing surreptitious glances at the folded newspaper on the chair beside him.

Dan appears to be trying to make the kind of cocktails they like; he is failing. He pours more gin, and then more, into a glass full of tonic till it runs over the top of the glass. He tries to pour some into another glass but by now his hands are unsteady and there is a widening pool of gin on the sink-top that drips very slowly but noisily onto the linoleum and rolls down the slight slope of the old floor. The first flies of the season have begun to write their unreadable messages on the ceiling, loop over slow loop. They buzz him and stick their feet into the puddle of gin and tonic. They shake their frail wings like infinitesimal birds bathing. He nearly knocks over one of the glasses with the dishrag.

"Oh, don't use that on the floor, Daniel, isn't that what you use on your dishes?"

Your dishes, they are. Louise, sensitive to the evasions and direct hits of mothers-in-law, takes notice. Not Laura's now but yours. She has never seen Dan looking helpless before, she values him for his unflappable assurance, which she trusts more than Billy's unflappable incompetence. Dan is—was—chief of the village emergency rescue squad and she was always sure people slept sounder nights, knowing that; at least she did. (Though there were plenty of terrible jokes after the accident, and Billy kept talking about the fire chief, years back, who got caught setting his own fires because he liked to put them out. That kind of disloyalty made her heartsick.) Dan is wringing the dishcloth into the sink as though he never wants to stop; maybe he's pretending it's his mother-in-law's stringy neck hidden there behind an arty Indian necklace that looks like a silver totem pole. Louise is a woman of few but passionate loyalties: she is ready to divide the world into villains and heroes if it will make her friend one bit more comfortable. What can she *do* for him now? The situation isn't clear enough yet to know if she can, they can, step in and do what friends are for. She will be uncomfortable until she sees how they fit here now.

"Danny, let me go see Laura, what do you think we came for? We can see you any old time." The brusqueness of this approach falls flat, it sounds absurdly tough. She is flushed with her defensiveness against these people who dislike Danny with severe bigshot bigcity meanness of spirit, and who are capable of sitting there this whole time without feeling the need to say a single word. They nod their heads when they're introduced and then they make no effort at all to help out in a tough moment like this. (Louise is trying to preserve her right to judge them back.) She walks across the room feeling the way she did once in a high school fashion show—punished for the vanity that encouraged her to show herself in public when she'd neglected, in private, to keep herself presentable. Her sandals flap. Mrs. Shurrock is watching her intently, puffing. Louise has never seen anyone hold a cigarette quite that way, her arm is inside out somehow, elbow forward, the butt hangs down as though it's in a long black cigarette holder. The arm position alone is worth $50,000 a year. Billy stomps on through the kitchen behind her, head down as though there's snow flying; where she gets flustered, he gets angry.

When they're safely in the living room on the way to the sunporch, Louise snorts heavily and says, "Danny, how do you stand it? They're so nasty to you—" She has her warm hand on Dan's arm.

But he looks at her, meeting her eyes for the first time since she hugged him, and she sees such weariness and a kind of helpless wonder in them, that she knows she's said the wrong thing. "Lou—" He is shaking his vigorous head at her, at Billy, at himself and whatever ghosts haunt at large in his house. "Look, don't forget, they're her parents. Whatever I think about them. I don't—what would you be like if somebody—" and he gestures vaguely towards the sunporch.

"I know but they never—"

"They never thought I should have got the time of day from her, right, but look what I got. And then look what I did with it."

"Danny." Louise is touched; her blue eyes brim. She thinks how Dan always sees wider, farther than she or Billy, how his sympathy bobs to the surface and pulls him, like a child you'd like to have—that is always her touchstone, would I like to feel *this* is the child I've made?—to the person who needs help most just then. She doesn't know that, these days, there's a ritual that Dan is faithful to, of announcing the most terrible possibilities concerning himself, before anyone else can. However effective it is, it happens that this is no ploy: he fears they are true, and he needs to keep hearing that. He has gotten to the point where repentance is the only position in which his mind, like a twisted limb, can rest.

He holds Louise at arm's length, far off in her own familiar world, and still shaking his head, he leads them in to see Laura.

Louise sees Laura and falls on her knees. Needless to say she regrets this the instant it happens, she is mortified and frightened that she has offended everyone in sight, but she is a loving woman, not well defended, and she is helpless against this. Laura is her good friend. Was. They had shared a number of things—a second-grade teacher for their sons (though differently: for Laura's oldest? of two and Louise's youngest of five), duties at the bimonthly blood drawing down at the church, hard-bottomed bleachers or side-by-side seats on the grass of the hillock at ball games, and not least in a place like Hyland, a strong antagonism to joiners' groups like the Rebekahs and the Eastern Star. (Louise comes fortified with reasons that camouflage her basic terror of being talked about—there is less possibility of being dissected if you rarely pass within their line of vision; it is only reasonable. Her weight problem, as she earnestly calls it—"her little pudge" to Billy, who doesn't mind—has determined more in her life than Louise can say. Laura's reasons had to do with being too smart and well educated to waste time sitting around exchanging recipes and gossip; she ought to join the chapter of the university women that met to discuss books and the world's affairs. But once Laura had said she didn't like being a part of any group. Another time she had said that Dan probably wouldn't like it, though she hadn't said why, and then tried to take it back with a shrug.)

But now Louise hangs on, desperate not to cry or cry out. She stands and smooths her blouse, the rolled hems of her shorts. Laura is lying on the couch the way one of those old stone queens would lie, arranged on top of her tomb (she had seen one once in the Boston Museum on a high school field trip; it was beautiful and awful at the same time). Her ankles, no, her feet, seem to be at an odd angle, disconnected, dangling. Her arms are at her sides; they look relaxed. Her hair is short and ragged, has it been chewed out in her grief? All that luscious heavy hair gone down the drain somewhere. She has always been jealous of that hair; it's never occurred to her that Laura might look different.

"Lor," she says with desperate casualness, as though she has seen her friend just yesterday. "You cut your hair."

Laura answers by smiling.

"Why," Louise will ask Billy later, buckling her seat belt in the car, "why is it I saw so much—I don't know, *pity*—in her smiling. I mean, pity for me? Did I seem so stupid or what standing up there on my two feet? Shouldn't I have stood there like that? Billy?"

Billy? Louise? There are days I dream in such gusts they would take me away except for the weight of the skin on my bones. I feel the flesh, it is smeared and heavy like a double coat of paint. A double coat of pain. I'd like to be taken away. But we huddle under the locked dark, it and I, flattened as a can under such a weight of empty air. You

*want to know why they didn't cut the killed part off, I
know you do. Leave just my head, which works? Works
double time. I would like you to visit my head, I'd keep
the cancelled body out of sight. Next time you come I'll
have it closed in a box, all right? With a padlock under
my chin like a silver bow.*

    *I have no hands but the inward. They do not reach
for you.*

Billy and Louise and the Shurrocks have left. At the door
each became subdued, as if distant matters had suddenly
flooded in to preoccupy them and keep them from saying some
final dumb comforting word. Dan had never given much
thought to it but he is beginning to see how much of what
passes for conversation is the simplest filler; like the down in
a huge quilt, it shifts and settles and warms. But Laura's
accident has gripped it like a giant hand and squeezed; there
is no movement, no easing. He stands on one side of the
obstruction and they on the other, fluttering absently, their
words, their feathers confused, insubstantial.

Now Laura sits on the sunporch while he opens cans for
dinner. She can come to him if she wants to, she has attachments on the rims of her wheelchair like hard tumorous
growths, like small fruits, that she can grasp, insofar as she
can grasp anything. Her progress is slow. By a fortunate co-
incidence, because the whole room is an afterthought, a
bastard sired on an elegant Colonial dam by an oblivious
Victorian father, the door to the sunporch is unusually wide;
her chair can get through, although there is a nasty threshold
that will take some seeing to. (The other doorways in the
house present problems. Whether they are insurmountable

or not is far from clear.) As to the front door: Dan carried Laura in from the car without her chair, carried her like a bride across the threshold of her first home; Laura suppressed a bitter comment and gave her eyes that locked blind look that conveyed anger and the unwillingness to see more than she absolutely had to. Once inside, having thought this out as incompletely as he's thought all of it, he looked around wildly for a place to put her down. In all the months she's spent at the Rehabilitation Institute he has never picked her up. She is heavy in a way he hadn't anticipated—no arms around the neck, no upward thrust, only that cruel downward pull of dead weight, all of it falling in different directions. He stumbled to the couch and nearly dropped her, nearly fell on her, crushed her as the forward momentum of her inert body dragged him down. "Thanks," Laura said. He removed his knees from her side: what gouges they must have made in her passive flesh. He muttered his apology, straightened her legs untenderly and went to get her chair. To do things ineptly, to stagger or falter, made him furious, his ears flushed red defensively, ears and neck and invisible chest; he came apart. All the scoldings of his chaotic boyhood broke upon him and made him want to be childish again, and mean.

When he came back with her folded wheelchair in one hand, as casual as he could be, trying to make it seem light although it wasn't, she was flat on the floor.

"Dan," his wife said in a voice that worked approximately like her fingers when she deboned a fish, removed all together its delicate feathers of spine. "Will you please remember that I have no balance. No way to correct the position you choose to put me in."

"I didn't choose!" he flared, as if in self-defense.

"Then you'd better learn to choose. If I break a bone—

you don't know what it would mean to break a bone." She could shake her head; she did it now, hopelessly, long, even swings like those of a steeple bell heavy on its rope.

"What do I have to do? Tell me." He was humbled. His heart pounded as if he'd been chased, at the sight of her in that flung pile between the couch and the coffee table.

"What do you have to do? What do you have to do?" She only shook her head; she looked as if she could let it swivel there forever, without will. "How can I say this, it sounds so stupid. You have to be my body. All right? You have to guess for me, feel where I am for me. *Why didn't they tell you these things?* Why did you steal me away from there before they could teach you how to handle me? This is no *joke*!" At least this was her own voice, only more desperate, close to cracking. He felt reprieved and rebuked in the same moment. Did she really believe he thought this was a joke? "I'm a baby, Danny, you didn't want any more babies but here I am, only I'm worse than any little squirming infant, don't you know that? Babies learn things, they get to be able to do it all, sit up, dress themselves. I'm not real, that's what I am. I'm your unreal wife who sleeps in a crib and has to be turned over and needs her diapers changed."

Dan said nothing. He shoved the cobbler's bench coffee table aside and went to his knees and lifted her carefully, digging his fingers into her sides because she was not unreal, she had give and depth and vitality, and he had been kept from her for so long. When he laid her down it was carefully, leg against leg like a corpse arranged once and only once for burial. He chose from her speech the only part he dared acknowledge. (Was he about to enter upon a life of cringing, skulking around corners hoping not to be seen?) "They were never going to teach me a single goddamn thing they didn't have time for all those months, babe. Couldn't they have shown me something about what kind of balance you do and don't have?"

"What do you mean?" When she lay on her back she spoke to the ceiling.

"Well, what does it feel like? How the hell can you blame me for not knowing? All they ever did was talk a lot."

She snorted at his injured innocence. "Well, sit there, then. Get in that chair and just flop forward—let go, just—limp as you can get, like a Raggedy Ann or something."

He tried to, sitting forward on the footrest of the big blue chair. He poised like a diver on the board thinking whatever it is divers think, he wriggled his neck and let go. The floor came up at him, he looked into the dust between the wide-spaced old boards. There was a hairpin down there. The quick dive made him dizzy.

"That doesn't feel too good." He forced a smile though only a frog could have seen him from where she lay.

"You still have about ten times more control than I have. All those trunk muscles—" There was something conciliatory in her voice, as if she had won a point, forced a wedge, and it made her forgiving.

"Honey—"

"I guess it's like a gym exercise, though. You stand up when you're done."

"Honey."

She didn't ask him what he wanted, she would not hear it but turned her head away at the end of a wide swing and left it there facing the wall. What he thought he wanted to say, a broad gesture to sweep all the irrelevant details away, was "Honey, I love you." He looked at the back of her head, where the tough little points of reddish hair lay their serrated edge against her collar. What would she do with his love, his greeting card, where she lay without balance? It was like talking into a heavy wind, all his words blew back at him, broke up emptied, milkweed pods split and shaken out.

"I need my leg bag drained."

He sat still. "All right."

"Grit your teeth."

"Stop." He had learned this, it was lesson #1, only he wasn't sure he was going to be able to bear it. *People do this*, was all he could tell himself, and continued to sit still. *People all over have to do this, there are so many messed-up people, and they all do.* But he felt unreal. The two people this was happening to right now he didn't know; he didn't even want to know them.

At the Institute, in bright impersonal light, the nurse, Mrs. Toko, had shown him how; called it her Procedure, stressed words like regularity, sterility, turgidity, flexibility— it was easy, it all reminded him of high school chemistry (though he concentrated harder this time), the endless opening of clamps and flanges, and twice a day the sterile solution in and out, the syringe like a turkey baster. She tried to frighten him into not forgetting to help empty Laura out, she never acknowledged how hard it might be, how damn near impossible. "It's all mechanical. Don't expect her to feel it. She drinks eight times a day, you do this eight times. She cuts down, you cut down. Don't expect her to feel it, just keep your eye on the clock now," she had told him as if he were a child who tended to forget to stop playing and come home on time for dinner. "Remember the body goes into severe shock when there's any blockage and the bladder is overloaded. You think it's only the bladder but if you forget she'll feel like she's got a bomb in her head, her eyes will pop, you'll see. The sweats, the shrieks. Some of them"—and she'd lowered her voice at the word "them"—"some have told me they'd rather die, after all they've been through, than have another bladder crisis. You never want to see it." She sounded like an old gossip telling about a catastrophe she's seen on her corner. "You're exaggerating," he'd said, hoping. Eyes wide, shaking her head mournfully, she denied it. "Dear, you never want to see it." He decided you'd have to be crazy to doubt her.

"Shall we do it here?" he asked Laura.

Laura laughed. "You sound like you've got something really terrific in mind." (The hearthstone, that unyielding winter bed; under the half-dead tree in the upper meadow, far from the house, both of them so white in the sight of the sun, with their clothes dropped all around like deciduous leaves— "Here?" she would always ask, skeptical. "You want to do it *here?*")

"You might as well stop thinking of this as private, pal. Everybody's going to have to get used to this if they want me around. The kids'll have to learn to do it too, because I'm out of business with my own terrific hand. They'll love it anyway, the smell, the wonderful squoosh under your fingers, right, all that yummy plastic to keep the waterworks going."

"Stop. I asked you." He was about to lecture her on taste, on decency; instead he ran out and brought back a pot from the kitchen, and fast, as though the ceiling were leaking.

"My good soup pot—"

"Look, it's all in the family, isn't it? I'll get all the equipment together, don't worry." He smiled; it was a funny line, wasn't it? "Your good soup pot."

He fussed with the clasp; the more agitated he became, the more inefficient. It was worse than undoing a bra. "Frostbite," he mumbled but she said nothing to encourage him. He felt punished. This was all to rebuke him. The warm bag that lay against her leg strained, softened and went limp. Slowly Laura's smile came over him, warmed him.

"Does that feel better?"

She did that shrug that seemed so normal. (Remember the kids when they were brand-new babies, he thought. How remarkable that they could sneeze and yawn and hiccup.) "It didn't feel bad. It didn't feel." She shrugged a few more times, eager, maybe, to use her one natural movement.

He tugged and straightened the bag, the tubing, and then paused, caught in a flash of perspective. His concentration had blacked out everything but the two of them sparring nastily as though on an ordinary day. There were no more ordinary days, though; the weight of unsaid words, the old ones, the casual ones, lay on his body like the lap blanket across Laura's legs when she sat up in her wheelchair. They would never be said, the ordinary fights would never be fought: why hasn't the garbage gone to the dump yet, how can it be you've chosen a six-pack with your friends over dinner with your kids. . . . There was only this hideous ganging up, a bully against an unarmed girl. Unarmed, oh yes. . . . Her thigh, nearly bare to his sight now, was thin but he would recognize it if it'd turned transparent. He ran his hand along the outside of her leg up and back, gently. The skin was warm, still pliant, the bones so long and familiar. As he moved his fingers, pressing down towards shadow, he imagined the tube that lay flaccid across her knee stiffening, behind its opaque smoothness turning golden with urine the color of cheap sauterne; as soon as the bag was empty it would tense and flutter and begin, slowly, endlessly, to refill. Dan's eyes opened wide and his lips flattened in an agony of effort. He was going to vomit, and if he vomited now, like this, at the sight of Laura's body, the robbed husk of her body, he was going to go out to the woodshed and kill himself. There was an axe; there were rafters and good solid rope. He has thought of this before, of course, he has almost domesticated the idea, the ultimate painkiller and no exaggeration: a violent bloody grateful nearly companionable

death: to ease his pain and to show her, show himself, he has
wanted to feel her pain and then double it, triple it, till he has
paid in full.

What he made himself swallow back was sharper than a
stone; it hurt his chest. There will be a scar inside.

She can wheel herself in to him if she wants to. It may
take an hour. He turns on the radio for company.

Hallie and Jon burst into the kitchen the way they always
do; the loose pane in the storm door rattles dangerously when
they let it slam. Dan's usual irritation rises in him, he opens
his mouth to tell them to slow down, cool it. He stops, the
paring knife clenched in his hand just as everything today is
clenched and awry. (Even the clock hands are bizarrely tangled,
it's 6:29, one of them is about to disappear.) He realizes that
the children are themselves again. The spell is broken, they
have emerged from the bewitching terror of New York, where
they were struck still and dumb as trees, stones; they are *fluid*
again. He has a distinct feeling, all through his hands, his
arms, of ice thawing: how, in the lock of hard winter, the
faucets finally trickle open, or the pump kicks on, warmed,
like a mechanical horse, by a heating blanket. This instant,
his children flowing past him in their natural rhythm, shouting, he holds in his body, the first relief he's felt in days. Then
it seeps back on him, the endless sadness and the shame, which
is like a color, a smell, an exhaustion of his muscles, the one
ice-lock that will not thaw. This time he feels his children
allied with him in their conspiracy of health. He has a brief
treasonous thought, which he turns away from: *Thank God
it was Laura because she can live in her head and I can't.* He
would take speechlessness, take stone silence, maybe even

blindness, but *not to feel*: he knows his life only by the taste of it, the way he turns it under his hands, feels the drill bit bite, the pieces mesh, runs his finger over an edge to see if it wants sanding. His wife he knows by smell and touch, not by anything she thinks or says; his children by the tension of their arms and legs bending, opposing, relaxing, in his grasp. He touches them greedily, endlessly, with something that is not sentiment but need. From the neck up, he thinks, has always thought, he's a goner.

Dan looks straight at the thought, which appears to loom and hover somewhere on the wall above the sink, where the tea strainer hangs on pegboard: Better that it was Laura. He can't decide whether that is too horrible to be indulged or is simply, not dishonorably, true.

Hallie and Jon have run in to Laura and are back in half a minute. They stand before him out of breath, arms dangling.

"What is your mother doing?"

Hallie giggles. She has recently turned eight; relaxed or nervous she giggles a large percentage of her waking hours and even, occasionally, in her sleep (and they stand transfixed, wherever they are, straining to hear that unlikely nicker). When she is laughing she doesn't need to talk, commit herself, make demands, *be* anybody in particular. She succeeds, too, in hiding a nearly adult seriousness from everybody except Laura and Dan.

Her brother, for example, is endlessly irritated with her. This time when she gives her characteristic irresponsible hiccup of laughter, Jon gives her a shove he doesn't try to hide.

"Hey!"

"Hey yourself. Don't laugh."

"I'm not laughing." She nurses the arm where she's taken his pointy elbow but keeps her aggrieved eyes on her father.

"You don't even know what you're doing then." Jon looks disgusted. From the first silent reunion with her at the Institute, Jon has been desperately trying not to be embarrassed by his mother, and the more he fears he's failing, the more his embarrassment shows. "What do you mean, what's she doing?" he asks Dan. "She isn't exactly dancing."

"Don't be fresh," his father warns. (That was his mother's continuous warning, appropriate or not. Half the time it meant, I can't cope with you this minute. Do me a favor and coop- erate.) He is lining up carrots side by side, jabbing at them with his knife, to see how many slices he can cut at a blow; the sort of playing at work that infuriates Laura, who can be grim before dinner. "She's not helpless, she can move her chair, you know. Did you ask her if she wanted to come in here?"

"I didn't think of it," Jon says dismally, looking at the linoleum. "Should I go back and ask her?"

Dan brings the knife down on the carrots: seven at a blow! "Just get me a saucepan, please. Hallie, set the table."

Dinnertime. The liberated woman considers her freedom. She does not want to be here, or anywhere she can imagine. She tries to see horses with their necks bent, how they are growing out of the grass, their ankles narrow as stalks. Searches out, in her memory, Danielli's greenhouse: row on row of the same flower forced for Easter, something lush and lurid, purple on pink, sharp little varicose veins. She tries to smell the flowers although they are not there.

What she smells is dinner.
I am trying to be somewhere else and failing.

Laura's chair does not fit under the kitchen table. "It would be nice to eat with you folks," she says cheerily, in the gruff wavering voice of a little girl about to cry, "but I think I'm going to lounge around here a few feet back." Laboriously she wheels herself into the corner. They stand and watch. "I'll need my tray, Dan."

"We could eat in the dining room, it would be like a welcome home celebration!" Hallie suggests, making her eyes go bright. Laura's face softens with gratitude; that smile, at least, is still available for the children.

Dan knows, though, that all the tables are standard height, and the standard is off a mean fraction by Laura's standards. The machine she sits in is hulking; it gleams, in fact, like the motorcycle of his dreams. The ironies are merciless, he never knew there could be so many practical jokes set out like snares to catch the innocent: all that Harley-Davidson dreaming gone soft in the cheek, the ass, turned into a Moto-Skil 500 Fully Collapsible Vinylette wheelchair with a six-foot turning radius. She can't even get through the dining room door on that goddamn throne. He wonders if she knows that.

He will dream tonight of taking a nail file to the doorway, and when that fails, using his nose which resembles a vole's, sharper and sharper, and making a neat pile of sawdust, like ashes. The life's work of a carpenter ant.

Winking to sleep in my chair here, my head bucking, a subway sleep, sometimes I think of my sister's friend Theodore's children. I am no longer to think of Theodore: forbid as best I can. (My sister told me never to remember,

*she spends her time forgetting.) . . . Last year it was, no,
the year before, a girl and a boy, their father's plane was
swallowed by a swamp Shame shame wanting to
laugh so the laugh throws a black cloth over my head
from behind How I want to pull my tongue out raw by
the roots except I have no hands to grab it with What's
rooted in a swamp my tongue is an oleander sagging
under a spider's weight They want to know (how often
he used to take them for example to the zoo like a
father who meant forever sunny Saturdays with cracker-
jack to feed their monkey hungers) if an alligator will
find him taste him he is sweet eat him Is that why
he doesn't come back (A man could be a hero to his kids
if they're young enough if he's young enough They'd
remember only his heels sticking out and the stubborn
lump he made in the creature's rough green gut) So I
am sending flowers in my head to my sister who would
have been his widow if they'd ever to the children to
myself though I'm no one's father and I fly carefully
around all swamps nonetheless and most days so far
I've been coming home lucky Understand luck is having
crouched after I lost most of my life like a dynamited
target my head in my hands but still me head. Still me
parts identifiable knowing at least how much one minute
lost. To lose one eye is to gain the other yes To raise
my head and hope to see three fingers shake in the wind
is to know two fingers would make a good hand. If only
that. Poor Theodore is all my body All in the under dark.
Ah don't*

She had been wheeled up to him the first time too, in a
manner of speaking: her parents were responsible for deliver-

ing her. She made the long walk from their side to his through a glade of pines, scuffing through needles the color of her own hair as if she had been constructed purely out of the forest.

It was the summer his Uncle John had rented out the little lucky Courser space they'd always owned (when they owned nothing else) on Pottery Lake, for campers and tourists and other no-goods. (John never took a vacation because he never worked; he held it against those who did as a sign of the weakness engendered by ambition.) Together they built little boat tie-ups—they weren't even proper docks, that took too much wood—and scuffed out some unevenly cleared lots between the pines and scraggly bushes. "They'll come and take 'em," John promised, "don't forget where they'll be coming up from—Boston, Hartford, New York, all they got to do is see some green stuff you can't put in the bank or flatten down with a mower and they'll buy, you mark me well." That strange courtly language of John's that got mixed in with the pig farmer's. He painted a little sign, so unevenly lettered it seemed quaint and fake, that said "Pottery Lake Camp Sites. Private, by WEEK or MONTH, Get away from IT ALL!" and hung it on the main highway that went through Hyland, right above a sign pointing towards a motel with TV in every room, as though to make a comment on civilization. John's arrow pointed east and led to another sign and still another, up the mountain road, from blacktop to dirt. The more remote the destination, John said, the better they'd like it. A cheap week's vacation in a leaky tent, for supper charred hot dogs and beans in a black pot, a long drive down for a movie on Saturday night: he had a poor man's contempt for self-imposed poverty. But the lake! The half mile of pebbles and soft dirt John owned, the only thing he'd ever gotten from his family that was worth a damn, fronted on such cool transparent water that entering it was like holding a magnifying glass, for no reason but pure pleasure's, to your feet. The white feet buckled and swam, seemed to move when they stood still, held fast in the pebbles. Dan could stare for half an hour trying to recognize his own white-green ankles. It was a pity these people had to pay $30 a week for the chance to lose apparent possession of their feet and see them crisscrossed with minnows quick as the sperm that made them, but Dan thought that if he lived in Boston, shoulder on haunch on calf, it would be a good deal.

He helped John clear trees that spring, rode around on a borrowed bush hog devouring the underbrush like William Holden in a tank, and they built a couple of long tall outhouses side by side the size of telephone booths. Inside their doors John tacked up maps with giant stars on all the restaurants and antique shops in Hampshire County, or very nearly. "When I think of some of them so-called antiques, seems the proper place to advertise," he told him, screwing in the hook and eye lock tight for the ladies. "Least we can hope the men'll learn to use the trees like nature intended."

People came. There were dozens of Massachusetts license plates, the same people who drove up to drink beer in hunting season and shoot their toes off, or their best friend's toes. Uncle John hunkered down his shoulders and set his lean face slightly crooked; his wrinkles deepened. He came out of the trees or the toolshed and entertained the tourists with his version of what he thought they expected a backwoods New Hampshire man to be. (He might have been wrong.) If he could have swung a maple syrup can in one hand and a bottle of dandelion wine in the other he'd have done it; he seemed to alternate cursing and silence; tried to glower from under his bushy unkempt eyebrows; Dan even caught him ruffling them one time, running his finger through them the wrong way.

John Courser was a man who liked a laugh; sometimes he laughed so hard, beginning with a high trickling giggle, he had to lean against a building or he'd stagger down. But he seemed to think these campers wanted a New Englander to be a cigar store Indian. If they came to ask him for something —a can to pick blueberries in, advice about where to go in Hyland to buy a tarpaulin—he studied the situation for a few interminable minutes, pulling on an old pipe he'd resuscitated from somewhere, then he'd give them two or three gruff words. Inside his shed he'd slap his knee and bellow with pleasure. In real life John could talk you into a stupor. Dan guessed that given half a chance—he'd been given none at all—his uncle might have liked to have been an actor.

The Shurrocks pulled up one morning very early. It wasn't a time for campers to be doing anything but starting their fires: soft curses rose as the sun warmed the tops of the trees, fathers lit and lost fourteen matches for each damp pile of sticks, they wished they were home in their wallpapered breakfast nooks with their electric stoves glowing pink.

The Shurrocks came to a grinding halt as though pursued. Dan opened an eye to the sight and sound of a car door slamming. He'd been asleep in a pile of pine needles, all beer and sweat and a complicated misery. His mother was dead that spring, he was a month out of vocational college and eager for nothing, he could hardly remember why he'd gone, let alone why he'd stuck it through; there were no jobs and he was stupefied by idleness except when he was working for his uncle, who let him wrestle with tree stumps and spread sand with a roller. There was a girl in Denham, the next town over, who claimed she was having his baby; maybe his was the only name she could remember. The town's youngest lawyer, who lost everything he touched—surprised he still has his collar buttons, John said—was trying to get his suspended license back ("DWI: dimwitted imbecile," said the lawyer, who knew at least a little bit).

He picked his head up to see who had driven through the half-lit forest at eight in the morning sounding like ambush and saw an older woman and a young one stepping legs first out of a sharp and shiny dark brown car; it was surely the kind that had no dealership in the state of New Hampshire. Laura Shurrock, in a short rumpled blue workday skirt, with her long red-brown hair touching all the way down to her dimples, stood and stretched, sticking her chest way out like a little girl about to do a backbend, collapse at the knees and touch ground with the part in her hair. Dan sat up in his pine needle bed. She wasn't beautiful; he couldn't have named her specialness then, nor could he ever. But he had very little in his life that summer and, worse, wanted even less than he had. A single blurry look at Laura Shurrock restored his hunger and his thirst, pained him for his lost time, and made him greedy.

Mrs. Shurrock had come towards him with the stride of a fourth-grade teacher whose students were overturning their chairs. DeWitt Shurrock sat, sane enough to be embarrassed for his wife, trying to look like a fine presence, an eminence beyond speech. He was at the steering wheel, though: he was the one who drove like a maniac. The good car subsided in the pale morning sun, settling the color of brandy.

Taken altogether it was an impossible situation to get involved with: the kind of situation Dan liked and appeared, recently, to have run out of. There had never been much space in him, much he would tolerate, between wanting and having. His will had been a miraculous instrument, like a lamp he kept in his pocket and rubbed, when he needed it, with

fierce concentration: it gave forth wonders. He would be cut
to ribbons, Dan thought, sooner than he'd learn these people's
names. The girl stood still for a long minute with her thin
arms raised, tight fists at the ends, listening to the starlings
squabble as though they were the well-advertised beautiful
birds of the wild north wood.

Dan rolled some warm beer around in his mouth and
spat it into the rust-red pine needles, fouling his nest. He
stood up, brushed himself clean, straightened his dungaree
legs, raked his dusty hair with his fingers, and went out to
claim Laura.

He'd prided himself that no girl was too bad for him.
Were there any who were too good? He rarely got close
enough to see but his philosophy (to honor it with a name)
was that all girls wanted the one thing he wanted, only some
priced themselves out of the market. Their loss. He made his
girls say "please" and "thank you," he gave them orders and
would not negotiate; he had the reputation of a hawk among
mice; a jailor who did favors for those who didn't plead. But
there was no place to go with that authority: he never even got
to see a girl with all her clothes off. The back seat of his car
was like a gym: the place where you went for exercise, or to
win the game. But half the time he couldn't remember the
difference between winning and losing. He never expected
beauty; he never got it.

It didn't take long to move in on Laura. (The phrase
had begun to repulse him. Later, when she was pregnant,
coffee would make Laura sick the same way: something was

growing inside and it changed one's tolerance for harsh stimulants.) But Dan moved fast, he circled and teased and got himself chased all over the court like a limber basketball player. In fact it was his hands that were limber: Laura said gravely that they were magician's hands, not because they performed miracles but because of the way they sliced and folded and arranged things with such clean practiced movements; they went right to the spot, they rarely had to look for it. It was the first of the things that impressed her, his plain and fancy professional hands. She watched him build a rain shelter.

"No big thing," he said; he felt bare in the rawness of his words.

"Nobody's ever very impressed with his own best points," she told him. (As soon as a girl was eager to be impressed, it was all over; she could put up with anything.) "That's good, too." She was as earnest as the girls he grew up making fun of. He thought he'd have to hide her from his friends. "All the people I grew up with live in their heads. My father doesn't know what a—" (she flung her hands around helplessly; he wanted to take them) "—a tongue in groove? tongue and groove?—are? is? Which is it?"

"Tongue in," he told her; then, his mouth already open on the words, suppressed the obvious next line which would have been sufficiently clever for the kind of girl he knew, like the pregnant cow in Denham: something about his tongue, her groove. He was appalled; he smiled at Laura and gratefully made himself quiet.

He began, in fact, to discover the virtues of quietness, the bottomless depths you could suggest for yourself without quite lying. He surprised himself: what was lying and what wasn't? The question opened wide for him, like arms he didn't exactly deserve to rest in. He devoted himself to mastering the signs of her uniqueness: less rather than more, gentleness rather than power; keeping quiet, just reaching out for her, but not demanding. Her hand, barely touching. The long crevice where her bathing suit tucked between her legs when she bent over. The distance between their bare arms so infinitesimal it drew the small hairs up like electricity. Admiring without touching—it was an exquisite challenge. He was sharpening his appetite, he told his uncle; getting the juices flowing. Any other girl did that to you, John said, you'd call it starving.

He had not come, after all, from a family of gentle men and it took a painful chastening of his impulses to learn subtlety where braggadocio came naturally. (Braggadocio was his high school English teacher's favorite word; she had beat him over the head with it. He loved it, that anything so flamboyant and mysterious and foreign-sounding could be called his natural style; it sounded like a compliment.) It wasn't that Laura Shurrock was the princess who slept on twelve mattresses and a pea. But *her* father didn't, summer or winter, piss against a maple in the yard, swat his children from one wall to the other, and die of drink or malnutrition or fury or one snow too many; whichever it was. She hadn't such a father but she was touched and not repulsed that Dan did. Thank God Kenton Courser didn't have to be coped with in the flesh anymore, she didn't have to be insulted by him: lacy drawers, narrow nookie, flat titty schoolmarm, he could imagine his father's booze-heavy Saturday night voice, call it up as a gutcrunching echo every day of his life if he let himself. Telling Laura about his father a little at a time, letting the old terrors leak out, the facts or the fear that lay just beyond the facts, straining to see him as a boy who must have planned, like he did, to have sons and must never have thought to abuse them, he found himself close to tears. What had brought him to such emotion? He'd never dared show a girl anything besides bare skin, hipbone, anklebone—was it his father who made him want to cry, or Laura who sat gravely listening, with her legs slightly parted?

She was wearing blue jean shorts; the half-invisible hairs on her thighs, like lights on the water, were silver. That wasn't the way the girls he knew allowed themselves to sit, they were preoccupied, all the time, with the arrangement of their bodies. Even when they weren't "sitting decent" (his mother to his sister Fran: "*Never* with your legs open, unless you're asking for it!") they were always aware, then, of their indecency: it was one or the other. They chose. With this quiet girl from Boston it seemed to be neither, her mind was on something else. (Her mind; he tried to imagine it and couldn't. What did it do out here all day near him, that mind, when his was on gears and rocker panels and wood sealer?) She had a slightly flushed, substantial look, he thought; not heavy at all but something weighted nearer the bone; maybe she was one of those people who couldn't float. Her thick reddish hair rode all around her neck like a mane, unruly. She kept it in a rubber band but it fanned out anyway. He guessed she'd never been to a beauty shop and what she had for it was lush and inviting, not like his old girls with those thinned-out greased-up gold-streaked piled-on wedding cakes they wore for special occasions and then, when you wanted to most, wouldn't let you mess. There was delicacy and force in her, and that serious listening quality, so that she was very quiet while he talked, she asked him questions and answered his meticulously, just as she sat in her own straightforward way, without coyness. She didn't seem to know or care how the Hyland girls pumped to keep a conversation going, filling in all the blank spaces, playing their desperate background music endlessly like human jukeboxes. Those were the girls his friends had begun to marry and to run from; after a few months they came and stood around with him and the other survivors and holdouts, staring at the floor, trying to be alone in their old familiar company.

By her listening Laura taught him to talk with the expectation that he would be heard. The first time he kissed her (terrified that she'd be terrified, or feel herself used or ordinary) he felt how tightly she held herself: stiff, without breathing, she clenched her eyes shut and seemed to work at the kiss. But it was concentration; it was trying to do it perfectly and feel it perfectly; she was only as serious about kissing as she was about listening.

He tried to step backwards to see himself whole, but that wasn't a direction he was used to; there was nothing to do but bungle straight ahead and hope. He didn't ask himself what he was hoping for. Laura had had two years at a college called Wellesley that sounded like a country club with a library instead of a bar: it was hard to imagine the campus she walked on, deep ridges overwhelmed with lush trees in purple flower; the galleries of paintings, the linen-covered tables with gold samovars, behind them, bowing, silent servants in tuxedos. She had fallen in love with her philosophy instructor, she told him in that same measured voice in which nothing sounded as stupid as she said it did, certainly not that. This little deepwoods vacation with her parents seemed like a wise cooling-off from what she called, chillingly, "an unwise relationship."

"Who called it that?" he asked her.

"Well. I'm nineteen." She smiled wanly at him.

"So? Up here nineteen's getting to be an old lady."

"Really?"

"Really." Up here, though, were a lot of things she wouldn't necessarily approve of: there was Lake Regions State

College that was like a locker room with a gym instead of a library. He never could believe it was a real college; that was the only way he could get himself to go. His teachers were frauds, coaches with fancy letters after their names, and as for the flowers she thought a college needed, the only kind anybody managed to plant were stunted little marigolds and the kind of petunias you see in front of Hyland Exxon. He saw Laura walking with her philosophy professor under the purple trees; he saw them pass out of his sight into shadow.

He was, in fact, a young man of ordinary tastes and it seemed hopeless to try to dissimulate with her; she would have found him out. Her philosophy man liked Heidegger, she told him, and he nodded bleakly, wondering if that was a place or a beer or a sport. What did he like? Tearing up trees on the bush hog. Swimming in heartstopping water. Bobsledding. He liked dogs, all his life he'd put a lot of love into them because they wouldn't laugh or push him away. He liked well-shined shoes; football that's more brains than shoulders; hot pepper sauce; cheeses that don't smell like someone's been sick in the room; all four-wheel-drive vehicles. He had never eaten an artichoke, nor heard a dulcimer. He fell asleep on uplifting music, though he liked to sing, and thought cars should be fast, not solid. The flag of the state of New Hampshire made his stomach sink with a churning excitement, almost a kind of pain, which must have to do with something he'd done as a child: carried the flag? damaged it accidentally and been punished for it? seen it in the V.A. Hospital where his father was dying? He wasn't patriotic, the word would never have occurred to him; why did he feel so unsettled when he saw the high-masted sailing ship against the sun? Once he blew his nose into a silk handkerchief and then and there decided that he would become rich, or wished he could decide: the feeling of luxury where you least expected it, of a private sweetness, meant more than the drape of any suit or even the chrome on a car. He hid this petty preference from his friends who would have thought him a pansy for it. And getting rich was never the point; getting halfway decent might be, if he ever got good and ready for it. He had always thought of himself as someone who got what he wanted: he thought Laura needed to know this, his honor demanded that he warn her so that she might defend herself if she wanted to. As a young boy, the youngest, he could charm his mother, whose experience of grown men had been nothing but mutilating. She would have given him permission to take the world but all she had of it was what he could find in her worn brown change purse, which reminded him of a tongue, of all her hidden places, limp and cracked. She worked nights at the paper mill all his life, all hers; she slept most of the day.

At school he kept a balance of terror, benign but effective: the annual lecture to the Society of Future Felons of N.H. was directed at his truculent head by Mrs. Hurley, principal. One day, to prove he deserved it, he had stood behind her while she reviled him, making motions first of picking her up off the ground, easy, and when that failed to get a sufficient laugh, of buggering her, with his eyes cast to heaven. He was smarter than his friends, played the odds, used his smooth face and eager goodboy looks, the persistent near-smile, the reassuring firm jaw, something clean about him that had to do with a soul that was subsisting on hope faintly warmed by his mother's love, and not with fastidiousness—something of this combination got him behind closed doors, dispersed his enemies, helped him to escape continuous punishment. There had been plenty of need for absolution and escape: he wasn't mean but he'd always been sloppy, had had a childhood, in close quarters, of breaking things, vases and bicycles, and once the top drawer of the only decent piece of furniture they owned; finally, of breaking girls, snapping their flesh like some cellophane wrapper to get at the sweets inside; and breaking hearts, that too. But there was some glamor in him, some obscure enviable energy that made his arrogance only appropriate; didn't he deserve, by taking them, the things he got?

At the worst his friends and he were vandals, irritating as the black flies that came in their season. What trouble and confusion they made was never intolerable. Hyland bored them; they had known each other, known the two main streets that met at a T and the leafy roads and old wooden stores forever: in another life. To keep their hands busy, their adrenalin in working order, they broke into summer homes and hunting camps. Once inside, the conversation was always the same: "Hey look at this!" to signify the discovery of anything worth ten dollars, and "Boy, you got to figure they've got another whole set of this stuff back home, right?" Dan's resentment was real; he never stopped being angry at the summer people and their endless duplications: his mother had patched together a set of china with one representative of every species of flower around the border. Even if the chipped plates in these strangers' kitchens came from the Ladies Auxiliary Thrift Shop he was angry; it was excessive. He and his friends would leave by the windows, would take the highways at unconscionable speed, occasionally in someone else's car. ("Danny's gonna jump-start his hearse," somebody once said.) They were all known to the cops, as the cops, and the cops' imperfect pasts, were known to them. But they were amateurs, every one of them; in spite of their noise and their showy toughness, small-town punks who didn't *need* weren't desperate. This was all braggadocio, that ticklish word: blood made the difference. But they had no blood guilt. They were puppies growing into their feet.

. . . .

Laura took him to Cambridge. One day near the end of her
three-week vacation, his license still impounded, he borrowed
John's abominable car and drove it well below the speed limit;
his hands clenched and unclenched on the steering wheel.

Within ten minutes of their arrival in a dark and noisy
restaurant in Harvard Square that smelled of deep fat fried
again and again, Dan felt himself growing critical, growing
complicated. A darkness stole across his vision the way a fever
dimly announces itself behind the eyes. He sat discovering that
disappointment and relief could live side by side, could tease
and be painful, and that he could watch them from some
small remove. He moved a step back into himself, brooding.
Finally he brought out his disappointment to look at it. "Half
the girls in Cambridge look like you, Laura."

But that made her laugh. "Is that an accusation?" She
was astonished: he was serious. "I never said I was an original,
Dan. A one-of-a-kind! Why do you look so hurt?"

He couldn't say why. It was taxing to wonder.

For one thing he found himself at a disadvantage: a
question of turf. He was as territorial as a cat, but he had
never known it. Across the room sat another girl, darker, but
with Laura's approximate profile: same bright scarf knotted
under her hair that added color to her face while it took away
softness. The gold hoops wobbled in her ears as she spoke,
and spoke with an identical earnestness—that well-fed, well-
read upperclass peasant look. She probably sat with lips and
thighs parted boyishly, like Laura.

"Is it what that makes you think about me and how boring
I am, or, somehow that I don't understand, what you think
about *you*?" When she leaned across the table the edge bit
into her breasts and left an indented line when she sat back

again. That must have hurt; he felt protective of her body.

He couldn't say what it was but it depressed him. He wished he had some beer. Probably these people didn't think it was proper to drink beer. He took a bite of a very bad muffin that disintegrated when he touched it. "Home cooking." He wet his index finger and picked the crumbs up with it; disgusted, he poked a clean circle all around his plate.

"Like sometimes when I'm shopping I think I've found a sweater or something that's really unique, you know?" She was eager to help. They all said "you know" the same way, he could even hear it as he sat here, the deep pleased voices of these Harvard people assuring each other that they knew, they knew, of course they understood, on all sides. "And then I find a whole tableful of the same sweater and—"

"Shut up," he told her with a new and desperate confidence, surprised at how trivial she sounded. "You're making it worse." He touched her chin across the litter of muffins and coffee stains.

"Well, tell me what you're thinking then, will you, if you don't like my analogies."

"Your analogies."

"My analogies. Stop that, that's a word I use. Don't be lazy." That was her force, to counter his: she could command him, and sternly. She was soft and hard, like those breasts she had leaned across the table, and not particularly conscious of being either. Probably the rest of these girls were too: it came with the green bookbag, the good teeth, large and white and stony. They all played instruments, these hard soft girls, and sports he barely knew the names of—weren't these the kinds of people who fenced and played lacrosse? "Shit," he said to himself. The word was comforting.

"I'm thinking I don't know a single goddamn thing, that's all, and I don't know why you're sitting here with me this way. Maybe a little about my own kind. But I'm not sure I even knew I had a kind."

She drank some cold coffee. "Oh yes you did, that's silly. You don't have to leave Hyland to know there are all kinds of people up there. You think you've got to call it sociology to know who your friends are?"

"Maybe." He put his head against his hand, meekly, and closed his eyes, a little sick. "I thought you were this miracle that walked out of the woods, I don't know, Sleeping Beauty or somebody. Unbelievable. This mermaid that got washed up a hundred miles out of the sea."

She smiled sadly but said nothing.

"But see, if you're not—" He shrugged, meaning the end of something she couldn't see.

"Well," she asked when he didn't go on. "Then what am I? I'm sorry to disappoint you so."

"It's not what you are instead. It's what it, it's what you can slip back into, this whole scene I didn't know existed. You just walk through the door—" He could see the woods slamming shut behind her, like the huge freezer door at the meat market where he worked one summer a thousand years ago, all the warmth outside with her.

"Danny." She took his rough hand this time and spread the fingers very slowly, causing a terrible consternation in his body and his soul. She closed and opened them like a fan, she was playing with him. "I think I've seen this in the movies. You think you're some kind of summer thrill for a nice sweet little professor's daughter. Do you? A little bit soiled around the edges maybe, just a wee little bit nasty, you know, rank and dangerous? Maybe to scare mama and papa into appreciating the philosophy professor?"

Jesus, he thought, and pulled his hand away. She was one step ahead of him in her conniving; that had never even occurred to him. *He had never been hurt,* he realized, plummeting backward, falling into a darkness in which there were no walls decorated with swords and lances, there were no dozens of people sitting all around him. He let his head fall into his open hand, trying to keep his cool by main force. "I'm no stud, Laura. Jesus Christ."

"Dan, I don't like to disappoint you but there must be, oh, maybe fifteen kinds of dangerous men in this city, I'd say. It's a small town too, even if it's bigger than Hyland. I'm not counting Boston. Dangerous boys, too." Her voice was mellow with mock patience. "But I don't know if you could even get into the heats. Is that the phrase? In sports. The final competition? So there's got to be something else."

He wanted to go home to the girls he scared, the ones who didn't set out their words like so much good china and then walk around the table getting all the edges lined up.

"Danny, don't sulk, please? Can I take you home and show you our house? You'll never get to see it if we don't."

He looked at her, stricken blank with hope. This was unfair.

"I like pine needles and nice warm Chevrolets but a room with a view of Brattle Street—"

"You won't need a view." He clutched her hand with a ferocity he failed to notice and she didn't break from. He was dizzy with the alternations in his, in their, possibilities; so that, leading him up Brattle, shouldering through the summer school crowds of women she nearly resembled, she felt as if she had a docile child by the hand.

It took him an hour to get over her house. The glare of it blinded him. Most of it was glass and polished chrome, but then there was a whole room of old wood and portraits, a library, he guessed. "Inherited," Laura told him. "My Victorian grandma. Mother has gone modern even though she can't stand the stuff, but she had to move out of her mother's house, sort of."

The force of it rolled over him; he stayed close to Laura's side for fear the distance, the sheer empty space and all it represented, would come between them just when he couldn't let it. It was not for nothing that his parents had protected him against the rich by teaching him to despise them.

All she could find in the refrigerator was white wine, mayonnaise, a jar of wheat germ that looked like a pound of sawdust, and a can of guava shells.

"Isn't guava bird crap?" Dan asked. He was just getting the chill out of his voice.

When she looked at him disapprovingly she was her mother's daughter. "Guano, you mean." There was no sense making conversation. She poured him a glass of wine which he drank straight down. "That was no shot glass, showoff."

He held up the glass for more. "I'm drinking to my mother's ghost. Once when she got laid off at the paper mill she cleaned up a house like this but the old lady died and they auctioned everything off. She went and watched them knocking down the stuff she dusted for thousands of bucks. Every piece cost thousands."

"Are you rubbing my face in this, as if I can help it?"

He was startled. "I'm not rubbing your face into anything. We keep getting confused about who I'm talking about when I get depressed." She poured him another glass. "My refrigerator always had a pitcher of dry milk in it. It used to separate into the water half and the milk half, you know? And a pack of baloney getting dried up at the edges because I was always stealing a piece and forgetting to wrap it up again."

"Pardon me if I tell you you aren't very subtle," Laura said.

He finished the wine and rang the rim of the glass with his fingernail. The sound was high and pure, the voice of a young girl.

She took him to her room, which was pink because it hadn't been painted since she was eleven, and busy with posters of the kind of paintings people said their cats could do by walking through wet paint. Once he had taken a girl to bed in her own bedroom, in her trailer; another time he had snuck into a dormitory at college and hidden under the covers while his girl tried to get rid of her roommate. When the roommate wouldn't budge, she climbed back under the covers and kept her hand over his mouth. Girls' bedrooms gave him the same fearful feeling as churches; to desecrate them was a special thrill.

Laura made getting undressed take twenty minutes because, she said, she had all that woods to get over, those animals cracking twigs behind the trees and she thinking they were all her father.

"I'd be more scared of your mother," Dan said.

"It's all the same, they'd mutter it all out and take me before the family tribunal."

"Are you serious?" He wasn't sure what a tribunal was but it sounded daunting. "Did they haul up your philosophy professor like that?"

"Ssh," she whispered. "You don't talk about other men at a time like this."

"But maybe you think about them." If she didn't, he did. "At a time like this," though: what a signal of arrival.

She pulled off his last sock and dropped it precisely on its mate. When she bent there, in midafternoon light, her breast rippled like the whole summer's lake water, shimmering. He wanted to walk away so he could just watch her move through the room, he needed an hour, a week of unabashed staring. He didn't want to be allowed to touch her. In her clothes she was such a good girl; now she seemed to him endless, round and womanly, pleased with herself and a little bit frightened, nowhere knobby or sinewy like the half-glimpsed chickens he dragged across the upholstery of his Vega; she was a new species, and she knew it.

"You see the disadvantages of a sneaking-around life." She didn't even have to whisper; her parents were reading *The New York Times*, sitting in beach chairs with their feet in Pottery Lake, they always did that as though they'd walked around the city all day and needed soothing.

"Laura." His voice was strangled with the effort at control. "I don't think I ever stood still with a girl like this."

She volunteered no history of her own. "You're growing up, child."

She was stronger and weaker than he in such perfect proportion he wanted to roar with frustration and pleasure. When he touched her left breast with the palm of his hand, keeping himself at a painful distance, both of them shuddered. Would he learn gentleness from her as well as silence? And the trust to hold on? He was not going to fall upon her, this torture was his pact with her and sex didn't even seem to be what it was about. He would learn from her, God only knew what he could gladly humble himself to learn. To begin with, there was this most staggering opulent unstolen pleasure in a life of small change. In the bold light of her bedroom window that opened onto plush well-tended city trees, he looked at Laura Shurrock's face, which was as new to him as the leisure to study her body; looked at her green eyes complicated with islands of brown; at the flush of her fair skin as she strained away from him, and she seemed to be telling him this was no ending. If he meant no danger to her, could he somehow mean safety? He was awed at her and at himself with her. She was coming back here with her parents in a week but first they would put the seal of their bodies on this quilt-covered bed in her parents' house. She seemed to be saying the stain, the seal, would not easily come out.

"Laura?" He calls her quietly because he thinks she may be asleep. The television set is droning just below the level of sense; it was Jon's gift, before his bedtime, to set her up in her chair in front of a show she had never in her real life dreamed of watching: con men chased cops chased women into all the dark corners of the picture.

"Okay?" Jon asked, delighted at his thoughtfulness. Laura looked at him as if he had already died, or gone away from her. Her long locked gaze, Dan is learning, they are all learning, is a form of hypnosis. The helpless are given a few nearly occult powers, as reparation. This penetrating glance is hers: she can get anything with it but what she wants. When she looks at him that way Jon comes and takes her hands—an adult gesture, Dan thinks—a lover's or a parent's gesture!— and kneels down in front of her. He puts his head on her knees. Dan trembles on behalf of the indwelling catheter but Laura seems not to worry. He will try not to worry; it is her body. (Or is it, if she doesn't feel it? Is it anybody's, then? Is it no one's?)

"Mommy," Jon says without looking up at her. "Mommy, I love you so much." As if it were in dispute; he doesn't know what he gives away by his declaration. Jon has never said any such thing before, not since he was very little, though he's a warm permeable boy who hasn't ever cared for the tradition of hell-raising that made his father a determined bum his first twenty years. He is on the firm side of frailty, of studiousness, he introduces a unique decency among his friends; neither hound nor hare, but safe and good. Still he would never tell his mother what he is telling her except for the grief in her eyes.

"Are you trying to make me cry?" Laura asks him, trying for jauntiness; it is her most futile emotion. (Perhaps one needs to be free to jump up and demonstrate jauntiness to be convincing about it.) She manages to touch his head with the bent back of her hand. He nuzzles against that pressure, pushes back. They remind Dan of young animals butting for greeting.

"No, I don't want you to cry," he tells her with great composure. "I'm trying to make you happy. Mom?"

"Mmm."

"I never liked the way you made my bed, you know."

"What?" She strains to hear him.

"So please don't do it anymore. I will." He laughs out loud, nervously, glancing at his father quickly, checking for approval or anger, some judgment on his wit.

"Is that a joke?" his little sister asks in a sharp appalled voice, clapping her hand over her mouth. She too is guarding her mother.

" 'Is that a joke?' " Jon echoes, his only nastiness saved, always, for Hallie.

Laura begins to cry, suddenly, silent, not for show. Her emotions these days change at the touch of a hair. The tears must run down inside her when she cries like that; they must puddle there and never dry. "Are we going to have to live like thieves?"

Her son hugs her knees desperately, needing comfort. "I was trying to be funny, Mommy, I didn't—"

"I know you were," she says gently, sniffling. Who will wipe her nose? It barely pays to cry. "Only you know I can't stand it when you children go at each other that way. You know—"

"Oh that." Jon is relieved. "Well, maybe Hallie'll grow up someday." He shoots her a look that promises: Later. Later you're getting it.

"All right. To bed," Dan says. "I'll come up and kiss you."

Set free, relieved, they run off into their ancient routine: wash, bed, kiss, book, nightlight. (He doesn't know if they need the muffled light anymore; but habits are needs, aren't they? Are real.)

Dan leans over Laura. "There's a tear on the end of your nose, madam. Is there anything you'd like me to do about it?"

She closes her eyes against him: Laura whose fine face is imprinted on the inside of his eyelids; her wide-apart eyes under such precise arches of brow; her firm, no-gosh no-golly nose (that's what he calls it). She does not have the face of a cheerleader. It can absorb a good deal of pain with dignity, or pleasure, or any emotion at all: her face is not petty. "We will not live like thieves, lady. Ever." He sucks up the tear into a kiss. "What do we have here that doesn't belong to us, please tell me that."

Silence from Laura, the set jaw, the locked teeth. It is already beginning to bore him, this listless abdicating silence.

"Do you know how happy your children are?"

"At what?"

"At having you home."

"No I don't know. I don't intend to lie to myself any more than I need to."

Her feet are flat on their foot pedal ledge, her hands arranged on the cool arms of the chair. He thinks, how strange to stay in the same position for laughing and for crying. "Goddamn it, neither do I."

"Dan, don't badger me."

"I'll badger you if I want to. I don't want to but I will. I'll hound you till you listen to me and relax a little."

"Dan," she says wearily. "Please. This is your firm, macho approach, I can see that, but it's transparent. I haven't become an imbecile, you know."

"You know what we're doing?"

"I'm sleepy. I need a lot of sleep." She turns her head vaguely towards the door, in the general direction of sleep.

"Do you know?" He is jubilant, he pulls her head back by her short hairs till she cries out. "We're having our first good old fight, hey. That was fast."

"You sound like you're on a situation comedy, do you know that? You sound like Dick Van Dyke."

"Well, isn't that what this is? I thought that's what this was all about, isn't this—" He looks all around him as though he's just discovered he's in the wrong room. "Oh, Studio *B*—"

Is he trying too hard or is she impatient with his usual volubility? She has been known to love him for this, which is foreign to her and which she calls gaiety; there is even a particular spot, the hollow in his neck above the collarbone, that she has made it her habit to kiss when he clowns for her.

He heads for the door. "All right, toots, watch your cops and robbers." He tells her this in someone else's voice. "See you around."

. . . .

Hallie is pretending to be asleep when he comes to tuck her in. No sense of how well grownups know the possibilities; she thinks she's convincing, an animal playing dead.

Jon, though, knows very well what he can fake and what he can't. He is lying stiff in his bed. Dan wants to sit down and comfort him, wants to tell him he knows it's hard, it's going to be harder still. He puts his hands down on his knees and sees himself from a dizzying distance: adult, father, composed and thoughtful. Up close, he's no better off than Jon but will not frighten him by saying so. And more: the first word he really learned from Laura, that summer in the woods, was *platitude*. She drew a little picture for him of a paunchy flat-footed bird she called the Duck-billed Platitude. To judge from the frilled candy papers all around, it had gorged on a hundred sweets; it was an appealing bird from a distance but if you looked hard it had menacing teeth and wavy lines around it, to indicate, she said, the smell of rotten eggs.

He sat for a minute or two looking hard into his son's earnest face. Let him try to learn words-without-words, let him master them early: another gift from Laura. Jon gave him the upper edge of a buried smile. It was embedded in the boy's face like a rock and Dan had to pull hard to get it out.

There is a bag of absorbent panty liners on the kitchen counter. He turns it in his hands; his anger nearly chokes him.

He is sure he doesn't know an uglier word in the English language than *prosthesis*. His first, inadvertent imagining when he heard it was of an artificial penis, something pink and rubbery, held on by straps attached by tubing to the hidden glands. He couldn't imagine Laura and the word at the same time without gagging. The catalog of inventions! What was worth it? The Queen Mary Tub Seat, the Swedish Grip Tong, the Bac-a-rac Bedboard. Less than ten ounces, made of sections riveted together in the center with a washer applied for smooth operation. The cock-up splint and the rotary splint, the flexor hinge hand-splint that lifts your wrist with a whiff of CO_2, kids love it, they'll come from miles around to see: if you can't order a normal parent, order one whose wrist lifts at the flick of a switch, like Howdy Doody. And oh, the toggle switch, piece of aluminum .040 thick, fitted with a rubber band, the flange with variable-width tubing, the duralumin reaching tongs . . .

(She said to Jon and Hallie in this very place at the counter, "Chocolate milk in your thermoses okay?" her head cocked for an answer. Flat feet she had trained to high steely arches from running on sand, from dancing. Arches off the cool brick-red linoleum.

"I don't think there's such a word, 'thermoses,' " Hallie said, looking up from her embroidery hoop. "Is there, Daddy?"

Daddy didn't know or very much care; he let it be. Laura shrugged and poured milk into the Quik, humming something with a thousand notes. The spoon hit the sides of the plastic glass, a dull click. She snapped the locks on their lunchboxes and moved her head in a satisfied nod, like a pat on the flank of some live thing.)

Prosthesis lived in a crack in the dictionary between *prosthenic* (stronger in the foreparts) and *prostibulous* (pertaining to prostitutes). "No, Mr. Courser, she isn't in need of a prosthesis," Mrs. Toko kept assuring him, irritated. "Why have you fixed on that? Prostheses take the place of missing limbs. Your wife—" Is only disconnected, he thought. The plugs pulled, the current shorted. "Your wife will have other systems of support." "Like a man in space," he said, imagining commands from Houston coming in to her, those crewcut midwest voices telling her when to move, to laugh, to pee. "Affirmative," she'd say and move not a single finger.

He had practically stolen her from the Rehabilitation Institute where she was not being rehabilitated. For one thing she never cried there, he wasn't sure she breathed or sweated. They pushed food into her and pulled it out. She sat like someone in a ward of what the children sweetly called "mentals" and studied the wall behind his head. He couldn't blame her: this was the place people—her fellow-wounded people— came to take heart, to learn to crawl and walk and jump (oh, to make leatherette purses and be proud of them, and birdhouses and pen wipers: she would love to make the least of them. And then there were the traitors who learned to drive). She was not going to learn. Not a single trick; only the movement of the plastic and metal and awardwinning-design lightweight aluminum: her surrogate limbs were going to school here, in fact had graduated. There was nothing more. Some of the moving parts belonged to the house, like chained-down ashtrays he'd met up with in New York, some of them he bought from the Institute PX when they left, they'd been made expressly for her and they were not cheap, and they did not even necessarily work, and some he'd have to find in Boston however he could. He thought, her own, her very own plastic prick to have and to hold, they'd take it home in a doggy bag, a Gucci-Pucci suitcase (he'd learned such things), an onflight underseat limb carrier, her very very own and his. See her learn to write her name in the air with the all-purpose patent-pending pseudo-dong: LAURA COURSER. GONE FISHIN.

She was sitting in an electric wheelchair in the lounge watching him argue with her doctor. Her neck was stiff and her body in its tight steel-backed corset was pliable as an old churchgoing Hyland widow's. She looked mildly curious as though she didn't know this man. Cowlick, clean collar, vituperation. Did he have a wife? A job? A subway token? What did he want with her?

"Before you go, Mr. Courser," said the very even-tempered doctor, as young as he and cool as a thug. His goldrimmed glasses flickered. They were opposed to his dragging Laura home, they referred to it as theft, they did not like impulsive or passionate outbursts, they were an Institution, had schedules and plans and he was not humble in the face of them. They were, it seemed, accustomed to being thanked. They saw nothing beyond their patients, who dropped out of nowhere, broken or bent. They pretended to have a deep concern for families but Dan felt untouched by it; felt invisible; did not, like so many others, "attend the patient," nor even borrow her weekends because they lived a hundred flights of stairs UP and he'd have a heart attack just getting her into the apartment. "I want to say—quietly, here please, let's not involve Laura if that's all right—" and they moved aside. "That I would worry a little—" pause because he was going to say something difficult and perhaps insulting—"that you appear to be as angry at Laura as you are at anybody else right now."

"Who—" He nearly stamped, knew he was being petulant, couldn't control it better than this since what he really wanted to do was roll on the tile floor and beat his head, which made petulance a triumph, this mere unmurderous rage— "Who should I be angry at then? Who?" His voice like a thirteen-year-old's, ripped down the middle, jagged on both sides. If he weren't such a child, Laura would say. ("Whom?" Hallie would say, her mother's daughter, the village grammarian.)

"No one," the doctor admitted, and smiled. "Well. Some people turn their attention to, unh, God at times like these, I suppose, but" (he looked around like a conspirator to see if he was being overheard), "but if that were your preference I trust you could have thought that out for yourself." His bought sigh. "No one then. But Mr. Courser, your wife has been here for months now, it's safe to suggest that it's time, you know, to start adjusting. She has her ups and downs, certainly, but she's trying. She doesn't say much, tell us much of what she's thinking, but she works out hard and makes a real effort, so I'd take that as a sign. A vital sign, you might call it. And so—you see, this marching off with her like this—this unprecedented *instant* removal from a safe and supportive environment. We like to get our patients and their families ready, you know. We have an entire department that is devoted to nothing but discharge planning, with all its little ins and outs, a thousand little details to make home adjustment more comfortable. We have a whole trained staff." He was being cheated, his forehead wrinkled like a small boy's, aggrieved. "And now, your anger appears to be—if I may—irrelevant. Do you know what I'm saying? Counterproductive." He looked down humbly. "Unkind, even. As if it were a punishment." But she dreams about crowds, Dan wanted to say, when she closes her eyes! They flow back and forth like water in a tipped plate. (He remembered her words exactly because they were so strange, this testimony she brought him from a foreign land.) People come to see her and they stand in the doorway a hundred deep. Would that make sense to the doctor, did he have a trained staff to see such dreams? All of them walking, moving, flexing muscles she remembered before the root rot got them. The cutworms. The slugs. Before her hospital gown, her angel robe, her shroud, her gunnysack. He wanted to take her away from the crowds, that was all. He was ready to take her back. They couldn't keep her. Before and after is all life is: that was the only lesson they'd learned together. B.C. Before Catastrophe. Or Before Courser. Before the Crusher. A.D. After Decapitation. The shop teacher learns a little philosophy between semesters of shellac and mitre boxes: Laura

before and Laura ever after. Unkindness to himself, to her—
that was the least of his offenses.

"Laura, bedtime."

"Okay."

"Up with me."

"Okay."

"Do you trust yourself in bed with a horny man?"

She could still shudder, though her anger and disgust
were identical. A wave passed through her like wind over
rippling water.

He could not apologize. "We'll work on a real bed for
you starting tomorrow."

"What about my air mattress?"

"I'll plug it in." Circulating air repelled bedsores; bedsores were something no one took seriously. You could work
up a real sense of righteous indignation against the spared,
the healthy. You could put up a flag and give lectures in the
street. In two hours her flesh would eat a hole in itself;
couldn't be simpler. It digested its surface as though anger
did it, hot acid pooling. Each bedsore meant a month, three
months, of healing. A permanent dent, a scar from the core
out. "Thousands of dollars if you can believe it, Mr. Courser,"
said little Nurse Toko with her little eyes. He couldn't believe
it, of course not; she only told him improbable things, she
liked to enlist what sounded like reason against the unfairness
of injury. It made her feel good: virtuous, superior to both of
them. Well, they were only free of her, not of what she
warned against: how every inch that presses down without
movement begins to die. Air, then, or water below her pressure points, those weighty bones, her shoulders, spine and

buttocks, that was all. "No one is light enough. If she had *wings* they'd rot," said Mrs. Toko smiling. Air, water and constant turning, chicken on a spit. The price of weighing more than dust is pain. He wished Mrs. Toko only the worst.

Now he puts his arms under Laura, ready this time for her uneven weight. They stagger on the dark steps, plunge towards the bedroom. He feels like a bear on his hind legs dragged forward by something—the hunter, maybe, who'll kill him later. They bump through the doorways, her shoulder against the jamb, taking his fingers along. His wedding ring slashes a long comet-arc in the paint. He tries to sit her on their bed; she could just as easily flap her wings and fly.

"How do we do this, honey? What should I do?" He is frightened, humble. Here they are again.

"I could fall on the floor for an encore."

"Laura—"

"Well, I don't know. Lay me down, I guess. You can't expect me to sit on the edge like a good little girl. Why don't you think about it next time?"

It occurs to him as he moves his hands to grasp her for pulling—he has shut it out but with this single action it's clear there will be no choice—that they will have to get out of this house. The house is so much his beloved place in the world, his rock, his name, that the air goes out of his body; he's fallen on his stomach into that old winded numbness of his child-hood. He looks at his wife appalled, as though she's asked for something he cannot give her.

Her head is on the pillow, not a good angle for it. It gives her pain. Before she can ask him to remove it, he has lain down beside her, both of them still in their buckles and shoes and belts and sweaters, like teenagers hoping to neck. She realizes after a while that he's begun to weep. As suddenly as

Laura folds into tears these days, it has caught him unprepared. His tears feel dry and rusty, it takes a long time for him to pump them up from the well they've gathered in while he's watched her cry and cry, with pity and disgust watched the skin soften around her eyes as if she'd stayed in the bath too long. His tears are stored very far down. But he gets the rhythm of it after a while; like making love with a stranger, it has its symmetries if one is patient. Soon he is sobbing like a small boy, shoulders, hips, he is bent at the knees with unbudgeable pain; he moves. He thinks if he stays here forever, breathing out tears, he will never have to face his life. Long after he feels nothing at all the tears go on, the circuit jammed open, comfortable. He understands how Laura finds them useful, how the shifting weathers that sweep violently over her are really a kind of movement, close to the center and far far back; she has nowhere else to go.

She can't put her arms around him but, eyes nearly dry, she murmurs, "That's better, Dan, that's good. That's very very good." Hallie on the potty, Jon on his first bike. He feels slightly sullied, as though he's masturbated while she lay beside him sleeping. And won't it come to that too, he thinks? The tears go on.

Then he gets up and prepares them both, blindly, for sleep.

He thought he'd been catching up with his wife through the years of their marriage. She was patient most of the time and he was hurrying.

He was hurrying the day they were sailing up under the flat face of the Palisades in Laura's cousin Natty Riggs's boat, his twenty-footer (the children in love with the bunks and the depth sounder, how effortlessly its green numbers flew past as though they didn't really exist). They ate hardboiled eggs dark with French mustard and pâté, and drank beer out of Natty's own barrel with its drippy spigot. When Laura and Janet Riggs went down the ladder and horsed in the water their voices were high and adolescent, Janet's because it always was, she was serving a life sentence as the last debutante in her family, Laura's because she was happy to be far from Hyland for a while. New York had made her walk swift and efficient, not at all a vacationer's stroll, but like a workingwoman's, and this kind of swim was one of the things she saw she missed— not a lake in New Hampshire with passive trees all around, so postcard-beautiful you ought to feel you were on vacation all the time and therefore never did. But that cliff of city down there just out of sight, that furious busyness, that endless-ness . . .

Because Natty made the mistake of asking, Dan assured him he could steer the boat, who couldn't steer, anyone who could drive, he could handle a caterpillar or a Maserati—he was hurrying then too, eager to prove a dozen and a half things to this stockbroker cousin of Laura's, when he grabbed the wheel and danced a little—was it a sailor's hornpipe? He remembers kicking up, feeling limber. He remembers the wheel was cumbersome, slow to respond. Whatever you did with it, you overdid. (Why weren't they anchored? Why was the motor on when there were swimmers over the side? Was Natty a sloppy sailor?) But he was the one who forgot the swimmers, who grabbed the wheel and gave the boat its rush, thinking the surge sounded—vroom vroom—like the fake sounds he made as a little boy playing power. He will not remember Laura's voice from beside, from under the boat, in the rotors, nor any of the next few hours. None of it, none of it at all, it is buried, he would choose to cover it with his own body if he has to, like a soldier falling on a grenade; only not to have to think about it, or see it, or hear it, again.

Laura knows a thousand things he doesn't now and he'll never catch up. A lot of them hurt, some of them hinge on a strength no one discovers unless the alternative is nothing; it is not transferable. Dan looks at her as if she's grown a new set of muscles stronger than the first. What they move is all inside, untouchable. They frighten him.

He knows a few things, though, himself, that he isn't telling her. For most of her stay in the hospital she asked no questions, she seemed to need all her energy to breathe. Then her words came back to her one at a time, holey, as if some grid laid over her brain let one word out of every five or ten slip through; he had to work to hear them. When he talked to her it wasn't to impart information so much as warmth, to massage her senses, to get her to reattach herself to him; no, at first to the life she'd nearly abandoned and only after that seemed sure, to him. The doctor told him he was her lifeline. He felt incidental, or worse: an irritant, a sty in her one unbandaged eye. No, said the doctor, even anger will do her good, even hate, recrimination, blame. They'll get her circulation up. So he was the sacrifice.

(How could that be, when so was she?)

She was a patchwork of bandages at first. It looked as though they had plans to electrocute her: the Crutchfield tongs held her head in place, massive and loaded with lead weights, stuck tight in holes in her skull. Had they drilled the holes with a squeaky drill, by hand? The frame of her bed was met with an identical frame and she inside like a sandwich filling. Every few hours the whole thing was turned over and she lay on her stomach looking at the floor. "You could read," he'd offered shyly. ("Danny, who are the people who do all that vacation reading you hear about?" And the children tugged and nattered.) "I'll turn the pages." Her laugh was as thick with bile as a belch. It came from under the bed.

Among the things he wasn't telling her was where they were living. Natty, in spite of his blazer and his stocks, and the irrefutable proof that Dan was a boast and a fraud, was warmer and kinder than his wife, who wouldn't talk to him. "That could have been me too, you stupid murderer," she hissed, and he saw that debutantes could turn as ugly as the next one; nor could she curse as inventively as the least thug in Hyland. "If I hadn't been swimming around the other side you could have gotten us both, you fucking ignorant showoff!" She poured drinks for herself. Was she the only adult in the room? Natty poured them for Dan and himself and apologized for Janet who, he said, was understandably upset: Laura was one of the few women she liked; she had a hundred friends she despised.

For a week Dan and Jon and Hallie stayed with the Riggses in Oyster Bay, where they lived in a house that was all striped carpeting, hypnotic, orange and yellow like a bathrobe. Janet circled him at a distance as though he might still be dangerous. Then Natty found them a place to stay. They hated the apartment but thanked Natty nonetheless, he had done the best he could, called everyone he knew and turned up this set of barren rooms only three long blocks crosstown from the hospital. It wasn't worth moving, once they were there. Dan had neither the cunning to find anything better nor the energy to care.

The front entrance to their building felt like a darkroom. The switchplate they grappled for just inside the door was crusted with fingerprints, three-dimensional with dirt; they weren't allowed to leave the light on. Dan watched the spark jump inside the cracked case each time he turned it on; it was live as a trapped firefly. The toilet was mossy, the paint on every wall looked like a map revised with a hundred new discoveries. Someone had pencilled the names of states on the bathroom wall. Jon added New Hampshire in a jagged square twice the size of Texas.

It—that was how they referred to the place, reluctant to speak of "home"—was up two dark flights that terrified the children for a month. (They'd been hoping for an elevator—the only one in Hyland was at the hospital, but if you were their age you had to be a patient to get into it.) Dan had always meant to sit down with pencil and paper and figure out how the steps could go straight up like that without turning—the building didn't seem deep enough. It was some kind of magic he didn't want to investigate, but he wouldn't have been much surprised if the steel basement door led through walls and caves into some infinite hollow place at the center of the city. On Sundays all eight million people could come out there and mug one another, or play ball.

Where the stair landing had its little plateau deep enough to stand on to catch your breath before you took the next flight, Hallie would sit down defeated. It seemed to be where she went to visit her mother; she would pull her knees up and stare angrily at them in the dark. There were metal edges on the step, at the top of the risers. She would run a finger along the edge till she got to a raised screw, then circle it a few times methodically and go on; then she would do it again. The first month or so Dan would carry her up the rest of the way. In the vague twilight under the bulb her eyes dilated, they were a witchy black he didn't recognize, empty screwholes bored between herself and everything outside.

When her leg muscles got strong enough to get her upstairs without exhaustion, still he would find her there. He began to see it was her one sweet hideout, her treehouse, her boulder. School was a torment, half in Spanish, half in a language she was presumed to know but seemed never to have heard before. ("What does it mean, 'I was eight before I was seven'?" she asked Dan. "A girl, Bunny, in my class says that all the time." "To the teacher?" "No, the boys.") She had no friends, no bike, no sled, no garden. The trees at home must have begun to turn, she told Dan once when he found her on her step. For her it was sufficient explanation of her presence there in the dark: that her home friends were in the playground standing on their heads, playing poly hockey. They were picking goldenrod and Vermont asters. Did they ever think of her? Her mother was down the block held captive by spikes in her head, turned with a wheel. Why did he tell her what Laura looked like? Dan thought it was just as well she couldn't go see for herself, it was a mercy, but he told her anyway, blurted it out. Why? he asked himself. (*Blurt* was the word for him, what he said and what he did. Courser the Blurt, king of the smalltown fuckups.) Hallie woke at night screaming her mother's scream. Dan sat up in bed, covering his ears, waiting for someone to lay warm hands on him before he'd realize it was not his nightmare he was hearing. Then, barefooted, he would run into the bedroom to comfort her, lay her down beside him, give her body warmth at least. At most.

So it seemed as kind as anything else to leave Hallie stretched out in the dark of the stairwell, her back to one wall, feet extended to the other, sneaker tips straight up the bleary green that was black as exhaust with unchallenged shadow. Hallie Lavender was what they called her when she was a baby because the name was sweet, old-fashioned, smelled good. Music. Now he left her alone like one more drunk in a doorway. Why not?

They had insurance for Laura, at least so far; his teacher's insurance, a bad-luck lottery they'd won. Flushed with sympathy, the school district was giving him the year on leave. But he needed a job for the rest of them: they weren't going anywhere for a season or two. Sure he could steer, who couldn't steer, anyone who could drive (and his little horn-pipe): he drove a cab, numb enough to do it well. Every morning before work he went to see Laura. For months she pretended to be asleep. It was easy to seem so when nothing moved, awake. When they took the bandages off her face he sat at the edge of her peculiar bed, or the edge of a Jell-O-green plastic chair, and touched her with his fingertips. If she was upside down when he came he found some other place where skin could be arrived at simply. Usually she wore no clothes under the sheet. Her shoulders were stitched and scarred in fewer places than he dared believe from the beating of the rotors. He traced a finger across her bare skin; she could flinch. Still those shoulders made him weak in the solar plexus.

He talked to her about Hallie and Jon but censored their misery; told her about his fares, about events he managed to strain out of the muck of the *Daily News*, knowing she'd rather he read the *Times*. When it was time to go he bent, careful to put no weight on her delicately restrung bones, and kissed her lips. The mummies at the Metropolitan Museum, to which he'd dutifully taken the kids—the mummies, he thought, would have kissed him back more warmly. "You've got more flinch to the inch," he said to Laura. "Aren't you jealous?—the mummies love me." He'd walk back to get his cab, pull a ticket off the windshield wherever he was parked, rip it down the middle, drop it in the nearest can or shove it in the glove compartment. Sometimes he made a plane out of it and flew it nose-first into the gutter. Then he would drive into the New York day, trembling until the violence of the traffic pacified him.

Spring came to New York earlier than to home. It was open season for suicides; the newspaper flowered with them, done in for once by their own hands in their own way, in jail cells and double-locked apartments, in penthouses and garaged automobiles. He had become a student of annihilation, a remote nonpracticing member of a brotherhood. Anyone with a real taste for despair, he decided, had to make it to the city; Hyland just couldn't support a habit like the ones he saw around him.

Laura had moved next door, to the Rehabilitation Institute that was an arm (the immovable arm!) of the hospital. Sometimes the kids came, but there wasn't much to do once they'd had their tour of the therapy rooms. They got jumpy and Laura got depressed; they sat and looked at each other blankly, their children's lives elsewhere, Laura's right here.

The day before Dan went and told them she was leaving in the morning—he issued the news like a holdup threat, there was no appeal but to hand her over—he had two encounters in his cab that made him rest his head on the sweaty steering wheel and breathe deeply enough to hurt, and breathe again. And hurt again.

A child of about eight rode with him crosstown, Seventy-sixth and Third to Forty-sixth and Eighth: she was on her way, she said, to acting class. She reminded him of Hallie, mostly in the hair but something, too, about the intelligent ready way she held her head, her small pointed chin. Except that she had a voice he'd never have tolerated in a woman five times her age—fake innocent, as if she'd learned to play a little girl, shrewish and nippy underneath. She earned enough money from one TV commercial, she told him, not even proudly, to buy his taxi out from under him.

"It's not mine to sell, honey, or I'd give you a good price."

"Tant pis," she said, tucking her legs up under her like a real child. "You know, you're not very good at timing the lights. I hope you're new at this."

And just at 4:30, at turn-in time, an elegant old woman pleaded with him to take her to La Guardia. She had stood on the corner of Twenty-ninth and Fifth with her matched bags way out in the street undecided whether to be angry or humble, arguing in a voice worn clear through with age or drink, or both, that she would miss her plane now, that this was the impersonal cruelty, the *very* cruelty, that had destroyed the city she knew.

"You're right, you're right, but I got my troubles too," Dan had called out to her. All he did all day was hear voices, words, the up-and-down of disembodied argument, and now when he worked he sounded like a lifetime New Yorker. How much convenient inflection he had borrowed from his fellow cabbies, the real ones, not the tender visitors—that shruggy, combative, casually suffering style, for which he had to open his mouth wide. The old woman was right, of course, the price of survival was exorbitant. Even with Blue Shield. He couldn't tell if it was higher for an amateur like himself or if he only bruised easily. "I go to La Guardia now, my friend,

I'll be home at midnight" was what he told her, enjoying the
alien sound of his inflection that protected him at work like
a uniform. "No way. You ever see the cabbies lined up out
there? I got kids at home, they need their dinner too."

He did, as he'd threatened the woman, go home and cook
dinner. It was 6:30, then it was 7:00 and Hallie wasn't home.

Jonathan had been with her at the skating rink in Central Park. There were a few places they would go, routes they
trusted on the subway. They ventured forth carefully like
Hansel and Gretel through the dark part of the forest, though
never holding hands. The rink, they had told him, was the
only place that seemed even a little bit like Hyland (the very
littlest bit, Hallie insisted protectively), only the crowds were
sickening, you could get knocked down, hit and run, and the
ice never felt right, it wasn't cold enough and it was shredded
by too many blades. Still it was made of more familiar stuff
than anything else in sight; they had had their own skates
shipped to them, like a letter from home.

They'd wanted one last run, Jon said, before it closed for
the season. And Hallie had gone off—he'd met some kids
from school who actually seemed glad to see him, they pooled
their money and bought hot dogs and one bag of chestnuts
between them. He had seen her talking with a youngish-oldish
woman, nobody familiar. The woman was sharing a bag of
something with her, he couldn't tell what it was from the other
side of the rink. She looked okay, he said. They were looking
at Hallie's skates. He was happy to see her occupied or she'd
have bugged him for a hot dog, and come giggling between
him and his—friends. She was cool, he said. No sweat. Dan
wanted to throttle him.

"Did she have any money to get home?"

Jon shrugged. His eyes were darkening a shade with the beginnings of concern.

"Did she know how to get home, for godsake, does she know where she's going? She's a little girl, Jon."

"I know she's a little girl." He gave up his vague defiance. "I was talking to my friends." He thought hard. "You told us if we ever got lost we could go up to a cop."

Dan didn't say anything about the hundred circumstances that could prevent an eight-year-old girl from finding a cop.

But Jon couldn't describe the woman. She wasn't young, she wasn't old. She was wearing a sweatshirt or something like that, with printing across the front, but he couldn't read it. She had longish shortish hair, no color in particular. "Well, was she transparent? Jesus!" None of it was the kind of thing Jon noticed—if she'd been a car, he'd have known her blind-folded. Dan felt himself break into a fever; not sweat, nothing he could wipe away. It was an inner burning, a terror for Hallie and an embarrassment for himself: what will I say, what will I tell them? Another mortification. *Nobody's allowed two catastrophes.*

Only a demon would ask such a question, he thought, put it first, worry about it now. He ran downstairs, through the steep dark right over Hallie's place in the middle of the stairway. Halfway down the block he realized Jon was running behind him, crying out to wait. Couldn't he keep his mind on two children at once? Laura was the one who was good at coping with emergencies, he was master only of the emergencies of others, of the whole damn town of Hyland. The Rescue Squad squawker on his belt erupted into alarms, fire signals, ambulance calls, sometimes it roused him out of bed, but they were impersonal, those crises, not of his own making. He loved fire calls at two in the morning at 20° below; the howling of the whistle sounded like a faraway train. And he could help grandly, it was his only philanthropy. His own emergencies reduced him—what was the word they used for Laura's spine? —*comminuted*—reduced him to fine powders . . .

He hailed a cab. It looked just like his own, his company's. He probably knew the driver. But he was lying low. He slumped in back, his arm around Jon, clenched, making deals with himself that he knew were juvenile and all one-sided: if I find her, if she's still there. Then what? Would he never leave them again? Could he forbid them to go out and live their lives? There were Puerto Rican kids in their classes who were imprisoned after school, Hallie told him. He'd thought they were running in the streets, nobody home to take care of them. Stealing hubcaps, purses. Whatever moved. "No," said Hallie with a little stamp of her foot, "those are *different* kids, these kids sit and watch television all afternoon in the dark. They look out the window. There's one on our block, Enery, sometimes I wave to her up in the window. She's in fourth grade. Probably that's what makes some of them terrible the rest of the time." Probably. Smart girl. He held his breath the way he still did when he passed the graveyard on Route 8, his childhood habit: *Nothing bad will happen if I hold it to the corner.* Help me, help me, he pleaded to no one but himself. Help Hallie. Last time he tried this—Help Laura—it hadn't worked.

They got off on the Fifth Avenue side and ran through the park. "Maybe they'll knife us and finish us off," he muttered to Jon, who infuriated him by looking up all the time as if for protection. Courser the Crusher here, kid, don't look up at *me.*

The rink was deserted. Its ruined ice gleamed dull and bluish under the streetlamps, scarred everywhere with shadows. It felt like a fairground after the fair's moved on.

"Jon, I could kill you for this," Dan said without looking at his son. He was scouring the horizon: blue-black trees, blue-black sky. The ESSEX HOUSE lights glittering out of nowhere.

"Why is it my fault, I only—"

"You only—" But then, "Sssh," he told him, finger to his lips so as not to disturb someone. Something. He didn't know what. "Never mind. Jesus, don't cry, what good is that going to do." He held his son against him, tight. He was not the one to throw stones these days. Wouldn't Laura laugh.

As dark as the park had been, the precinct house was aglare with light, all its bulbs naked. There was an endless clatter and dull commotion, metal chairs on wooden floors and heavy feet in official black shoes, all of it amplified by Dan's desperation. The desperation made him strangely quiet, though; he must seem cool, even indifferent. He watched himself being inspected, saw the questions revolving in the bleak routine-glazed eyes of the interrogating cop, whose name tag said O'Heare. Drugs? he was silently asking himself, riffling his little deck of nasty possibilities. Foul play? Dan's open shirt collar was being assessed, his grey slipover under his parka. Money here? Kidnapping? O'Heare inquired after his wife. "In the hospital," Dan said. "That's why we're here, we really live in New Hampshire." Country cousin, O'Heare must have been thinking. Poor bastards don't know what's out there. Who do you think gets raped, gets taken for a ride, gets rolled? That Puerto Rican mother across the street who pens her daughter behind the window, she knows. "In the hospital," said O'Heare and wrote it down slowly, dutifully, pressing hard to get it through all his copies. "Sick?"

Dan looked away. "Accident. She's crippled."

"Un huh," O'Heare said and took another quick look at him.

"What was she wearing?"

Laura? A sheet. The cop looked so weary, Dan asked him, "This kind of thing happens a lot, hunh—kids disappearing—?"

"Coat? Dress, slacks?"

He raised his hands in despair. "I don't know, they get dressed themselves, I'm already—I go to visit my wife in the morning—"

"Her blue jacket," Jon offered, standing on his toes in front of the high desk. "She didn't have her hat, she left it in school."

"What else?"

Jon hung back. "I don't know. Pants I guess. Dungarees. I didn't notice." He put his heels down on the floor again, defeated.

O'Heare made slash marks on his multicopy sheet. He looked exasperated.

"Well, Jesus, would *you* know?" Dan asked him. He hadn't planned to defend himself. "Do you know what in the hell your kids wear in the morning? If I asked you right now, would you know?"

It may have been a fair question but the policeman would never acknowledge it. It didn't take very many words to turn relations gritty in this place. He would not like to have seen what O'Heare was thinking about him; he and Janet Riggs and Laura would all agree he was a dangerous man, to be watched. Count the accidents, don't count the good ordinary days of his life, they would whisper. Something's the matter with a man things happen to. If they didn't find Hallie he could imagine O'Heare going to his house and giving orders to search the apartment. Under the bed, in the closet. Behind the locked steel basement door he pretended held back the other eight million who knew how to take care of themselves.

They rode home in silence. Jon went to sleep in Dan's bed, looking for comfort. Dan drank two six-packs in very little time and fell asleep in his least comfortable chair. He woke up so engorged with beer he almost didn't make it to the bathroom. But there was that single blessed minute of reprieve between waking and flinging back the toilet seat, letting go, before he remembered Hallie was gone. Everything was *before* and *after*, okay, it was true but he thought he'd already learned that lesson. His life was becoming one long catastrophic event punctuated only by numb forgetting while he slept or dealt with his brainless body. The sound of the beer hitting the side of the bowl was like a hiss of disapproval.

He made Jon go to school; he was too sore for company. Skinless, he sat beside the phone. He called the Rehabilitation Institute and asked the nurse to tell Laura he had a bad cold. He called the police who told him they had found a girl aged approximately eight—found how? alive? whole?—but it didn't seem to be a good match. He hadn't had a picture to show them, how did they know what would make a good match? He was about to be belligerent.

"Does your daughter have a gold front tooth?"

He breathed again.

"You don't have to call us, Mr. Courser," they said. He didn't tell them he had no trust in them.

He stood at the window looking down on the street, its many shades of grey, real and accumulated. Which building held the captive child after school? Could she see him from where she was kept packed away like a precious stone? He was touched, thinking Enery, Energy, Enery, seeing her pacing in her cage. Who in the world, except her parents, would think of that kid, whoever she was, as a precious stone? He would; he volunteered, deep in his stricken parts, robbed and helpless, to stand watch with them over their child.

He slept, woke with his teeth clenched so hard his whole jaw hurt, slept again, going off in a sickening etherish wave of excess sleep that was useful only for forgetting.

At one o'clock, after a good deal of fumbling, a key turned in the lock and Hallie walked in looking at the floor. She was wrapped in a faded blue and white Fordham sweatshirt, her jacket gone. (So was her undershirt; it was a blessed while till he discovered that.) She answered him in monosyllables that had the quality of shock to them, or extreme guilty sullenness, how could he tell? She was as uninformative as an adolescent girl when her father provokes her with questions that aren't his business; or that she wishes weren't. Hallie who was no hider. He wanted to examine her, to run his fingers all around and in and over her delicate little girl's body that was neither a baby's nor a teenager's. As gently as he could, trying to suppress his anxiety, he asked, "Hal, will you come see a doctor with me? Please?"

He got the response the doctors down the block had hoped for when Laura was in her twilight state—anger, at least, made her quicken. "Daddy, what's the matter with you? There's nothing wrong with me except I'm sleepy. That's all."

"Didn't you sleep last night? Didn't they let you get any rest?" His jaws ached with anger.

" 'They,' what 'They'? I don't know why you're flapping around like that."

He wasn't flapping but he made himself sit down and be quiet. But waiting didn't help. She lay down on the couch, turned to the side so that her back was to him, her face hidden in the crook of her arm, and was instantly asleep. She looked, from where he watched, like a small, cozily rounded woman.

From where he watched, in fact, everything was floating off, just out of reach. His friends were a lifetime away; after today it was more than one lifetime. How could it be they'd been part of him forever? It was easy to forget why they were here: a day without his visit to Laura and even she drifted off to the corners of his memory. Before she died his mother had complained of "bits and pieces" floating around in her eyes; they weren't anything, she said, just rods and circles and dark shapes splitting off everything she looked at. It was her sight that was disintegrating, that was all. When he closed his eyes, faces, whole moving bodies, and Laura unmoving, shifted nervously behind them, cruising like fish in a tank. It was no dance, he knew; it was his life disintegrating.

He had to go to Laura and plead with her to tell him what to do. He was out of choices. Her sweet lap—hers and his mother's were equally beyond him now, foreclosed, untouchable in their various grown-over graves. *Was she going to live in public forever?* That was the question. They didn't allow laps over there. Deltoid muscles, biceps, triceps, laterals and pectorals, but nothing so intimate and undiscussable as a lap; nor anything so demanding of care or openness or ordinary affection as a husband. No one was allowed to need but the patient, why could he not understand that? Why did he fight them? They invited him to nurse her like the martyred mothers who lived in, or just about. Thank God he had a living to make. Her lap? "Her lap is functional as a shelf now, you see, where she may rest her hands and her devices."

She was theirs. No one's first and after that theirs.

When Hallie woke it was getting dark, the room seemed to be sinking into a vat of blue shadow that rose around it, slowly penetrating. Dan slammed doors in the kitchen, Jon was watching a screen devoted to Martians and cows who seemed to be sniffing each other with equal suspicion, and no wonder. Hallie walked into the kitchen in her stocking feet. She had no air of mystery about her, only a vaguely chastised quietness.

Dan put a pot of water on the narrow stove, for the endless spaghetti, and took her gently by the shoulders. There was some authority he could still muster, though he was down to the dregs. "Hallie Lavender, if you'll look right at me I'll tell you something good."

She thought about it, afraid, leaning her forehead into his buttons.

"Hal—?"

She squinted at him, trying not to look straight into his eyes. Now she had her portion of guilt, he thought. The year the Daniel Courser family of Hyland, New Hampshire, giving each other a shove where they could, learned to grovel. And God knows what else.

"You need your mother, sweet girl, don't you think I know that? So we're going to go get her tomorrow. And then what do you think?" Before her next of kin disintegrates. Let her doctor and her therapist join hands and howl! Before we all turn into Missing Persons. "And then we're going home."

He never broke promises. Now they would have to.

The sun does not come into the kitchen in the morning; winter at the breakfast table. Dan nurses his coffee mug, hands splayed around it to get some warmth. Shadowy as it is, it's better than East Twenty-second Street. It is eight o'clock; he is exhausted. The alarm has ripped through him three times since midnight, once when he was swimming in an endless pool, losing a race to a girl he'd known in high school who was built like a boy and in the dream swam naked, as the boys did. As she passed him, flooding his face with water, her breasts pulling up out of the pool, she turned and said a word to him but he didn't hear it. "What?" he called out. "What did you say?" but the alarm was dragging him up out of the water, dry.

I am dreaming: Riding to the funeral parlor together, a family-full. I almost knew their faces. The car thick, muffled in silence. That blank echo of snow just stopped falling.

Mother was going with us, we would wait for her to finish her dying when we got there. She did not complain.

They met her at the open door and took her away gently into a room as though she were the mother of herself, who needed comforting. We in the lobby, then in one of the chapels, an aimless animal milling, rehearsing the funeral before her death. They, helping her across the last single minutes of her death expertly and discreetly behind the door.

A man came walking across the endless carpet to us all. He took my hand and held it at a distance, he walked far out in front. The back door, a screen-slam. The coffin door. Somebody says they built these houses with an eye to everything. There was no surprise in it. We had brought her here.

The graveyard was the lovely shadowy old Tremont Street burying ground I've walked through a hundred times, thick with the dark and modest stones of Boston's famous families, Adams and Hopkins and Chauncy. Endless roar of cars gunning at the stoplight. A net of exhaust fell across us as we walked, we were greying everywhere. My deepest mourning that she would be buried here in a wind of candy wrappers.

She lay on top of the coffin, tilted, on a mound of grey

*carved flowers, but on her side, curled almost, comfortable,
a hand under her cheek. The sight of the arms, familiar,
still vibrating warm in old blue blouse-sleeves with cuffs I
remember turning twenty years ago and I heard a cry from
my own throat: No, I have lived with my arms all this
life! I have spent the whole of my sight looking down at
them, their shape, the way the little hairs lie.*

*And it was real, I was here, my arms bent sleeping.
They were stiffer. Heavier. My wrists were hardening to
stone. Someone, weeping suddenly, made a widow-sound,
a move like lunging to throw herself in the gravehole, and
I blinked my heavy eyes open to see who had ever loved
me so. The cool air hurt my face. Are there embalmer's
holes where the blood's sucked out? I know there was
only a cold space for a nose.*

*Then that voice crying out, running forward. Rough
arms around me, small, raising me from my hard bank of
flowers. My lids blinking against the cold. My pained face
forward to see. "You're alive!" Shaking me. "Mommy?"
Sitting up slowly there, all ruined holes, seeing the streaky
red then green of the streetlight at the corner, I sat all by
myself. No chrome, no plastic, no cold shiny eternal equipment umbilical to keep me up. I could sit and sit unen-
cumbered, I only had to die first for a while.*

*Waking among the stones free, my bare arms poked
pale out of the rolled sleeves. The wind, finger by finger,
was playing my face like a wooden flute.*

Laura lay beside him with a pillow behind her, a pillow
between her knees, her ankles. She was awake, staring into
the dark. He turned her to her other side, rearranged her legs
and put the pillow back beneath the pointy bones. In the

watery light just showing around the edges of the window, this was no more real or unreal than anything else in the world. If he bore down and thought about where he was, how Laura slept beside him, pieces of a jigsaw puzzle dropped and carefully put back together, a few small pieces lost; how if he lay up against her clenched in the good old way, melting back to sleep, he would burn a hole in her skin. (Mrs. Toko would shake her finger and scold.) Well, it had already begun to come loose anyway, when his mother died. How could he live in a world that she was not awake in? It unravelled, row after row of certainties, expectations, assumptions of how things should be; the threads came loose and dangled, connecting nothing. Nothing, apparently, had to be. His mother, Harriet Wardwell Courser, small and a little round, not the dieting kind, short-haired, nervous, kinder to her children than to herself, was and then was not. The world rushed on either way. Now he thought of her mostly at night; hauntings like that must become the ghosts grownups believe in. A chill sun is going to crack through any moment; it will wash the yard with light. The children will get their bowls of Cheerios and go watch a cartoon. The world does not consult you to find out if you think it's real.

Laura is still exhausted from the trip. When she wakes; when, that is, she acknowledges that her eyes are open, the morning ritual will begin: swipe of the washcloth, teeth done with an electric toothbrush, basin held under her chin; two kinds of elimination, one coerced, the other accomplished in a dozen separate steps, a matter of purging and making pure, of tinkering. He boils water in the biggest pot, to sterilize the irrigation equipment. He suspects it is no longer sterile when he gets it to her: doesn't air contaminate? Then there is the business of dressing. She can help by flinging her shoulder about like the jib of a sailboat, can facilitate the matter of pushing her arms into an orange and brown blouse she has directed him to pull out of her valise, which is still packed as if she is only stopping over.

This time he thinks it out first, carries her chair into the kitchen, picks her up knowing enough to dread the walk down the narrow stairs. "This is ridiculous," he mutters as he balances his shoulder against the inner wall, panting. "What would happen if you weighed twenty pounds more?" (Watching her at the pond with the other women: how compact she is, no stomach kneaded out of shape by the babies, no veiny pulpy thighs. Bending over Billy's rowboat, looking for Jon's sneaker, the perfect arc she makes. "A dancer's responsible for every part of herself," she had told him early on, "no outlying provinces unaccounted for." She'd wiggled her fingers and toes. Billy sits holding an oar across his lap. Dan gets the back view, tight and smooth, and Billy takes in the deep shadow between her breasts. He is too proud of her to mind; in real life poor Billy has Louise. After he's had enough of a look, Billy pulls Jon's sneaker out from under the seat and hands it to her, barely smiling.)

Dan makes breakfast silently, concentrating. There is toast, which she can pick up between thumb and forefinger if she raises her hand precisely. Everything depends on flexors and extensors. Without them, he thinks, vaguely amused, what would there be? No wars, no bowling.

Her hands are better than some because she wears a strip of plastic for a brace—color of old-fashioned eyeglasses, color of his mother's, in fact, never exactly the shade of anyone's flesh; when they rest on the arms of the chair they appear to be at peace, waiting, not heavy with immobility; that broken-winged crippled look shows only in movement. She manages to get the toast up, though she makes angles Dan would rather not have to look at. She manages a certain neatness he can barely aspire to, though, with all his limbs flexing and extending. She pats her mouth with her napkin; approximately her mouth. A few crumbs remain, and a gloss of butter on one cheek. He has seen her do all this before, silently, sullenly, at the Institute; she has shown him how she does it with the expression that might be seen on some captive's face when her master stops by to see how the stone-chipping goes. Now the first square patch of sunlight passes into the kitchen just beyond the foot pedals of her wheelchair. The children have gone out to play on the lawn. They seem to go out a lot. He should take them into town today to see their friends. (It is a school day, he remembers. Later then.) It takes her fifteen minutes to eat her piece of toast and wipe her cheek. She sips her coffee lukewarm through a very long straw. Once, at the Institute, when she picked up a glass—however she managed to, in her paws—the weight of it tipped her over.

"I'll give you your choice, Dan," she says to him now, looking at the sun patch that's about to arrive at her feet like a spotlight. "Laugh or congratulate me, either one. Nothing you can do is worse than sitting there pretending you think everybody eats breakfast this way."

These words are the most inviting she has said to him in months. Every part of him lurches as if the kitchen floor has become a deck in rough weather. There is a cold wind blowing on his feet.

"Goddamn kids left the front door open," he says and rushes to close it.

When he comes back he tries to do the last half hour over again, this time without the awkwardness. He would say he knows the risk; nonetheless he tells Laura, "Well, you always wanted to slow down, honey. Second cup of coffee, a

little music. You want some music?" He makes for the radio,
smiling. She will know bitterness when she sees it.

But she is looking at him as if she may or may not know
him, though he is standing in her kitchen, leaning his elbows
on the counter and twisting the dial of the radio, stopping at
the overexcited voices of disk jockeys, getting them perfect,
right into the throat of the noise, moving off, then, into a
long spill of Muzak.

"Lousy," he mutters and turns it off. "Save you the trouble
of objecting." His face is redder than she has ever seen it. He
looks straight at her. "Damned if I do and damned if I don't,
right?"

Laura's eyes narrow a little. She knows him. "Get a taste
of it," she says.

Secretly I breathe in, hold, breathe out, hold, breathe in.

*Dan's head darkens for me. Fading color, a nimbus
around his shoulders, light withdrawing. Stipple and shadow, black against white, flashing. White against black.
Goddamn him, I will not faint in my own kitchen. I will
not faint. When I was two or three or four years old, I
would hold my breath. Everything darkened. The way the
movies go dim before the curtains open: light sucked away.
I would do it to myself and then I'd wake up gasping—
maybe it was only a minute—but I'd be safe, on the other
side of whatever made me angry. It was a going blind.
My body going blind.*

Even if the sun barely penetrates the kitchen Dan loves
the room; he loves every room in the house and, after a boyhood of wardrobes and boxes and piles of clothes against the

wall, loves every one of its numerous closets. Every time he has stashed something in one of them or in the basement or the high solid attic, he's said the same thing: "They'll never get us out of this place alive. With a crowbar, in a coffin, but not walking." Could this be the same man who came through the jimmied windows of those camps and exclaimed over the opulence of those second sets of dishes? Everything he had he stole into then; now—before the qualification of the present —he has had Laura, has had a job going into its seventh year, and a reputation for energy if not precisely for steadiness; he has a house that still astounds him. His wife and his house, in fact, seem to him to have come on the same lucky gene: given more than earned, though not *entirely* given. Good luck is as perplexing as bad, he is willing to consider that—responsibility may be braided somewhere into it, obscurely; or may not be. (Laura has told him that an ability to think two things at once is a form of higher thought, intellectual capability. Some of his Neanderthal friends, she says, can barely handle one. Does she respect confusion and uncertainty? She uses the word "ambivalence," or "ambiguity," the word "complexity": it is apparently the highest compliment she can pay anything, that it is forked, divided, irresolute. That it is *debatable*. Dan has lived two-thirds of his life among emphatic men; maybe the women are always something else but the men, right or wrong, meant what they meant, brooked no uncertainties. People who hesitated were flabby, half-assed, some physical mockery of men. They stepped hard and frequently smashed what they stepped on.)

The house was in the family; the family, like most, had branches so unlike one another it seemed inconceivable they shared the same roots. Many by now were total strangers. Dan knows there is a Courser in the legislature; there is a genteel painter of great local fame, Queen of the Gift Shoppes, named

Check Out Receipt

Cincinnatus-Kellogg Free Library
607-863-4300
http://kelloggfreelibrary.org

Wednesday, May 10, 2023 3:02:30 PM
08197

Item: A20521276295
Title: Tender mercies
Due: 5/31/2023

Total items: 1

Kellogg Free Library Hours
Monday: Closed
Tuesday: 1pm-7pm
Wednesday: 1pm-5pm
Thursday: 1pm-7pm
Friday: 9:30am-11:30am/1pm-5pm
Saturday: 9am-1pm

Aimée Courser de la Petre, which gets the Courser pronounced Coor-say. Then there was Kenton Courser, long gone, and Uncle John who had an automobile seat for a couch and pigs living under his trailer.

Dan lived, he guessed, somewhere near the exact middle of the spread of the Courser fortunes. (What was his work, seven years in the shop department at the Hampshire River High School? Neither white nor exactly blue, he called his job grey-collar.) The year of their marriage, his Aunt Jemmie had taken a cursory look at Laura; had recognized her fine "lines," studied them, Laura complained, like those of a horse; had identified, or so she thought, an ally against the more wretched, if democratic, tendencies of the Working Coursers, the nonworking Coursers, the farm and mill Coursers; had rewritten her will to bequeath her house to the newlyweds on condition that they make no significant changes beyond what was minimally necessary to secure their comfort. Then, rather than put herself to the trouble of dying, she removed herself to an alternative home in Palm Beach, where the winters were more considerate of the limitations of age. To Dan and Laura in the vigor of their youth and health she left the boorish New Hampshire weather and the house. Once in a while she wrote them cheerful postcards, Mediterranean blue shoreline and unreal Everglades birds hanging out their wings to dry in the perpetual sunlight; she inquired after the health of the house as if it were some dear chronic invalid relative entrusted to their care. They wrote back in more detail than she hoped for, and sent pictures of its unchanging face. Only the children, sitting on the rim of the well or balanced too precariously on the stone wall on one foot apiece, were allowed to change: they were true to her will.

Aunt Jemmie's house was very old—only 120 years older than she, not so very impossible to imagine, really—and it must have been elegant from the start, must have belonged to a family with pretensions, otherwise it would never have had such high ceilings or been set so far back from the road. It was still and always would be referred to as the General Bolt house by the Friends of the Hyland Historical Society. It might be a Courser place forever, Dan could remake it into an igloo or a hacienda; still it would revert—snobbery, pride, he couldn't say which but it redounded to his credit one way or the other and delighted him. General Jonas Bolt had ridden out to a single battle in the War of 1812 and then, for obscure reasons not accounted for in the Town History, ridden right back again without having dirtied his uniform. Possibly he didn't deserve to be remembered as a general, but as a builder he had accomplished a work of such nobility of lines ("like a horse?" suggested Laura again) that there were times, angles, from which Dan saw the house—say, from the garden, looking up from the turned row that was receiving a handful of carrot seeds—that made him stop and stare, humbled. It was no cottage but a monument. A fine, ample, unpretentious, unadorned, thoroughly conventional monument of its time, probably, but anyone who'd built as much as Dan knew true proportion when he saw it, and grace, and permanence. General Bolt had seen to the raising of the giant summer beam and the laying of the fireplace arch in the basement that looked like a quarter of a Roman aqueduct. He had buried his two wives in the back pasture under what was now a crude tractor shed, and so the house stayed his, and deserved to.

Dan had rarely been troubled by concerns with history and the ironies of time passing, but the house and his rightful, legal, documented ownership of it were enough to impress and incite him to learn what his history teachers had despaired of teaching him.

He could see the general, who was really a farmer, bending over his own row of carrots, of feed corn, broom corn for his wife and daughters to gather together to sweep the hearth with. He could see the wagon parked in the shed, and the same mountain, unmoving, teased by clouds, out the twelve-on-twelve side windows.

Somewhere along the line the Bolt and Courser families joined; eventually there were a dozen Courser houses and this was only one. It had got away from the family for a while and was brought back into the fold around the turn of the century. Widowed Aunt Jemmie closed off half the house and raised two daughters in the rest, and they went west with husbands. (She'd had no sons, praise her, since sons were the ones who held on to land.) So the dark horse got it, the youngest nephew, the one who had married class back into the family. (Clearly Aunt Jemmie thought Laura was insane for marrying a Courser, but that madness was the only short-coming Aunt could see.) John, his brother, fumed and kicked stones, but it was John's misfortune, perpetually, that for every stone he brutalized he had only a bruised toe to show for it. He inherited the smallest of the Courser houses, a straightforward little Cape with no charm and no elbow room.

Dan installed a dozen lightning rods, rewired, replumbed, painted the whole huge hulk with forty gallons of primer and good barn-red paint, reaching from a terrifying ladder; sanded the floors; polished the innards of its central chimney till the old handmade bricks gleamed. He listened for voices in the walls, discovered an 1850 newspaper stuck sideways to the back of a closet and read it off with something like pride, as though he'd excavated for it: *Dr. D. K. Boutelle, dentist of Concord, was discovered mortally wounded at the side of the Manchester and Lawrence Railroad Co. tracks approaching his native town, on the north side.* CHOLERA INFANTUM—*No mother need ever mourn the death of her child by that infant-destroying complaint when* TEETHING *in warm weather!*

There was a choice of rooms for everything. He felt like Goldilocks, deciding all the time. The first few times he and Laura made love there, he speculated, filled with a wonderfully augmented, magnified, strangely anonymous ardor, on the sexual habits of General Bolt and his first consort Molly, the wife of his youth. "They must have slept up here, it's the logical room for the Parents of the House, isn't it? Even then?" A shrug from Laura. "Eight kids, cold winters, all that nursing, all those *clothes*—in and out, before she knew it, I'll bet. Consider yourself lucky, woman."

Laura seemed to find such inquiries blasphemous, or just plain silly. "Poor woman died at forty-one, honey, can't you let her old ghost rest?"

"She's had a hundred and seventy-five years to rest."

"But she never thought the kind of thoughts you're thinking, you terrible man. You're part of the Licentious Generation, don't you know that? Women like Molly Bolt, Beloved Consort, weren't allowed—"

But Dan said "Bullshit" to that. "You think we discovered laughing in the dark?" It was the only instance he knew where he opted for complexity and shading and Laura, strangely modest and unmoved, let things be: maybe because they were his people? The secret lives of his relatives, the passions beneath the nightcaps and flannel gowns, the stirrings of dream and feeling in those suppressed hardworking dutiful people who were also—elegant? ambitious? "Human," he said to Laura, disturbed and stimulated, profoundly so. "Human."

Laura was amused. She thought it was that he had been deprived of family history and was making up for it with clichés. Kenton Courser was not an ancestor worth speculating on; he was more like a derelict son. But Dan said no, that wasn't it. The house had spirits in it, the residue of all the love and work of two hundred years. The candles dipped, wicks trimmed, tomatoes canned, turnips buried for the winter. Thousands of *everything*, year in, year out, everything chafing: feet on the doorstep that had still not begun to wear it down; feet on the hearth, the thresholds. The size and shape of the rooms memorized, moved through. The black wrought-iron brace on the front of the fireplace would never buckle. Never: if the house fell in around it, it would hold. The cellar stairs, those half-logs, pegged, still spiny with splinters. Maybe it had to do with working with your hands, Dan said, with tools, with all the stubborn materials you had to prod and make into their own best shapes, going with the grain, building to last. If every movement or passion evaporated in its instant. . . . He thought of his mother who ate dinner in her apron, whose red hands never healed.

"I think I hear religion nudging the old Courser atheism somewhere," Laura teased him. "Don't tell me your Daddy went to hell for nothing."

"Not religion but, I don't know." Some kind of memory? "Listen, why are you laughing, that's not fair. Here I am trying to be serious, but you only like it when I'm serious about *your* subjects. Jesus, Castro. Ingmar Bergman! Why are you making me defend myself?"

So he was left alone with the extra dimension of his love for the house. Laura appreciated its size, certainly, its appointments, the fine presence of it, turned towards the sun on its small knoll above the road, so that it was easy to drive past and never see it. At night, lit up, it was like a great ship breasting the waves, a ship on which a party was always raging in full light. But she seemed purposely unsentimental about its history. She had the house off Brattle Street, maybe

one house was all you reasonably had the energy to love? Dan
fingered the forged iron, the door hasps, tried to date the
feathering on the living room walls (made with a cross-cut
saw, which means renovation after 1850?) and went on medi-
tating on the imagined personalities and faces of his ancestors,
dozens of Bolts and Coursers, Voigts and Conners, with a
fierce pride. He shared the house with them. He was their
loving tenant.

Amputation: to cut away the thresholds. To hack at the
doorways. The front step? The stairs (there are four stairways
in the General Bolt house, two steep, two gentle). The kitchen
doorway is like the neck of an hourglass, wide at both ends,
pinched in the middle. The house is on a hill, a curve, far from
anything but woods. (And the hill and curve just severe
enough so the town has placed a sand barrel on its side on the
margin of the uphill lane. When there's enough snow down
to need it, it can't be found under the drifts the plow has
made. He sees Laura rolling down the hill in the barrel; at
the foot of the hill, the cars stop at the blinking light to let
her through. "Oh it's only Laura Courser going shopping,"
they say. "Look how she gets around. Isn't it *wicked?*")

They would do better in Uncle John's trailer, pigs and all.
Dan looks out the window at the dwindled woodpile. One of
the early Coursers (when this, where he's sitting, was the
summer kitchen, the keeping room) was blind. He had knelt
in the soil and fingered his way down the furrows, trying to
get his crops in straight. He sang in public with two blind
brothers, his first wife left him, his daughter stayed. There is
the possibility that he killed himself; it is unclear, shadowed,
in the box marked COURSER in the temperature-controlled
records room at the Historical Society. Laura has sharp eyes

for him, but look, he had her fingers! Collaboration over time. What a match. In the long history of the world they've only missed each other by a blink. Unfair!

She will wheel herself down the long living room soon and come to the kitchen door, between cabinets, the neck of the hourglass, and she will want to pass through. He drove a truck one summer and got it caught in an overpass. How they cursed him. He skinned the whole top of the truck off, peeled it back and left it naked. Jesum Crow, said John, next time want us to lift the bridge? Rich Laura—but this is cruel and he chases after it to throttle it down—will get stuck in the eye of the needle. He chases the thought (which comes with a flash of the Shurrocks' shameless library) but he cannot catch it.

I sent Jon to the basement to look for the blacksnake family that comes with spring. "Too late," he said, more or less, "or too early or moved or died." I'd have gone down to visit the snake mother, shiny as water, and her long babies. Shown her myself on my stomach, how close we've come.

She always liked to stay near the wall but it wasn't enough, Jon. Nothing is.

John Courser is taller, thinner, more pallid than his brother. He has a high narrow forehead and a worried manner. To Dan he has always looked like an unhappy intellectual. In fact he is a severe and nervous man as he was a severe and nervous boy, not much fun, prone to secrecy, headaches and an improbable morality. He is no intellectual. As it happens, though, his frown impresses employers, bank managers, all those bureaucrats whose job it is to read a man's reliability in the set of his features. The consensus seems to be that anyone who looks so burdened must be tending to his business. He has not done badly; in fact, having convinced these people to give him mortgages, loans, credit ratings, John has begun to have some confidence in his powers. Most of his life it has been his clown brother who has charmed himself behind locked doors. John owns the gas station at the foot of Route 8 and Mill Circuit Road where he is reported to be able to fix anything on wheels, cheap, honest, fast. The station has John's cheerless look, though. Laura hates it and insists it isn't snobbery: the place, she says, is blighted by its earnestness, as if adornment were cheating. For all its business, it looks abandoned. John has the unfrivolous zeal of a fundamentalist, but no religion and not much holy joy.

This morning he is at Dan's door. He has not bothered himself to distinguish between concern and curiosity. If he plans to be kind it will only be for Laura's sake.

"Hey Buz," his brother says, the door half open. "How'd you know we were home?" (Buz is short for Buzzard, the name John gave to himself as a child because he had no hunting luck, never caught anything, never even got anything to slow *down.*)

"Danny," John says, getting right to it. "How's your wife?"

John is embarrassed to say Laura's name and always has been, so that Dan has sometimes wondered if what ties him up right there is a little charge of feeling, like a shot of scotch, warm, sudden and over with.

"She's fine." He shrugs. "Considering."

They are standing at the threshold.

"Can't I come in and say hello?"

Dan makes a small uncontrollable movement of defense.

"She's—not altogether up yet, I wouldn't—it's quite a production."

John drops back. "Oh. I tried to wait till a decent hour."

"What if I call you. Maybe you and Donna."

"I'll be at work."

"Well, later. Tonight."

John takes a long look at his brother, trying to imagine how wrecked Laura could be that he needs to be so pathetic and evasive and insulting. The idea of Dan's guilt arouses strong feelings in him which make him sigh, a long irritated exhalation, like that of a horse. It is more complicated than comforting to have your worst fears confirmed. "Dan, look, let me say hello to her. I've got to see her sometime." He forces through his clenched reticence as simple a smile as he can manage. "Doesn't she need some cheering up?"

"Why in the hell are you so eager to see her?"

John realizes now how tense he is, how every part of him is a fist. He is shocked at the bareness of the question. "She's my—she's your wife, fella, do I have to have some special reason to want to see how she is?"

"I just told you how she is." Dan wants to say "Off limits to you now, isn't she, baby." He wants to say "Don't gloat in my doorway, Buzzard. Aren't you glad I finally got mine." It occurs to him, though, that John will not gloat in Laura's presence. He is not that unkind.

"All right, come say hello. Maybe she'd like that, she doesn't have much to do."

"Thanks," John says, but he's not adept at sarcasm and sounds grateful. He follows his brother in.

Dan wants to inflict what pain he can; he says nothing to prepare John. Laura is on the sunporch facing the windows that are silvery with light. Her idleness is like an occupation, it takes her full attention. Dan watches his brother stiffen at

the sight of her and hopes two things at once: that he manage
not to make her unhappy and that he say some outrageous
thing that will earn him the right to be k.o.'d right there,
bloodily, arm pinned, knee in his gut. When they were teenagers John broke his collarbone and would not be sorry.
They'll settle up someday.

John and Laura are talking. Although there is a chair to
sit in, John is squatting in front of her, holding her hand
quite casually; as if it isn't hard to touch her. Laura's face is
pink and mobile, it makes the face she shows Dan look like
a putty mask.

She seems to be telling his brother, quietly, there were a
thousand more things she could have learned if she'd stayed
in New York. John is a mechanic; he is asking mechanical
questions. Then he says something Dan can't hear. From the
back his head bobs as if he's nodding.

"Well, he did a real Dan," she answers and the two of
them laugh shyly. The characteristics of a "Dan" appear to
be familiar, ridiculous, a matter of public history. He feels as
if he's eavesdropping.

John gives him the big brother's eye. John would frown
if he were feather-tickled on the soles of his feet. "Sounds like
somebody told you to get out of town by sundown."

"You could say that." But he is going to hold his ground.
He has swallowed the evidence: Hallie's defection, his helplessness. "I did what was best for all of us." But this has no
conviction in the absence of the facts.

They have closed ranks. John kisses the top of Laura's
cropped head (though he has never before ventured near her)
and raps her shoulder reassuringly as if she were a pitcher in
the middle of a bad inning, but one to whom he's just given
the advice and the spirit to get out of it alive. He walks to the

door without a word, looks at Dan briefly, knowingly, and leaves.

"You seem to know each other pretty well."

"This is really the time for your routine jealousies," Laura says without much passion. "You still sound like you've borrowed a television script, a really rotten lousy one, from some kind of show we never watch. 'You seem to know each other pretty well.' Why don't you leer at me when you say that? Imagine our secret passion, all these years." She hangs her head, chin on her chest, a massive movement in her rapt unmoving. "All this thing is proving to me is that you don't have any style. No style at all."

"I didn't know you married me for my style." He offers his weak defense stiffly. "But if you want to talk about style, I always thought my brother wasn't one of your favorite people." He is feeling more and more exposed: why is he standing on this ledge, caught in a high beam?

"That was when you were. And now that you're not—"

What? he thinks. And now *what?* Who finishes that sentence, and how?

He stands beside her, facing the same window through which a bleached sun sends its harshest light. He watches, weary, as she tries to do her little dance, the closest she'll come to one, her weight shift to relieve one sitting cheek and then the other. She straightens her arms to their full length, elbows locked, and leans forward on them, hangs there. Air, nothing, half an inch of cool relief against her flank. The stomach muscles she doesn't have must quiver; the memory of them. She is gasping with the effort.

"Do you want some help?"

"I don't want anything, thank you."

Her dignity has no dignity in it, it is mere blunt courage:

stepping down hard on sharp splintered bone. Something is stalled but is going to begin. His impatience tells him that if it doesn't happen naturally he will make it happen. Even endings begin. He knows she would leave him if she could. He knows it's supposed to be the other way around.

Why did I have to survive myself?

Let me be one of the casualties no one would dare call "courageous" and "noble." Courageous and noble hurt too much. . . . Let them put me away somewhere and mourn me and be done. I could rest, he could rest, some-one would turn the key and separate us once and for all and then I would be his late Laura. Non compos mentis. Non compos corpus. Fondly remembered.

Everyone needs to know where the escape door is. Short of starving, I couldn't kill myself if I wanted to.

Short of anything I couldn't kill him.

The house, lit, does appear to be the scene of an endless party. Tonight there are a dozen and a half visitors warm inside; the driveway is as packed as a parking lot.

The party is an accident. In the afternoon the children can't wait to be alone with their mother. Partly to oblige them, partly to regain his breath, Dan goes out after lunch to do some shopping, to buy the paper whose typeface has been replaced in his memory by the agitated style of the New York *Daily News.* The children have insisted they can take care of Laura; she is their new project. Hallie is planning entertainment for her, Jon refreshment. They go at their responsibility with the intensity of rookie babysitters. To start it off precisely right Jon walks his father to the door, the host of the house. "Don't worry, nothing can happen," he assures his father. "Just don't stay away too long."

"Gotcha." Dan rumples his hair, which is not his gesture but the kind that belongs to fathers who wink, who are called "Pop" by wide-eyed apple-cheeked children on soundstages. "Hold the fort."

"Dad?" (But Dan will not wink.) Jon lowers his voice confidentially. "Can you get us something?"

"What do you need, Jonathan? Shaving cream? *Playboy?*"

"No, I mean—you know, something—good."

"You're talking about a payoff. Listen, pal—"

Jon is caught somewhere between fear and embarrassment.

"You expect me to pay a tax every time you do something considerate for your mother? I don't know which'll happen first, I'll go broke or all your teeth'll fall out."

"No, not for that." Jonathan, behind the storm door, is suddenly shy. He shrugs. "Just—because."

"Oh, your charming smile, your honesty. You highway robber." You earnest eager honey-flavored boy, you hybrid winner. Why not? What the hell. "A Milky Way for you and an Almond Joy for Hallie. Will that hold you?" Jon, who knows he and his sister deserve something they had better not ask for, smiles.

This afternoon the trees are in bud, lime-green: it happens all in a day. Everything will fall into place now. New York is a feeble dream, a distant memory he can easily convince himself never happened. (The day before yesterday, no, three days ago, when Hallie was gone, he couldn't remember Laura's face.) Anything can be beaten down with enough attention to the path of blacktop just ahead. Provided you stay awake, you don't crack up first. And keep in shape. When your guard goes down, everything competes to be called *real*. Me, me, no, me. He sees the kids at school breaking their arms to be called on—oooh, oooh, Mr. Courser! imitating real pain. But reality doesn't have to be picked out of the class, there it is suddenly. . . .

On Main Street he makes his habitual U turn into the angled parking bays in front of Hatfield's Books & Stationery. There is an impatient rapping at his window, a big face staring in, anxious, flat-up like a child's at the bakery. He rolls the window down—"Not one but three signs up there and they all say 'No U turn' "—and round-bellied Benny Sheehan in his worn blue uniform stops midsentence. "Danny! When'd you get back? Jesus!"

So it begins. Benny walks him in to see Jay Hatfield as he would escort an apprehended thief across the street and into the police station. He does not know how to walk any more without hovering.

Jay Hatfield, with a new mustache, is stacking boxes out back but comes to him so quickly Dan thinks he must have left them hanging in midair like the Road Runner in his cartoon. He talks quietly to Jay and Benny, who are outraged that the Bickfords got to Dan and Laura before they did— how did they do it, that's the mystery and it's worth a good deal of speculation. Dan feels himself waiting. He has a net out and people are swimming into it. How obedient they are. Well, he's the only show in town. Imagine New York. He sees Second Avenue, his least favorite place to drive, all the Bumper Cars hightailing it downtown, rolling, free falling from left to right and back again, lane to lane, braiding traffic, the fire lane clogged (Hallie and Jon worried a lot about the fire lane, they put a lot of energy into praying it clear and open just in case. He wondered if all children were as sensitive to the imminence of disaster.) But even there—a month ago he was walking the kids on Fifty-ninth Street, they were standing in front of a vendor who had a car-trunkful of stolen meat, and was selling it faster than radios and leather belts, before the cops could discover him—holding up each great red rack of it like a newborn baby by the heels—and there were Natty and Janet Riggs, pretending not to see them, turned to look into the window of a store they would sooner die than shop in. Dan saw their faces in the window, muffled but undeniably theirs. He smiled and hoped they saw his reflection smiling, turning away.

In Hyland, the rate at which they swim up is daunting. Or it's because he knows them all: Miralee Guyette throws her arms around him with an emotion he finds half touching, half absurd. She rests her head on his shoulder. He reassures her: "Miralee, hey, it's okay. Nobody died, you know." He has tried, his whole life long, to get close to that chestful she's lugged from the seventh grade on; she with her tiny innocent face that seems not to acknowledge herself from the neck down. Her hair is an artificial grey—strange. It's impossible to get close to her across that fortress of bosom, he wouldn't have guessed. Chet Guyette comes in behind her; the door swings mightily. He raises a hand as if to say *"There you are!"* puts a long arm around him, gathers him in the way he must his wife for comfort, large, commanding, forgiving. There is emotion in the air, a fierce charged elation. *He's back, Danny's back*—but the faces cave, one by one, after the easy moment of greeting. They are so glad to see him, sincerely, and so surprised, that they forget why he's been gone. Then they remember.

After a while it looks as if Jay Hatfield is giving a party. Dan stands beside the counter holding a newspaper which Jay won't let him pay for. (How insulting good people's good will can be. One needs a home-grown ingratitude to understand how it's going to make its victims feel.) There is an air space, eye space, in the middle of the crowd which is the place he stands in. He is relieved to learn he can breathe in it, at least. They ask such kind and timid questions, but thank God they are still here, these people he's logged a thousand thousand hours with, and they still love him. He watches the love hang from a distance, crystals of it, hard, permanent, apparently unkillable. He wonders if it has anything to do with him or only with the space he has always stood in, *Danny Courser's place.* Or is that him, all there really is of him? He didn't fare so well out of it in New York, he didn't cast a shadow.

It is his gratitude: in response, before he can stop himself he has called out "Listen! Everybody! Laura wants me to invite you all over to the house tonight. She said if I saw anybody. . . . Come on and see she's not so bad off as you think."

They demur. He insists.

They are relieved, delighted. He tries not to think about what he's done, he is like someone overspending at the store, running up such debts anyone with sense should stop him, ask if he's got the wherewithal. He is the man the bartender should have ejected. Jay is the bartender, but he is rubbing his hands together; for a quiet man he can't get enough of parties, he drinks himself into total silence, smiling, shyly touching the women, nodding at their husbands as if he's only doing his duty.

"Call Sandy Mead. And Roger. Call Gordy, huh? Is Annette around, that whole crew out there?"

Miralee promises they will bring food at least. "Dips 'n' desserts."

"Like a wake," Dan says, coming back down.

"Silly, like a picnic." She is laughing, backing away to get started in the kitchen. "And some cakes, cookies, petit-fores. For Laura, petit-fores."

Her husband gives her a pursed look. *"Miralee."*

Let them check out Laura and back away some more.

"We'll bring the beer. And remember. Don't fuss, Danny, we know you've got your hands full. Just open the door for us and then relax."

"Laura will be tickled," he says and leans against the swinging door with his shoulder. (Look Laura, no hands!) "Thanks, Jay," he calls back, tipping the paper beside his head like a hat. He has left them in there to talk about him.

He takes a long time shopping: the children will be upset. But he's afraid to go home and tell Laura what he's done. Instead he invites a few more people at the A & P. They can't wait to come, can't wait. He stops off at his brother's station and invites him too. John, at least his white eyes, gives him an incredulous look from beneath his chimney-sweep's dirty face. "Did Laura really say—" but then he stops. "Donna's got bowling but she'll break it," he says and goes back under the grease rack.

Hallie and Jon meet him at the door, jumping like two-year-olds, but he's forgotten the candy. Standing in the center of the kitchen, imagining himself in the space again with all their friends—his friends—around ("For Laura, petit-fores," that bitch) he lets it become a surprise party. She's never had one before.

Sitting still has nothing to do with resting. They are at odds. I am at odds. Trucks change gear passing the house, just at the mailbox they do it, grinding and gasping, the only thing I hear facing back towards the garden is the sound of huge animals climbing out of breath.

I see my husband then running around the side of the house that muffled way I remember, sitting a little on his heels, that crouch that feels noiseless. He is holding a two-by-two in his hands in front of him, cradled, a scepter. His

*shadow runs out ahead, swings sharply as he turns and
stops. The woodchuck, brown and still as a stump, is busy
fattening on last year's parsnip greens, cropping down the
row. (What ever became of last year's garden? The season
drowned with me and all that green.) This one is pudgy
and its back is turned. Dan moves up a foot a minute, he
never ripples the grass. I don't know about his face, from
behind he all flows into the club. He raises his arms as
slowly as I do. Holds and holds and I know the animal
will feel him, smell him, stop, turn, run, but it doesn't. It
crouches like something small at prayer; it will die gorg-
ing. Dan makes a noise like a Samurai, I can hear it through
the glass, and (I close my eyes) bashes the bent head. (It
squeals. I open them.) And bashes and batters it—his heels
come right off the ground—until the squealing stops.
The two-by-two is bloody halfway up. He kicks the carcass
with his toe and then turns and is angry, his face is angry
at the woodchuck. Maybe it should have saved itself. He
is walking back carefully now, picking his way through the
unplanted garden, its muddy rows, putting his feet, his
sneakers, down precisely as a horse's hooves, for the sake
of their whiteness. I have to recognize this man. He has
killed woodchucks before. "It's us or the woodchucks," he
says each year and I agree, their blood baptizes the peas,
the carrots. He does it with a gun like game, stands behind
the broadest apple tree to hide and fire, more cowardly
than clubbing. But I look hard at his angry face, angry
myself. He drops the square club in the barbecue pit, without looking lets it go and comes on walking. He disappears
around the side of the house. One day he will never come
around into my sight again.*

. . . .

Their house has no doorbell. You do not even enter at the
formal center door; maybe you did in 1790 but now there
isn't so much as a path across the grass to get you there. You
enter the mudroom alongside the kitchen, which used to be
the wagon shed. (It's one thing to own a beautiful house,
another to put on airs; they would all have to be different
people to want to come in by the grand entrance, looking for
a place to lean a baseball bat or put down a bottleful of
insects.) As to the doorbell, Dan has always thought (he's
impressed by Aunt Jemmie's purity in the matter) doorbells
are so—anachronistic, Laura ventures. Just out of place, he
answers, whatever else. Of course he could install one, *Jon*
could install one, but imagine General Bolt with a little canned
"bing bong." ("Oh, imagine your General Bolt with a dish-
washer, honey, a shower, a dryer, a blender. Do you think he
blew up his hair like whipping cream every morning the way
you do?" But she kisses him as she says this, just at the bottom
edge of that layered froth of hair. His spotty vanity amuses
her, she condescends to it whenever she can.)

Instead of anything electric there is a long string of golden
sheepbells Laura bought in Greece one summer. They hang
by a ribbon on the heavy mudroom door, a mild affront to
the portion of the Hyland populace that has reason to call on
the Coursers. Inside, the house is lively and foreign, as the
bells warn it may be: a rug from Chile and one of those
strange stringy hangings with knots in it from somewhere.
Colombia? It is all Laura, the interesting unmatched furniture,
the hanging pots that look like they've been dug up in the
yard. There are no ruffles and there is little shine on the sur-
faces. It is not taste to be proud of, their friends think, nor to
make the house proud, but they seem happy enough with it;
even Dan who grew up with scuffs and unmatched furniture
of no particular period seems happy enough. He has a collec-

tion of stolen road signs, spiced with a few stark printed direc-
tives from the Walpole jail.

For an hour, from 7:30 to 8:30, the sheepbells have been
jingling, the door opening on another and another. Billy
Bickford and Louise, proprietary, are leading the guided tours.
After the first few arrivals Dan decides to be in any room
but the one in which her friends first confront Laura. He has
seen Miralee come laughing in—she seems to fan the air into
action around herself—and turn before his eyes, before Laura's,
to a pillar of sugar. Dan would have preferred salt but she was
not consulting him: on her own she oozed hope and delight
so strenuously that Dan wanted to put her out of the house.
Had Laura become Miss America? Dougie MacDermott appears, breathless, all angel blond curls. He has tried to become
a musical comedy star and has gotten as far as the Laconia
Summer Theatre (going to Broadway, his friends say, by the
North Pole route); has grudgingly taken on the role of
Hyland's star furniture salesman in the meantime. (Laura:
"What's the difference between Dougie and Harpo Marx?"
Dan: "Dougie's sexier? I don't know—what?" Laura: "Dougie
can't play the harp.") Dougie goes down on one knee, arms
spread, in full theatrical cry. He seizes one of Laura's hands
from its limp curve on the arm of her chair and tries to kiss it.
Noble try, Dan thinks, the ass. They are astounded, call out,
come running: she is falling forward. She lands with her head
tucked to her knees, tucked to Dougie's lap like a woman
overcome with an unseemly passion. "Is she fainting?" cries
Miralee, leaping backward as though she's seen a mouse.
"Help!"

Dougie's cheeks turn tomato red. Dan has never seen skin
color so spectacularly; it's awesome. (Surely they could find
a use for such a skill in the movies? If they filmed him in
black and white his cheeks would turn up in Technicolor.)

Dougie tries to help Laura up but he is awkward, his eyes are fevered with embarrassment. He is afraid to touch her now.

"Here," Dan says, gathering up his wife. For the first time there is some comfort in her half-familiar body. He lifts her in a kind of hug, knee to knee, and settles her back in her chair. Her shoulders are shaking.

But that's laughter, as it happens; she is going to keep him off balance one way or the other. "You can't jerk me around like that, Dougie, I can't defend myself the way I used to!" She tells him this cheerfully, without malice. "Of course it's the thought that counts, right? So thanks. Nobody's tried to kiss my hand in a while." Dougie goes on blushing, his cheeks look painted.

"Come on now, do I have to cheer you up?"

A wan smile goes around the circle.

"Look, give me your hand," she directs, and with a massive effort of shoulder raises her whole arm off the arm of the chair. At the end of it her fingers are locked in a gentle curve. "Five poor parsnips hanging in the weather."

"What?" Dougie continues to look as if he's been struck a hard blow between the ears.

"Oh, some poet who didn't like his hands anymore. I think they were getting old." She would never have invoked a poet before, not in this group. Well, they can all walk; let her have her advantage.

Dougie, alarmed, grasps her hand lightly, holds it now like glass.

"Listen, if nobody's going to laugh with me, I'm going to get very lonely." It's the cajoling voice she uses to jolly up the children. "I told Dan we'd better learn to laugh be-cause—!" She is also, he supposes, entitled to her bit of make-believe, an edge on the soft voice they know her by. But she does not look at him.

"Here, now, look!" She demonstrates her ability to drink from a long straw, to move her chair an inch a minute, to write her shaky name four inches high, splayed like a daddy-long-legs across the page, with the aid of her metal-rubber-plastic do-hickey, which she straps on herself, slowly, slowly, using her teeth. Her cheeks are pink with a low-burning excitement. It is unlike her, the whole show is, she seems to career, a little drunk on something, only in slow motion. Anyone who entered the room as Dan picked up the dropped paper the second time and, expressionless, replaced it on her tray would think the people in the silent circle were watching a magic show, or a high-wire act. They are skeptical and hopeful and eager to be convinced.

Laura smiles straight ahead and Dan sees that she hasn't been proving her triumph with this show of expertise, but her failure. "That's it, folks, that's all there is, there ain't no more," she declares in a small voice, smiling, sweating hard from the exertion. They argue her down, assure her that it is remarkable, this repertoire of tricks a monkey can do, and swing by its tail to boot. Her eyes are shiny as, relieved and appalled, her friends pour their admiration down on her.

Oh friends, let me explain myself. I don't know what you see. I am the same woman but for small differences. For one thing I complain constantly, it gives me something to do. My voice raises reassuring welts on my husband's skin, otherwise he might forget me. (I will try not to complain to you.)

For another I have no IUD or anything like it and another I never had dandruff before but they give it out in the hospital so I got some.

For one more where you can't see I am falling for-

ward   almost always falling forward though what meets
the eye seems to be sitting tight. I spend time every day
remembering how, disgusted, I watched my grandfather
without his glasses groping, twitching his hands over sur-
faces like a blind man looking for clues, working his tongue
on "Help" in case he needed it, his eye sockets mulched
pale by the heavy hornrims. He would stuff the folded
glasses in a beach shoe and deflate like the beachball at
my feet. I'd lead him to the water, in to his waist. He'd
flap his white arms then, wings of an oversized barnyard
bird put upon by something smaller, quicker, that bit at his
feet. Then he'd raise his face to the sun because he didn't
have to see it to know it was there.

   Whether you want to know or not, my whole blind
body is nowhere that way, hanging withered in space, and
now when I close my eyes it is falling forward, weightless
but somehow   somehow falling

   and if my house began to burn, General Bolt's beloved
pile of ancient tinder, who would save my children   lady-
bug   I'd be falling pitching down
   Would I have to hear them catch and burn?

There is a corner of the living room where Laura has
perpetual lights that make her plants flower. Violets thrive
there, coleus comes up garishly bright, the mottled green
of leaves is exaggerated, unreal. Dan thinks it's obscene, city
folk's impatience: things ought to grow when they grow,
flower when they flower, die at the end of their season. But
she is always dragging in weeds from the garden, in the short
voluminous months when they outdo their more modest,
permanent houseplant cousins; she pulls things out of the
woods and watches the collapse, the wilt, the seedtime and

browning. *Nature is not your enemy* is what he has tried to
teach her, but it isn't your patsy either and it will not be
pushed around. But she has grown up with flower shops and
out-of-season vegetables at shameful prices, why should she
believe in such limits?

The argument, at this point, isn't worth waging. Who
says nature isn't the enemy? The lights are on and he will
tend the plants as he tends her. Let the flowers burgeon for
their mother who loves them but who has no hands.

Dougie MacDermott is standing in the dark corner far
from the center of the party, with his hands splayed out in
the fluorescence as if it were a faucet letting down warm
water. Dan feels as if he is talking to the hands, which crumple
to fists and open, crumple and open.

"You look like you could break something, Doug," he
says kindly, and leans an arm on the awning that hides the
lights.

Doug keeps his hands open in the wash of light. They
are unexpectedly wrinkled, their furrows dark with shadow.
Dan thinks of two young sisters whose deaths he read
about one time, whose hearts, the doctors had found, were
ancient: the gnarled hearts of old women, and no one knew
why. Why are your hands so old? he wants to ask Dougie,
pity seeps up in him, accessible these days as Laura's tears and
his own. You don't do any dirty work, you move dressers and
click lamps on and off for your customers, and write out
receipts on carbon sets, why do you have grandfathers' hands?

But it's the light, this ghastly illumination seeping like a
gas. He stretches his own hands out beside Dougie's, they
stand side by side like men at adjoining urinals.

"Jesus, Danny," Doug says bitterly, and points with his
chin in Laura's direction, out in the light. "Isn't it all broken
already? What's left to break?"

Dan moves closer. Dougie's life has never particularly interested him; he's lived with his pretty, funny face turned elsewhere, he can tap-dance, he can juggle and recite Shakespeare in a thin voice, he reads *Variety* in public. He has no wife. Dan doesn't even remember inviting him to the party. Where does this sudden feeling come from?

"Dougie, I don't know. I don't want this to feel like a funeral—"

"My grandmother had a stroke," Doug says. "This was so long ago—but she was an old woman, there never seemed to be much sense pushing her very hard, you know? I mean, for what? She knew she didn't have long anyway. But Laura—"

"Well, Laura's pushing. She's had plenty of therapy and she'll be having plenty more I guess. And a nurse, she'll have to have somebody in with her, I'll be back at work sometime. I'm trying to get something to tide me over till the school year starts."

Dougie nods absently. Then he straightens his shoulders, pulls his hands out of the light and says abruptly, "Do you know I've always been in love with her?" Dan can feel him smiling into the dark.

"Laura? You serious?" He feels an odd pride as if she were his eligible daughter.

"Always, Danny. Since the first time she came into the store and took one look at the trash in there and I thought she was going to be sick. And, see, I agreed with her but nobody was supposed to know that. I mean, you know, it's an appalling bunch of . . . well, anyway, ever since then I've had a real thing about Laura. You can tell her if you want to."

Dan stands in the half darkness, bemused by this confession. "Why should I tell her? Wouldn't you be embarrassed?"

But Dougie shuffles his feet and says, with the conviction

of a child, "Why should you be embarrassed about loving somebody? It isn't shameful, is it?" He shuffles some more. "I'll tell you, she's always popping up in my dreams."

"I think I ought to be jealous." How Laura would laugh.

"No, nothing like that, they're really the most ordinary dreams, I mean very decent, altogether too decent. Once she was teaching me how to climb a mountain, we were both wearing these ridiculous knickers and goggles, we looked like Lindbergh and—I don't know, Amelia Earhart. Listen, Dan—"

Dan listens. Dougie's real voice, animated, is much more commanding than his stage voice which sounds like it comes out of a kit; he wishes he could tell him that.

"Danny, can I come over sometime, maybe, and sort of— just sit around and be with her, do you think? If she wants company? I mean, would that bother you?"

What a strange blend, he thinks, of old-time shut-in visit and new-time horny neediness. Don't you have any kids your own size to play with? he wants to ask Dougie. But a part of him is touched, is trying to be touched, instead of pitying. Behind that—his head is like a railroad flat, room upon room of feeling—he is simply angry, insulted: you don't consult somebody's husband, no matter what kind of time you want to make with her, innocent or not. *There is no innocent time.* How in the hell can he ask permission?

"Look, you don't have to ask me, Dougie. She can have her own friends and they don't all have to be women, I mean, Jesus, if you want to come. If you have time . . ." But look, he wants to add, no soothing the sweated brow with lavender and bringing little bed robes and custard. And likewise, no touching the goods.

Dougie shakes his hand fervently. They have agreed to some kind of deal on good terms. What bizarre comfort the invalids can give each other. If he is jealous it is for the rough piece of his own pride Dougie has torn off in his smooth hands without even suspecting.

"Holly baked them for you," Marian Hatfield tells Laura, offering a heaped plate of cookies and learning then and there the slow motion Laura moves through. She will tell her daughter Holly that Laura looks as if she's under water. She moves like the doctor in that movie they saw about the new way to give birth to a baby, all gentle, all slow, and then they bathed the baby endlessly, remember, breath by breath. How she brought her cupped hand over, lowered it deliberately as a crane, fell on the cookie, grasped three or four times with thumb and forefinger until she hooked a firm edge, brought it up so carefully and, leading with the top side of her hand, by the time she got it above her mouth and down and in, she looked like she had no appetite. Her eyes were full of tears. So were mine, Marian said, but I thought, We do what we must and what we can and God only measures how much we care. "Oh God," Holly will say, "God gets into everything. You shouldn't have to care that much about a tollhouse cookie." "Why not?" Marian will ask, not because she is pious but because she is practical. "What difference does it make. Care is care."

What's been lost?

He has no right to an opinion. He can feel his little toe, he can pick lint off Marian Hatfield's shoulder, casually, a long pink thread. He can feel a fullness at the crotch at the sight of Laura's profile, her sweet unchanged breasts that must be warm under her blouse, above the armor of her corset; something like orphans they are, abandoned. He is entitled to an opinion nonetheless. What are these wives, he thinks. What are they *for*? To wax the kitchen floor, then strip the wax, then wax again? To lie on their backs (or otherwise) and make the lights go out? Is she for standing on her thin cross-country skis, smiling, with snow on her blue hat, salted across the front where her hair sticks out? Standing with her back to him in dungarees, the way the belt pulls a little low across her backbone? Something tough about that; she likes to think it, once he caught her posing in the dresser mirror, thumbs in the loops, dragging on them. Buttoning the kids up and down—they manage that now. Sitting in the big chair reading, her feet in the speckled wool socks, legs slung over the side like a sixteen-year-old on the phone.

Is it her pinescented ammonia he loves, her dustcloth? She's a lousy skier, he looks for excuses to go without her. Is it her piccalilli, her frozen squash? She heckles him for the basketball he watches, but likes it, likes the heckling, sometimes they end up scrapping and fooling around and finally warming up a little in the breaks between quarters. Her father doesn't know a backboard from a backgammon board. Well, she can still heckle. Her fingers on the holes of her recorder, flattening down; she makes a double chin and cross-eyes to check them. She can't play while she's laughing. He hates that dinky sound, he calls her Little Toot. Her fingers playing him, certainly, but even that is no sum of Laura. Wife? As wife? The room is thick with wives. What are they? What is she to him that she can no longer be?

Only the losses to herself. . . . Her self flies up in front of him where he can't catch it. Who cries when she cries, who feels nothing? Feels the perpetual dull ache of skin against bone? Grey. White. Black space. She's always had a passion for saying about husbands that they see their wives only as wives; appurtenances. Moving parts and a motor called duty.

Not what are wives, my husband: who are these women?
These people. Now he feels this detaching: stands in the doorway running his index finger round and round the triangular
churchkey hole in his beer can, winding himself up like a
spring watching her. "You're all alone in the end, don't you
forget it," his mother had said one day, viciously, squeezing
cold water out of a rag to put over the eye Kenton Courser
had bashed. "For better, for worse, but I don't know who was
ever really sorry to lose the company they married." He
doesn't really remember these words, not exactly, but he remembers his confusion about how this had happened, this
blue eye socket, purpling fast, and what she meant; remembers
the grey outside the window, late fall surely, around 4:30,
5:00, dishwater dark. That was the worst time of day for him
and his brother—the time they came into the low tight house
and stepped on each other's feet, breathed the same air—Fran
doing her homework, good girl, he and John snarling in the
corners . . .

He goes across the sunporch to Laura, very purposefully,
she sees him coming and he knows she stiffens. But he stands
behind her chair, lays his hand as casually as he can across the
back of her hair, smooths it. He feels her straighten her
shoulders as if bracing for something.

*I smell it, I can spend hours only smelling it: spring com-
ing up on summer like last year, all the last years. Sweet,
ripe, what is it? Smell old melting snow still, just the way
my fingertips still feel. Lodged in the brain cells whole, all
of it is. If Dan with his stiff neck, stiff back, ever touched
me above my breasts where I edge towards feelings like ice
thinning out, do you know I would feel it everywhere.
Memory is not only unkind. Memory is a muscle too if you*

work it. It still bends and straightens though not always at command. That seems to be my secret. Will he ever go out of himself and his mourning, his loss, to guess it: I am still here.

Louise, still sitting knee to knee with Laura, is suspicious of the young teacher who thinks electricity is a fit topic for study by both sexes. "So then he held up a lightbulb and said 'Tell me, does this say *boy* on it anywhere?'" She laughs meaningfully. Laura smiles. (Every one of Dan's students is a boy.) "But I told Pammie if she really doesn't want to make a motor I'll go talk to him and see if he can't find something a little more useful for her to do. What's she going to do knowing how to make a motor, will you tell me? I think the truth of the matter is, a man teacher doesn't know what kinds of things little girls do."

"Well, not only that," says Marian Hatfield, dragging a frayed string of connection as far as she can and discreetly dropping it, "they care so little these days, do you know they told Jamie, not outright but in so many words, that even if he keeps up his grades, it doesn't matter how high they might be, it isn't going to matter because they have a new quarterback who just happens to be the son of the assistant principal, you know, that took Ed Brandt's place when he moved over to Keene."

Dan rubs the back of Laura's neck; she moves her shoulders comfortably in spite of herself. This whole long year he has learned a new kind of thinking, or had it forced on him, his mind is loose and busy with random firings. Was it the busyness out there, the unpredictability of the city? He's seen more moving images in a year than he'd see in a lifetime in Hyland. Now he finds himself somewhere in the middle of a memory of a movie he saw in New York that was a "glimpse" of a Hollywood that might or might not exist but that Louise and Marian and even he like to imagine: everyone bouncing from big pill to little pill to bed to sanitarium, and then to Forest Lawn, or whatever it's called, before their time. Mourned in the headlines but *we know*. Movies like that are supposed to make you feel a little safe and boring but very virtuous, contented, close to the warm center of the good earth: your death will be ordinary, shovelling snow, pushing back your chair from a Thanksgiving meal in the bosom of your family, yessir. Imagine Laura whipping him with a belt, needing to slam his flesh into wan excitement; imagine the things he can't even imagine.

He curls her hair around his finger. He feels hard and clean with gratitude and garden-variety lust. Clear water. Her voice, telling a story about a practical joke somebody played on a nurse and the way the nurse lost her temper, breaks his heart. He is sure that is what it feels like, a real spilling over inside his chest, the way an egg, sunnyside up, runs down when it's pierced, warm and thick. It is only her voice—not what it accomplishes, not even the stories it tells— that makes him feel like himself. Its suppressed Boston that suddenly blooms wide when she comes to words like "bahth-room" and "hahf." To this day he is unprepared for it, that fake classiness that's frozen closed by the time it gets into the mouth of New Hampshire—it is a condition he lives in. Familiarity, love, voice music, they are conditions, like the temperature of air, the barometric pressure. He would like to wrap himself in her voice the way he wrapped himself in her robe, one time, where it hung in the closet on East Twenty-second Street, its sleeves buttoned around air, and pressed hard to absorb whatever it might still hold of her. He felt like a teenager with a crush and at the same time like a pervert with a secret fetish: both. Both sides of innocence, and in the middle nothing.

"Laura, I think maybe we've got to go in the other room for a couple of minutes," he whispers. She's been putting away as much beer as Louise, which is good exercise for her but only if it comes out as fast as it goes in.

"Where are we going?"

"You know, come on."

"No, I mean where, not why."

The old sticker. He feels as if he's dropped her again.

The chair doesn't fit into the narrow downstairs bathroom. There are people in all these rooms. Either he lugs her upstairs or—"Come, let's go outside!" he says and pushes her chair to the kitchen door, scoops her up (the laborious careful scoop that puts him off balance) and, leaning her whole weight against the storm door, unlatches it and moves down the few back steps with her towards the garden. "You want to fertilize a little patch out here?" Now what? Will he trip in a woodchuck hole, fall into the compost pile, pitching her forward onto the coffee grounds like a banana skin?

He sits, trusting, on the small stone wall that separates the upper from the lower tier of the yard, the grass from the apple trees, and pulls her down with him. Unbalanced for a second, he rights himself; she's not the only one who's off center. (Well, she is his center of gravity. Is it any wonder?) She is bulky as a grainsack on his lap. "Now, m'love, if you'll just let me get up under here." He holds her back straight, thrusts a hand up her pants leg to throw the switch, nearly capsizes more than once but holds her, holds the damn hose, twists it open. Half a six-pack sizzles out onto the grass. He can see the bubbles standing on the grass, little fish eyes. "Aren't you high from all that? Jesus."

"Mmm hmp. Don't stand in it."

"I'm not." Doing all this with one hand while he supports her weight with the other is exhausting. He moves her on his lap and she sits hard on the tenderest part of him, but like a stone too big and centered to be eased off. "Laura."

She doesn't answer.

"Laura, laugh with me a little, huh? Here we are, two adults."

"Is that what we are? I thought we were one infant with a woman's brain and one stalled child—"

He is holding her in his lap: Edgar Bergen and Charlie McCarthy. What was his name, Jerry Something and Farfel, the big dolls always a little irritable, being misunderstood all the time, or misunderstanding, which was it? Somebody always saying "No, *no*" but which one did the contradicting, the man or the dummy? They seemed more alive than half his friends. His brother called him Mortimer for years, Mortimer Snerd the stoop. The feeble-minded noisy one.

She seems to shift in his lap. Possibly he relaxes a little and she sways. Her face stays tense, absorbed; whenever her body is in a new place she concentrates like a cat, learns what she needs to know and only a little bit extra. Body, body, body. The dinosaur was all body, no brain; at least she sees herself as woman brain, infant body. "Listen, this is not the time or the place but I want to tell you—if we're going to go on—"

If she turns her head she will have to speak into his forehead. She chooses to look straight ahead. "Go on how?"

"Go on. Like before. Like we've always gone on."

"I've never thought of us, before, as going *on*, we were just—"

"Oh, forget that. That isn't what I'm talking about. I have got to have—" He stops. It is too unreal, too grotesque, he can't speak. There are real people inside his house, eating date nut cookies, looking for napkins in the kitchen drawers, turning on the bathroom light.

"You've got to have some respect. R-E-S-P-E-C-T, Baby what you do to me!" She sings that, a frail-voiced Aretha.

"No, you don't have to respect me. Only I don't understand how we're supposed to go on living under the same roof with you despising me every minute, day and night. Again and again—I mean, I know I'm not in a position to ask you for anything, except you've got to tell me how—Laura?—how in the hell I'm supposed to get from minute to minute of the day with you treating me like that. This doesn't have anything to do with forgiving me or approving of me but does it ever occur to you, in the middle of everything you're going through, that maybe I'm in some kind of pain too? Does any of that—"

She manages, with the closest thing to no movement at all, to indicate impatience: a matter of breath. "Do we really have to straighten all this out right now, while I'm sitting on *nothing* and the house is full of people? Is that thing firmly closed?"

He tugs at the tubing. "It's closed."

"You know, sometimes I think the worst thing about this—being a 'crip,' did you ever hear them call us 'crips,' that was really lovely—is that I can't get up and walk out on silly conversations like this one. It is just getting to be so damned hard to say no and have anyone listen."

She is bearing down hard inside, he can tell, and he is sorry to have pushed her to it: her right knee, suddenly, goes into a spasm, bounces the way a whole child bounces when she desperately needs the bathroom. Slowly like a dancer making a grave movement she raises her arms and puts her hands on her knee and tries to press; most of her weight does not apply. He puts one hand on hers and closes his eyes and pushes downward the way you would hold something under water, leaning hard, as hard as you can, against its instinct to rise. It is more than a flutter they have to kill, it's a hard wild knocking, it is something other than Laura; it is Laura. The tighter she holds herself, the more in control, the more she is liable to flow over. Her energy froths and spills, and feeds nothing.

"The clonus kid," Laura says bitterly, meekly. She is going to cry, her whole face blurs even before the tears.

"Don't, you don't have to be embarrassed, it's no shame. Laura? My lovely Laura?"

"Lovely." But for a moment she relaxes against him. The twitching subsides and she falls back from it, triumphant to be returned to immobility. "Danny," she says against his temple in some small person's voice.

He takes a breath so deep it seems to scrape along the pickets of his ribs. Then he carries her into the house, a man flying through clear air empty-handed. If not "yes," hasn't she said to him, in her desperation, "maybe"?

The pressure of the roomful of people, making a constant noise like water. He needs to be alone with her to get on with this beginning.

He lowers her into the chair as gently as he can; it will always be awkward. He cannot see her face as he wheels her back, parting small tides of friends. This is tantalizing, harder than courtship.

No, your friends cannot contain you. I always knew. Their intentions are so good, I am embarrassed for them, touched. They hold my corners in their hands, my most visible edges, the loose eyelashes of my experience, a circle cut out of my belly like an old Bavarian peasant-clock. Dougie

*holds three fingers between his, and tight, as though that
were all of me worth keeping. The three small square-
nailed fingers of my left hand. The frail bread of my body
I try to break and share with these laboring guests across
the strewn sunporch. My words are crumbs, not very filling.
They want to see me dance.*

    *What my friends know is probably a metaphor naming
something I resemble.*

News drifts up like snow against the house.

Freddie and Annette are not here; they have had their
last fight. (They like to do it in public, they've always in-
structed their friends to laugh and their friends have been
obedient.) Freddie is the size of a jockey, which makes him
a bantam cock, nervous and jealous, the leader of the laughter
at himself; Annette is so perfect she is not quite real, every
feature drawn with a delicate brush. No one quite takes her
seriously. (She is the girl Dan went to in her trailer—they
were sixteen—and found her so frail, so narrow, she was like
a child with a lurid heart. Who was corrupting whom?) But
they've had a soft accepting spot for each other ever since, a
brother/sister conspiratorial warmth. Freddie is anxious with
Dan, it's even worse because they were once good friends, in
trouble together, had to walk the line for the Hyland police
again and again, touch their noses. "Friends I trust the least,"
Freddie would say. General Tom Thumb and his lady. She's
filed for divorce, Freddie is gone, no one knows where. One
of the kids went out on the highway, walking east, to look
for him.

And Roger Mead has bought a used Mercedes. Georgia,
his wife, has opened a Carvel stand; Roger's waiting to catch
the pieces when it falls. "The zoning board gave her a hard

time on the store. I said, don't worry, it's only gonna be a temporary nuisance."

Jay Hatfield's daughter Martha, at college, is going out with a congressman's know-it-all son. "Yeah, I keep telling Marian, he's like Georgia's Carvel, only a temporary nuisance too."

They are solicitous of Laura, who is in turn solicitously grateful. They bring her more cookies than she can eat. She eats them and then closes her eyes, letting them puddle in her lap. Miralee has a friend whose cousin is a nurse who works with—pause—does therapy. Marian Hatfield's mother does too, but she's probably too old if there's lifting involved. There's lifting. Louise looks like she's guarding Laura and her chair against further harm; she is not a grandmother yet, she has not had a chance to use this particular look of happy busy power since she had a child in a baby carriage.

Paraphernalia, Dan sings to himself, par-a-pha-nail-ya. He feels mellow; almost normal. All his instincts are not so base: the party is right, it's what she needs. For what it's worth. What he needs.

"You know what I really wanted to be, don't you?" Jay is asking Dougie MacDermott. "A minister. I don't remember why, to tell you the truth. But anyway my father kept saying 'That isn't work, that's talk!' He said 'Why don't they let the ladies do it, I never understood why they don't do that, and we'll do men's business.' "

Dan listens to the laughter, men against women like voices in a dishevelled chorus, but neatly divided. Laura used to wander over to the men, she made everybody nervous. If they were telling blue jokes they stopped and looked like their mother had caught them at something. Whether she wanted to make them itch or not he never could guess. Some part of him enjoyed her daring, she was provocative the way

these other wives would never be, these boiled potatoes, sufficient, tasteless. His friends expected him to prevent her, though
—the part he could have done without. There wasn't much
he was going to prevent her from doing. (The only resemblance he'd ever found between himself and DeWitt Shurrock
was that neither of them dared ride their wives when they
didn't want riding.) When she came and stood among the
men, or sat, or hung in the doorway listening, pretending to
dry a dish, pretending nothing, commenting quietly but firmly,
he ignored her. He only half-hoped she'd go away but meanwhile he pretended she wasn't there.

"And the dreamy things they were wearing, it was like a
fairy book, all laced—"

"Say the tax goes up another eight cents a thousand, all
right, just say for argument—"

"They can't use the phone book, they don't know how
to make change of a dime, I swear to you, I'm not exaggerating—"

"Marshall's has them. Not in every size but they're always
reduced, it's a permanent sale so what do you call it—"

If he closes his eyes, it's Before.

Then will it all have to happen again O Lord to bring
them to this day?

He aims an empty beer can at the wicker trash basket and
heads for the kitchen to get another. Then he goes to find
someone he can talk to about the Patriots' season, and the
Red Sox's coming up.

But they will not let him. Jay Hatfield is not smiling and
patting the women; not drunk, that is. He is in one of his
vigorous argumentative moods, not precisely in disagreement
with anyone but so much more vehement than his friends that

he sounds thoroughly, endlessly, fed up. He is wearing his incessant grey unbuttoned sweater and sits very straight with his hands on his parted knees, licking his pepper and salt mustache, which hangs over his mouth like bangs. He looks like a man hard at work.

"Are they making you pay taxes on all that money, Danny? That's what we're wondering."

"All that—you mean the money you folks raised." Dan colors to his hairline. The HELP LAURA! dances, bake sales, the raffle of the patchwork quilt, initials sewn in every square. The Saturday matinee of *The Gnomemobile* whose profits went to the HELP LAURA! fund. "Oh God," he says and covers his face in mock horror, "I never even thanked you, all you incredible—"

"Nonsense," Jay snaps out, businesslike. He is such an old schoolmarm, sweet and sour by turns. "You wrote us and we put your letter up on the post in the store, you don't have to roll around on the floor to make your gratitude felt, you know. That's an insult to the dignity. People understand, your friends are prepared to understand a lot more than ever you may imagine."

"Well, but still."

"But now, Laura, she must have been pleased, you never told us what she had to say about the way all her friends came out for her."

Dan sighs. You will always be caught, always, and no matter what your intentions someone will be hurt. The secret that charmed his growing-up was that he never knew that when it might still have hobbled him. "Jay, listen—I don't like to have to tell you this, I know you're going to be hurt, but—look, I guess I never did actually tell Laura."

Good try, he thinks, but saying it is not so disarming that it keeps Jay from pain. "Oh, Danny," his friend exclaims without reserve, and raises empty hands from the business of his knees. Jay runs his store, but his biggest sideline is being good in public. "Danny."

"I couldn't, I couldn't. You can—you said people can understand all kinds of the damnedest things. I know how much love and kindness and generosity went into all that effort, believe me, I can remember some of those times. When the Sharps got burned out, I remember what we got together for them. And the Madigans. You know me, you know how it made me feel to get all this help. But Laura—look, don't blame her, I just thought she wasn't ready to accept—we never even talked money."

"But Danny," Mick Tobler says (Round Mick the Mad Plumber, wide as a barrel, his cowboy belt a single stave, who douses for water with a plastic stick and plays music on the job to draw the water through clogged pipes by "Hydronomic phono-attraction"), "this wasn't just money like some insurance policy paying up, you know."

"Look, don't you think I know, Jesus. How could I not know every one of you—"

"Don't argue with him, Michael, you don't argue some things," Jay tells him, his judgment made and filed, secure.

"Jay." He is going to keep his temper, he will not stamp his foot like a petulant boy. "Jay, did you ever think how sometimes when you deal with some kind of problem with Marian it's sort of more like politics than anything else? You know? Nobody ever says it'll be like this but it is, with our wives, right? Sometimes you're not lying exactly but you're telling her only so much, or you're waiting with the whole story?" He subsides, out of energy.

"Still, Dan."

"Still nothing. You don't know. *You don't know.* And don't ask me to explain what you're not going to understand either. You saw the little signature trick—if you could tell it was her signature—and the straw, the way she gets the chair to do ten inches an hour in there, and she's smiling and she deserves to be proud of all that, but you've got to trust I was trying to deal with a psychological state. Here's a woman who's so reduced—" He lowers his voice, as though it's a secret. "So reduced she can't—"

He sees them huddle in that tense edgy elation, the same breathless attention he saw when they watched Laura do her tricks. It's the tension you take to the circus. Who can blame them? It doesn't make them any less decent, they are outsiders, that's all. He's in and they're out. (Jay used to tell him that about the war: you've either been there or you haven't. "Don't even *try*, if you never saw the floor of a foxhole. Did you know it looks just like a goddamn grave inside?") Their wives don't have their asses hooked to their elbows by clasps and plastic tubing like a Rube Goldberg invention.

It's true he does remember his emergency crew leading the fundraising drives after every calamity, what a fine pleasure it was: you set a goal, $2,000, say, and then you compete with it, like a kid trying to outrun his shadow. What a simple contest, a noble game, and everybody the winner. Charity the cornerstone, the bottom rung, the layer of straw to keep the cold away; it gives you a couple more of the easiest inches in your kids' eyes. He remembers the Madigan fiasco in fact: little Sean Madigan, Sean a second grader with Jon, a lip reader, a showoff, a hanger from trees and gooser of girls, a pest (like Dan at eight): Sean thrown in a watery ditch, his undug grave; his sister wandering in a daze looking for help on a rainy night, and Skimmer Joe Madigan pickled as a fish, pinned in his pickup off the road on a mild curve, his neck twisted in a hangman's fracture.

So Hyland discovered the Madigans: made piles of canned

goods and brought them over in Jay's station wagon while
Joe lay in his hospital bed; exclaimed in horror over their
shack that had been there through a hundred winters with
nobody ever exclaiming before. Dan and his men had gone
to insulate the walls, a gift of the town (making a connection,
not necessarily the right one, between the family's poverty and
Joe's bad steering), and the day Skimmer Joe came home from
his ward and found Roger Mead the paperhanger in the same
room *with his wife* (Roger festooned with rolls of donated
cabbage roses, a pot of glue on his arm, trying vainly to match
up the unmatchable flower petals), Joe chased him halfway
to Route 8 with a brick in his hand.

He should have been grateful, they all intoned, the loyal
ladies and debentured gentlemen; even the ordinary onlookers
shook their heads. Skimmer Joe wasn't made for gratitude,
though, nor for looking like a damn fool in the first or second
place: bad enough to have broken his neck. Dan remembers
being angry, wanting his pound of repentance, if not precisely gratitude. Half a dozen family men had spent their
weekends out here unrolling asbestos batting for this joker,
laying rat poison, closing the hole in the porch floor so the
kids wouldn't break *their* damn necks falling in. He is more
civilized than Skimmer Joe: they are waiting for their thank-
you note, co-signed; it's not a lot to ask.

All he can do is close his eyes, cover them with one hand,
not coy this time. "Someday she'll thank you, Jay, you'll get
your thanks. Someday there won't be so much shame in it
for her."

"Danny, I'm sorry," Jay says sharply, irritated at the sound
of Dan's irritation. He is remembering the round collection
box that stood, steadily filling, on his counter. His daughter
Holly handlettered HELP LAURA! in poster paint with small
blue flowers twined around it. Maybe he is sorry, though. "We

weren't trying to put any kind of pressure on you. I was just surprised is all. Because I'd have thought it would be good for Laura to see we care about her. That can sometimes be better than any medicine. But you know best, Dan, no doubt about that. You're in the only position to know these things." Still he wears his affronted look, a certain stiffness in his long body that he doesn't know is there. A really big man, he is thinking, is not reduced by having to be grateful—Dan knows Jay would feel that way. But the problem is that it's Laura they're talking about, and who knows how to measure the requisite space gratitude ought to take up in her hollowed-out body? Who dares approach her to take the measurement?

He is always underestimating Miralee. She wears that bright inviting expression that was intended, in high school, to make people want to confide in her. She was proud of the number of friends she had, but even Dan knew nobody had that many, not friends. The word was never meant to encompass a whole football team. ("Carry a *Reader's Digest* with you at all times," Miralee's mother had told her, "and you will never have to search far for conversation.") But she has had her reverses: her three or four lost babies, the Korean child, surely a gain, not a loss, but slight and withdrawn, on whom she and Chet have spent most of their stored-up social credit. Oh, that plush maternal bosom that will never nurse a child, what an irony: for touching only. She's sobering fast; maybe that's what the bottled grey hair is about. A sign. The flag grief left on her pillow, ordered her to fly. . . .

"Danny," she says to him at the bottom of the stairs. "Let me talk to you a minute."

"Yes, dear." But he regrets that false solicitous voice; she is serious. "Yes."

"Is it going to be all right?" She leans close to him so that she doesn't have to whisper.

He sighs then. "That depends on what 'it' means. *You* know—"

"Yeah. Or what 'all right' means, oh I guess I know plenty. But not this. I just mean—doesn't she get too terribly depressed? And you too?"

"You'd better believe it." He takes her hand. He is trying to be as grave as she, not make the quick dismissing answer: honor the effort, this is no high school senior. "Miralee, I wouldn't know where to begin with the problems. Hers, mine, ours."

"The kids'."

"The kids'. You name it, it pinches. Or aches. She's very brave, though. She shouldn't have to be so brave."

"Well, she's got no choice. Why do people think it's so damn wonderful to be brave?" Miralee says this very coolly, stiffly. Dan can sense a shadow of resentment in her, something just grudging. Did they not take her seriously, give her sufficient sympathy in her cruellest days? The last baby tore loose and bled away after six or seven months. She was at a wedding and the baby stopped, like a clock, she said. It moved and then it didn't move any more, it only bled. She went home before the ceremony. Then wouldn't come out of her house for a month. She was home, Dan supposes, learning about the differences between choice and no choice: facts, not opinions. Not hopes but actualities. Two points on a line, but the line is broken.

Dan takes his friends for a tour of the bearing walls. They study posts, the cabinets, the lintels. He knows more than they do about the way the house is supported, what is dispensable, what is not, but he is a doctor who wants another opinion; it isn't tonsils they're talking about. Roger Mead, Sandy's brother, round-faced, a weight lifter, hard as a boulder, works for a construction company that has built two houses whose roofs have collapsed under snow. (And not much either. Ice and snow, all right. But those are the expected conditions, the starting line up here: you don't build for 365 days of continuous sunshine!) Roger shakes his head as they make their slow circuit. Upstairs he kicks a post that still shows the marks of the adze, the honorable traces of a workman dead two centuries. "God*damn*, houses like this make me want to hide my head," he says, again and again with slight variation. "Jesus, what they knew."

"You know it too," Dan tells him, leaning on the post, "and a hell of a lot more. They just won't let you do it. These guys weren't trying to make a bundle, they were only building houses. This place got built for somebody's son."

"Comes to the same thing. You know their axes never rusted?"

But the men agree. There are some walls that could go, a few. Doorways widened. Some rooms that will be off limits forever, immovable objects on all sides: fireplace, stairs. "They showed us these movies at the Rehabilitation Institute about how well all these graduates of theirs managed, but Christ, they all lived in California, I swear—you know, all these posh flat-out ranch houses with glass doors you could open with a fucking push button!" Here there are nothing but stairs: the kitchen could be rearranged but what about a bathroom on this floor? She can't go outside every time they have company and she has to pee. The house has become an endless maze, every turned corner leads to a wall.

"All right, don't blush about the toilet," Jay says, "these are facts. Everybody needs a bowl to piss in, Liz Taylor, Raquel

Welch, everybody. You think they do it in thin air? Their hairdresser takes care of it?"

Dan blushes anyway, if only because he brings out the father in Jay. But what a subject for friendly masculine discussion. (He is fastidious; half his best qualities, says Laura, are undiscussable.)

"Hopeless, you think?"

"Dan—lookit. How do I say this." Jay is the spokesman. He stands straight in his natural dignity, he needs a vest and chain. When he speaks his nose lengthens. "The question is how much can Laura do? That's all. Even if you rearrange the kitchen, you build a lot of new cabinets, all right—can she use them, will she want to? You've got to be sure you've got a woman here who wants to do dishes, okay? And chop onions. I mean—do you know these things before you start hammering and sawing away? Have you asked her? I'm sorry but I have to say this. Do you know what you're doing or are you just hot to get your hands on some wood so you can feel like you're doing something. Because we all know you can do *that*."

Dan stands looking away, listening. His jaw is tight, his teeth are locked on anger and humiliation, he is doing the hornpipe again, kicking his heels, gunning the motor, tearing Laura to scraps, feeding her backbone to the gulls that work the river patiently. He is nine years old.

The others jump in, glad they didn't have to say it first. Mick the plumber says authoritatively, bringing up the rear, "You find out every Christmas there's some gifts nobody needs."

"What the fuck do you know about it," Dan whispers and then touches Mick's shoulder in shame, knowing the anger was meant for Jay whose eyes would not have widened, then narrowed, as Mick's do, to take in the pain.

Laura whispers, "Dan, I'm very tired all of a sudden."

He has to ask them to leave. They apologize for staying too long. "No, I'm glad you stayed, it meant you—maybe you had a good time. Only she's got special needs, that's all, she gets tired like a little kid all of a sudden." It's all right, it's all right, don't all fall down.

He wheels her as close to the front door as they can get. She can't wave except with an awkwardness she will spare them, but she smiles a great deal, and nods. Things become formal, they all become anonymous: Visitors Departing. Paintings have been made of the scene: lamplight inside, snow out, a sleigh pulled up and waiting. One horse paws the ground. Cheeks are dutifully pecked, a few emotional hugs of the sort people execute at funerals: Here, they say, let me press some strength into you; I know it's futile, it's comfort, not a cure, it changes nothing. But let me do something before I escape.

Laura's knee begins to bounce again. They stop and regard it. No one says a word. Laura looks at it as if it were a fish flopping in the bottom of a rowboat; she thinks it's as nasty as the next one. She gives Dan a desperate look.

"Watch this, Magic Dan goes into action!" he cries out, a casual business, he pushes back his sleeves, rubs his hands together and pushes down, feet aligned, both hands tight. If she could pound that knee to bits, punish it, disconnect it. Betrayer. His face red he bears down with all his weight and it fights back. He feels as if he's suffocating it under the pillow of his hands; an extra shake to make sure it's dead.

"When I get tense," she says in a sweet false voice to her astonished friends. "See—I'm so glad you came that I guess I get upset that you're all leaving."

The rest of their lives, the rest of Dan and Laura's, seem to loom at the door. This is the sickroom after all. His brother looks as if he's swallowed something rancid.

Go, go, Dan thinks. Dismissed, good people, thank you. We are alone here one way or the other. Good night, good night, Dan says, God bless.

The door closes on the last of the earnest helping people. He stands stricken, his face in his hands in spite of himself. He hates her, hates her, he wants one of them to die. Escape is not enough, is not possible, he would have to leave her behind watching him go. "If you ever divorce me," she used to say, "please take me with you." The logic was perfect for its moment. They will make a pact, stop breathing one after the other, scribble a note: *Dear People, good people. It is not enough. You are not enough. What do you think we want, why do we want it? Before is all that's left and there is no more of it.*

He wheels her to the center of the room and with a small hard breath of desperation, as if he's boosted her up to safety on a high rock, he leaves her there. She can't get out of the kitchen to look for him, the cabinets come nearly together on both sides to keep her in. He very nearly runs.

For six months after Jon was born she could get no more than an hour away, an hour back: no one else could feed him. Dan remembers trying, the baby rejecting him fiercely, spitting the bottle back with amazing vehemence. He waited for her breast, shrieking till he was blue. He took it back into himself when she finally brought it; one of his limbs that had tried to get away. Jonathan Michael the hairless tyrant, the more he needed her the greater his power. Tethered, she'd say, the year I learned to walk bent at the waist for speed. But she would smile when she said it.

. . . .

He turns on the television set and resolutely watches
I Love Lucy, which he has always despised for trying so hard
to make him laugh and failing. The show is as old as television. Its tape is full of static, a snowy haze lies over the clown
faces, softening them to something less seen than remembered.
Before for Lucy too, there are so many befores, and Desi who
is no longer her husband. This actress sidekick dead and that
funny man a wizened beast now, well pensioned in some
Beverly Hills nursing home. Lucy knocks down a whole
bookcase searching for a dime for the parking meter (who
would trust her with a car?). She raises her head from the
rubble with that familiar round-eyed stare, somewhere between blank terror and blank stupidity, Henny Penny's face
under a dandelion mane. The audience laughs on its tape, in
its box, echo of real laughter on another day, brought on by
something funnier. Brainsleep. He warms his hand between
his legs.

He comes back from nowhere, rested. The test pattern
holds, flatter than flat, humming to madden a dog. Muscles
that flex need release; he has been clenched for hours. Hate
doesn't enter in, strain is the toxin. Why can't he remember?

Laura is asleep, one arm over her chair, chest open as a
cat's in the sun. She is so far away he can hardly see her.
She has left her body on the shore of the long evening,
cast it off like resistant clothing and is swimming free. Float-

ing. She must be as buoyant in sleep as she once was walking, dancing, in her obedient bones.

He wonders what she dreams. Instead of terrors—all the things that could happen have already happened—maybe she dreams she's dancing. Tumbling. Diving. Tying French knots, three times around the needle. Plucking the tangles out of Hallie's hair. Dreaming backward, the way dogs dream when you see them kick in their sleep. What a curse, to float into the backwaters where you can never go again. Like dreaming of someone you loved so much who's dead—reaching, trying to touch. His mother slowly dissolving under the hill. All you have is the lifeless body, and the body is your own. He aches for her, her losses, a dark slow red ache, deep in the pocket of his chest where he can't put his hand over it, any more than she can put her hand on anything.

There is the slightest burnt-sweet smell around her, a nimbus. Old friend catheter, her chaperone, her limb, her root.

If he were Laura he would never go to sleep.

Two o'clock he turns me away from the moon   Move it for me Danny   if you love me   Can't I take anything with me onto the dark side?

Get this straight, kid (like a man with a wet cigar he would say it) The moon keeps moving   Any way you face you're going to lose it   Jon is getting pubic hair now What do you think of that?

He turns her over, this time facing away from him. So familiar that precise length of spine. Whatever its incapacities, its failures now, they are secret and subtle and it is dark. He

arranges her pillows at the chafing points, but when it is time
to replace the one at her back he substitutes himself, lies the
whole length of her and places his hands gently not hungrily
over her breasts. He waits for her stiffening but she is pretending sleep. She is wearing a flannel nightgown which took
him ten minutes to struggle her into because she is always
cold, mortally cold, she says it almost with satisfaction. Some
quads' thermostats get stuck on one side of normal, some on
the other. If she were always too hot, what would she do?
Sit on an ice cube? "How in the hell could we really live in
New Hampshire? Oh, winter's going to be a real circus." He
thinks again of the films they showed at the Institute about
Adjustment in Albuquerque, Phoenix, Tucson, where maybe
the sand shifts but the wind doesn't blow.

The worst thing, that widens the rift, is that there are so
many things he cannot tell her; or thinks he can't. Can't tell
her, Lor, I feel like a kid at the movies, the way I used to slip
my arm around some girl's shoulder, sort of sneaking, a little
at a time, and we'd both pretend nothing was happening.
Victory as a vise grip; arm as C-clamp. So (can he say it?)
we're back to about fourteen. He tightens his hands on her
warm breasts (one of his arms, the under one, will surely fall
asleep) but they will never rouse themselves for him. Missed
by an inch or two, the fatal line, the snow line. (Cold from
the feet up, Dan, she told him. The hemlock seeps that high
and no higher. But no lower either.)

"One of these days," he does half-whisper, undecided between threat and seductiveness, "I'm going to turn you over,
Laura, and show you how much of you is left."

There is a pause in which Dan hears the charged silence
of a blank spool on a tape recorder ratcheting round and
round: the sound of empty air on an open circuit is nothing
like silence. Wearily her voice begins. "Listen, you can do

whatever you want to with me, we both know that. There's nothing I can do about it." Her steadily bled voice. It is white.

"That's not what I mean, my dearly beloved wife." He drops his hands, his body softens. His knee is tight against her air mattress, which yields like flesh. "You're talking about legal rape. That's not what I'm talking about." If this woman was a miracle the first time she came to him, yielding, the next time will need another name. Salvation, maybe. Absolution.

He holds on, though, he is going to be her pillow, like it or not. He curves to her from behind, a question mark. She can't feel him there against her, except for his breathing in her hair, his shoulders bent towards hers; she feels, he supposes, what the table would feel if he lay himself across it, what a mannequin would feel. So they say. No one will make him believe it, though, unless there's no difference between living and dead; nothing alive is that simple. She turns her chair from time to time when she sits downstairs because the changes of direction, the movement, are good for her. If she sits perfectly still for too long her energy sparks over, it seizes her and shakes this hand or that leg. Matters of nerve endings and blood pressure, chemistries too complicated for him to know, but he trusts them and their sovereignty. He will lie against her, warm no matter what, and someday she will melt.

I only want to be warm, I said. (Bring this lady a tea cozy, slip it over her head the way you do her blouses and let her ears stick out.)

If we needed ecstasy to live, wouldn't the streets be clogged with corpses as if the plague had come?

. . . .

Meanwhile his dreams embarrass him. In this dream, which he invites, half awake, he knows he is ashamed, sneaking, hoping not to be seen. His X-rated movie: he has brought a huge crowd into the bed with them, familiar and unfamiliar faces, but mostly limbs and naked anonymous parts, superb, athletic. There is a cat sitting on Laura's face when he turns to her, the cat is opening and closing her paws, the way theirs did when she nursed her litter, an ecstasy of feeling, almost a moaning without sound, paws opening, closing, opening, closing, the nails lengthening for an instant as the skin draws back. They are in the middle of a river, on a stony spit of land, making signs to the shore. He and the cat are there, lying together on stones; where is Laura? Grass grows between the stones. He stands entirely naked, smooth as a small marble statue, a miniature with the modest genitals of a young boy. He bends and picks up the cat, which leans against his chest then, nibbling at his hairs, gently at first. Some of the hairs are grass. The cat begins to pull them out in clumps like sod, with a great effort, arching its back, sinking its claws in his skin for purchase. His feet are in the river; naked he worries about his cuffs. As the hairs pull loose, his chest glowing a marble white, he feels, surprised, the long familiar rising begin, from the scrotum up, irreversibly. Which one of them is melting? But the feeling is on the opposite shore, he can't reach it. He is in the middle still, wet to the ankles, and the tidal swell is somewhere else, coming towards him. Asleep, drowning, he can't pull back from her in time, and when he wakes with a gasp he is too late. No joke, Dan thinks, lying in the mess he's made, the back of Laura's gown sticky, Laura making angry noises, no joke, I'm fourteen. A year or two later and you don't have to do it in your sleep anymore. And what does that make Laura, his dirty dream? His pinup, impossible, looming, used?

No matter what it makes her, he is her husband (he thinks this amid a dozen conflicting angers that tug at him like currents) and he'll be damned if he'll apologize.

Someone was chasing me through my sleep with a butterfly net. The rim of the net was falling, the shadow coming down cool, but I turned without warning and flew out from under it. Rising against the depthless blue I clapped my hands and they rang blue and purple, shimmering like moire, like cymbals. I shuddered in flight and looked down into the iridescence. Some kind of good news in that flight, but I had to wake up.

Oh so many ways to be helpless in your body, Danny, so many ways. Look. Both of us are subject to fits and spasms. Just like that. Irresponsible riot, trunk and limb. Dream without end.

Your body has its way with you or without you.

"Range of motion." In the morning she lies back on the bed (he has placed a towel over his gluey adolescent stain the way the children used to when they wet their beds: dry till morning, then, only the stubble of terrycloth for punishment).

He is showered, extra clean, in his chinos and a T-shirt. His body is supple, contained, lightly muscled; he is not as small as the marble boy in his dream. Although he might go about his business half-dressed any morning of his life, there is something just possibly self-conscious about Dan's bare arms and flat solar plexus this morning. He feels himself to be in costume, or almost so. Flaunting, or merely free of constraint. He is not trying to be cruel, only he has to know that he is strong, surely not *needy*. Could this vigorous young man, taking long strides from here to there (he asks this vaguely, without words) be the pathetic victim of wet dreams against his wife's turned back? Would any circumstances forgive him if he were? This morning it seems damned unlikely; so says his firm walk from bathroom to bedroom and back again.

She is cold again, so cold, she has demanded that he put two thermal shirts on her. "You'll sweat," he says, "exercising. It's warm in here."

"Good," she says. "I'd like to be too hot for a change."

He lifts her leg.

"Farther," she instructs him.

"How do you know? You can't feel if I'm doing damage."

"No, but you've got to push as hard as you can. You're supposed to be stretching muscles that want to contract. So you've got to find the last point I can go to and then push against it."

"Okay." He holds her at the ankle, gingerly. The hair on her legs is soft and blond; it always has been.

"But not too far."

"Okay, I'm trying. Jesus. I wish—" He pushes, feels the spring of resistance before her leg is straight up. Like thwanging a guitar string, a vibration, a tremor of distress.

"You wish—"

He shakes his head, runs for cover: he wishes he'd had time to learn more about this at the Institute. She said she didn't want them to live like thieves; every time he suppresses a thought, a word he can't say, he steals from them and puts back nothing. He pushes vigorously now, invited; perhaps too hard. "How will I know if I rip something?"

She smiles her new smile of self-loathing, self-satisfaction. (Was it always a possible smile for her, under the surface of her sensible kindliness? A superior smile? Was it, he asks himself but he can't answer.) "I guess you won't."

"Terrific. Does it matter?"

"What? You mean, does it matter if you rip something?"

"Well—" He lays her heel carefully on the sheet and takes her hand, coloring from the neck up, trying to be matter-of-fact as though he hadn't said that, or meant what he said. The catheter runs out to the edge of the bed, the bag dangles over the back of Aunt Jemmie's antique parlor chair, a vivid yellow against faded brocade flowers.

He and John used to bend each other's fingers back like this till they got a satisfying shout of outrage. He tugs. What would make her shout? He doesn't want to be here when her fingers turn to claws. He uncurls them and pushes, trying to impress them, to make a difference. When he pushes her fingers back to the shouting point, they go white at the joints, thank God, like anyone's.

Hallie is playing jacks on the kitchen floor. All she learned about being alone in New York she has brought home with her. The night she left the skating rink with the odd friendly woman was as much a night alone as any other (or so she has reported, mildly, in her own good time): she had a meal, she had a bath but made the woman stay in the living room, she tried on some other girl's clothes—they were too small, except for the shoes which she could not keep. She used a sweatshirt for a robe and wore it home; even over her blouse it felt good inside, soft and worn as fur. There wasn't much talk, only a lot of looking; the woman smoked and stared and once in a while she stroked Hallie's hair. All this fed her nothing, only made her miss her mother. She told herself that when she opened the door to the apartment her mother would be there. The woman said she could make it happen if she believed it hard enough. She has made something happen, something like it (though she was probably dreaming of her mother whole). They are here and she ought to feel good about it, Dan says: They are here, first thing, for her. Now she seems a nearly sufficient companion to herself, calmly going about her games, playing both sides.

"How about calling up Cara when she comes home from school, or Wendy or somebody?" Laura asks her at lunch. Hallie has finished and has turned back to her ball and jacks. Laura holds a large slice of apple firmly like a child who's just learned how, the whole fist committed, and watches Hallie at her feet, a woman in a rocking chair regarding her crawling baby.

"Not yet," her daughter says, "I just like being here with you." If she weren't smiling that particular smile—a good deal of sweet indulgence and a tiny fear of being caught at it, her eyes, as in bad books, bad movies, very nearly shifty—Laura would not pick up her intention, she would be pleased at the hope of intimacy.

But Hallie does smile that way, awkward dissimulator (silence and absence are all she practiced on her father, she got no experience at lying), and Laura puts her apple down and sighs.

Her daughter looks up, sees she has been caught, smiles again, this time apologetically: this time a saddened smile, no teeth. She throws the ball up again and it gets away under the refrigerator, to which she can turn her face.

. . . .

*I used to rollerskate with Hallie, strap the wheels to my
shoes with the metal wings that only the key could move.
We'd hotfoot it downtown over the cracks in the sidewalk
bumping, regular, like a train, thwack and the whish of
open space and tha-wack again over the cuts in the concrete. Hills on two feet, bent at the knees like cross-
country skiers. Bent at the waist uphill against the incline.
Once I was a Pied Piper with half a dozen hooting kids
behind. Dan hid his head when we went out, imagine, con-
cerned with the seemly, the unseemly and the something-
in-between. I haven't any reputation to undo, I told him
and you—little thug of the Hampshire County District
Court, vandal graduate, o cop's hot dinner gone watery
and cold—you are so good I don't know who you are.
Where is my pushy boy?*

*Step on a crack   break your mother's back   Hallie
would sing. I hear the echo now. She cornered well, stopped
on a dime, turning in a tight circle, her calves snapping
stiff. Was somebody listening who heard the dare? Did
Dan step hard on the crack to keep me home?*

There are a few transactions Dan misses by virtue of
absence, weariness, inattention, even indifference. This one
appears to be lost to the sports page, which is open on the
table beside his plate, but in fact he is thinking about the baseball season, the relief it will be to run, to sweat, to get out on
the field where the only horizon is the fence, and the score-
board, that tipoff to their massed unreliability (never funny
at the time, only later, over beer, those basketball scores:
seven innings, 26 runs!). He hopes it's not too late to sign

on with the Hatfield team, they usually get set in late winter. It comes as a shock, sickening and reassuring both, to realize they could never deny him his place on the team now. If he showed on the Fourth of July they'd shake up the lineup to fit him in; if he made an error an inning they'd forgive him. Compensation for being pathetic, like a free pass to the poorest kid in town. They won't even have to discuss it among themselves—outrage is rising in him, adrenalin courses around his body these days at random, looking for a fight. His uniform will glow under the lights with the phosphorescence of specialness, of exemption. Probably they'll resent him too, this stranger they've silently agreed to coddle. Like a stain of darkness and not light, their graciousness, their pity spreads and spreads; the children will have it too, and cruelty at the bloody edges.

The girl from the newspaper is such easy prey. She is the niece of the editor, which makes her combative, tense, unduly independent. Or perhaps she has grown up on Brenda Starr and, latterly, Ralph Nader. Either way, she comes uninvited to do her interview with the Coursers as if there were some muck to be raked.

"This is not just going to be the usual pap you see in the old village paper," she assures Dan, coming in at the door fast, a quarter of a step behind him. "Sometimes you can barely walk around the office for all the goo in the aisles." She is on his heels. When he turns to look at her for that remark they nearly collide.

Her eyes widen with possibility when she sees Laura. Laura in turn looks her over slowly from head to toe (dungarees and a mussed pinkish Indian shirt, high wedged sandals, very straight clean earnest good-girl hair: a confusion of impulses). The girl, who will not smile, clearly does not like to be studied. She is here to do the studying.

"How did this happen?" she demands, more brusque than a doctor new to the case.

Laura laughs at that. "Well, now, I don't think I caught your name. Or which of the papers you're from?" (Whoever has come has scooped their competitor; that's laughable enough.)

There is the exasperated sigh of a dedicated worker slowed down by someone's rank inefficiency. "Phoebe Landgraf," she concedes. "For the *Bulletin.* Now—"

"Why don't you sit down, Phoebe Landgraf," Dan suggests, smiling behind his eyes to Laura who almost invisibly smiles back.

"Thank you." Not grateful, she sits in the wicker chair, very still. It is a creaky chair that likes to relax and give its opinion of the sitter in little clicks and raspings but it is silent beneath the absolute Miss Landgraf.

"New on the paper," Dan says neutrally.

"Yes, rather new. Now Mrs. Courser, you were going to tell me how this happened."

"Was I? All right. Very simple. An accident, a boating accident. I got caught in the motor and it broke my neck."

"Among other things," Dan offers. This is the first time any of this has seemed remotely laughable, a weapon, a shaggy dog story, a toy mouse, anything but what it is.

"Among other things," Laura agrees. "Too many to mention."

"How ghoulish." The girl wrinkles her nose in fastidious distaste.

"Well—ghoulish. I've heard it called a lot of things but never precisely that. You never, uh, tend to look at yourself in terms quite like that, do you think?"

Phoebe Landgraf sits still, pondering. "I only meant the event, not you."

"Thank you," says Laura smiling. "I wish I could make such a nice distinction between myself and the event."

"Mrs. Courser, will you ever walk again? To be perfectly honest?"

Laura looks at her as though from a great height, squinting. "The essence of hard-nosed journalism appears to be short sentences," she says coolly. "In one short sentence then, no, I will not."

"Well, what makes you so sure of that?"

Dan is fighting very hard to overcome his desire to show this young woman to the door. He has a better idea. "Stand up," he says to her, "and put your damn notebook down."

Obediently she does so and stands, a little anxiously, before him. He takes her right forearm then; reaches around to the back of her and, leaning hard (resolute, angry, and shocked at the closeness of her thin body in its cotton shirt; she is one of those concave women with baby breasts that he tends to think of only as rich, as if the rich had enough without needing bodies), he turns her arm in a wrestling hold that he remembers from the high school lightweight team. It doesn't hurt to have your arm pinned that way but you can't move your hand at all. The poison dart, they used to call it: soundless, odorless, painless, deadly. He rarely found the right place on a moving target. "Okay, now move your fingers."

She takes in a sharp bewildered breath. "I can't."

"Sure?"

She twists away awkwardly, and uncrumples her blouse. Her cheeks are red and she is staring at him. "Yes, sure."

"Okay then. There are some things you know, that's all." He sits down again innocently. Arrogant little bitch.

But the feeling of her drawn-back body, tensing at his

sudden attack, his warmed him dangerously. Laura is studying her blue polyester knees.

Miss Landgraf resumes faintly. "Have you ever thought of—I'm really very curious—have you always been sure it was worth going on in this state?"

Laura opens her mouth and closes it again. She leans back and stretches, her best movement, casual-looking. It is the energy of her anger that makes her move. Dan can feel it sparking, blocked. Her arms rise as if she has surrendered.

"To be perfectly honest again." Dan the Defender. "That's a hell of a question, do you know that?"

"No, look, I'm not trying to be offensive or prying or anything. But the alternative to this kind of question is Toni Sargent comes up here, right?—the Comings and Goings in Town lady with her glasses pinned to her good old pink sweater, and she writes 'Mrs. Daniel Courser is home with us from the hospital again up on the Mill Road, looking rested and rarin' to go. She thanks all the residents of Hyland for their bouquets and get-well cards.' Is that better?" She is sitting up straight, flushed angrily, happy in defense of her defects.

"Yeah, as a matter of fact," Dan says, "you make Toni's column sound better than it ever sounded, if you want to know the truth. Listen, it's a good thing to try to write a real article, you know, with real pain in it and real problems. But you've got to get yourself a little finesse, I think you call it. You don't just climb up into somebody's bed of pain and start rolling around in it just like that. Jesus, you come in, we don't even know your name, you start asking my wife if she ever thought about killing herself—"

"Would you like me to leave," she asks, says, standing wearily. Her eyes are full. God, Dan thinks, they collapse like dandelions, even the toughies. He wonders if her pride can

bend enough to allow an apology. "I've never had any experience with——" She looks at Dan, confused.

"Cripples," Laura offers. "Or did you mean people?"

"And I didn't know you were going to be so defensive."

"Look, sit down," Laura says bleakly. In spite of her sharp-
ness she does not like to dislike anyone; Dan has always
thought—since *she* can entertain opposing thoughts at once—
that she's the most generous critic he knows. "Let's give you
a little education in ghoulishness."

Uncertainly, Phoebe Landgraf sits. She has the grace not
to pick up her spiral notebook and her pen.

"You want to know what it's like I'll tell you. A little
monologue. After an accident like this, first all you want is
light. And breath, nothing else. And then noises all around
to make you believe you're still alive because you doubt it,
but that comes later, when you're already coming out of
yourself a little." Because she has to sit so still Laura sounds
like a woman on stage, alone in a spotlight; it is a pity she is
embarrassed by the dramatic. "Okay? You with me?" She
asks this softly; the girl nods, perhaps forgiven.

"Then the noises begin to make you crazy with nervousness. And you want the parts that still hurt to stop hurting,
your head, your neck, your shoulders, but they're all full of
stitches so they smart and itch and then all they do is ache
endlessly. Endlessly. A hundred degrees of pain, if you con-
centrate on it, it gets completely unreal—you just blank out
on it as pain, it becomes something else, some—I don't know,
some uninvented new thing. I don't know what. Nothing I
would recognize from my other life." She can scratch her
nose; she hits it with the side of her hand. "But you see, when
that stops you want to know what about all the rest of you
that's been cut off, taken away, flushed down the toilet." She
is almost merry with the animation of this guided tour. "When

you're alone you try to move, just a half an inch, maybe. You try to trick yourself into moving. Every twitch feels like it's the beginning of something. It takes incredible concentration and energy, you want to go into a complete collapse every time you work on a finger. And meanwhile every ten minutes somebody's in there poking or prodding or stretching; they don't even want you to sleep because your lungs fill up as soon as you stop concentrating on them, so you're up all night and all day and you never know which is which—and then—" Laura is watching Phoebe Landgraf listen.

Can I expect to tell her how for months I thought I was asleep? In every direction warm stone. Mountain and green growth of blanket. A hundred years, I thought, and I would stir, and the maids in the scullery, the lawn-tenders and the horse-boys: the castle would blink and wake. The doctor was the prince and he would kiss me up and out.

But I almost died. They made such noise saving me. And they began to say You have to stay awake. Only a minute's sleep. I remembered the lovely doze between contractions then but look what came of that, Hallie and Jon—sleep for strength, not each time a little nip of dying. The body, mine but not mine, breathed slowly, heavily, in its tunnel between sheet and sheet. Pores opened and would not close, closed and would not open. Someone tinkered all the time and after a long bleeding the surface looked whole. Anyone can see it went on being, it was only incapable.

Warm tears, familiar blood. Blood felt the same finding its easiest course down everywhere, the new notches cut, a whole streetmap flayed from my face. Fontanel drip-

*ping the freshest tears. The nurse would come. "Tears?
Why tears? My dear." Prepared (her orders were) to be
firm, not pitying. Firmness is support is improvement is
unmaiming. The book says. Though in my case I think
they closed the book early on. "Take out the death supports. Let her live." I think that's what they said.*

*I never told the nurse my plan, my fear, my secret
resolution: to lift this anchor, some particle of it, one day.
A finger would do, just to begin. Today, I thought one
ordinary morning, right now, after the breakfast tray had
gone back on its little sneakered feet, and the nurse that
came with it to tell me to open wide the way I told my
babies. She would laugh, though she had orders to encourage; she knew I had only that withered root she shook out
every few hours, turning the soil, turning the whole bed
over and over. It was not in the book that I would move
the blasted root through which my life ran out the wrong
way, into the ground, draining back into the white muslin
ground.*

*Words cost me too much, some unkind parts of words
ran for a long time just beyond me. Mercury rolling always away. I never talked to Dan, I had nothing to tell
him anyway so far on the other side of every real thing.
"Please." Just that exhausted me, the shadow across my
tongue. My head, which moved, fell back damp, sweat
cooling. Sweat in the alleyways where those tears rolled.*

*She bent over me, warmth and blue shadow across me,
eclipsing the fluorescence that made static in my head, and
leaned, pulled down the sheet, and I watched—someone
else, someone in Kalamazoo, no friend of mine—I watched
me moved like a tree limb I once saw in a steam shovel's
mouth. Carefully raised in the clenched pickets, carefully
lowered, branches up saying a dumb stiff goodbye to the*

head I came from. Bleeding sap without pain. She replaced one arm, for example, on top of the blanket and I felt it coming down on me. Top of my ribs felt it from underneath, here but not here, precise. She left, packed up her stewardess smile with her blood pressure tubing and left my line of vision, which was fixed.

Ready. I didn't know which finger. They had my wedding ring. I had no husband I ever wanted anymore but I thought, that finger of mine has no more distinction, it could be any one. Which was the quickest to move once in its life? Thumb, fat housewife finger, cinched at the waist, built like my grandmother? She did things. Would she flick her head just once for me? Or quick wit, accusing finger, the sharp one who makes up for its shortness with precision? Did. I put off a decision. Dozed, their breakfast fist in my stomach. This was November.

I woke like a child about to make a journey, excited, afraid. Index finger was the quickest once, acute. J'accuse: that finger. Hereby elected.

I would not watch it. Turned. Lovely quiet swivel of my head, like pouring water from cup to cup. Arm lay hand palm down on the blanket looking emptied, innocent. Not as it is, stubborn. I thought the blood must have rotted black in the veins by then, I tried to think the rhythm, systole diastole   thrust and withhold   thrust and withhold. The only scars, they said, were going to be at the shoulder, a small straight line—quite handsome, healing a stern white like furious lips—behind the elbow, below the useless left nipple, just missing the heart. Like a mummy, whole outside and empty in: a taunt.

Green blanket rising like water all around. If a fly landed on my knuckle he could eat it like a lollipop. But I told myself, I tried to call across the downed lines of my arm, Get ready. On your mark, the order's coming. Remember the way a dance of fingers felt. Liquid. It would take a slight push against the tension, the spring of gravity coiled down, always from this position it took a thrust. But the blunt point would feel the air lighten. Sorting the orders: finger on that side, that, the inner side, pull from under, tight underneath, the nail raised towards light. That much farther from the pull of this earthweight. I kissed myself goodbye, bon voyage, you shall fly. . . .

Flint-spark, command, panic. Tighten. Finger, if you live. Everything in me curled head to chest inside, eyes averted. Just up for a second, wag that blunt head, then have a good sleep. But there was space all around, the whole world of air began at the tips of the finger's tip and continued up and all around. The empty space of the room, sixth floor, fourteenth floor, the empty sky outside the dusty window and down to the street, up over the fogged city, up and up, galaxies, infinities of sheer air, all of it weighing, pressing down on me.

I gathered myself for a shout and pushed the current of all that wishing through my arm again, a second time. And no. I was too angry for pity. But no. So they were right, doctors not princes with their electric probes not kisses; their cattle prods, their needles. They knew and made no secret of the vacuum inside me. I hid in the dim green blanket they call apple green. (I will not blame it for sounding, in the mouth of the nurse, like hope: "The walls are butter yellow, we call them, and the blankets apple green and periwinkle. To give a little boost.") There was a kind of twanging I couldn't hear, couldn't see, almost could not feel but it rushed back: echo, afterimage of the impulse. Something rode back up the arm to the shoulder, fading like a twitch. The twitch that used to answer the doctor's knock on the knee, reflex casually fighting back.

Miss Phoebe Landgraf, you come and talk sweetly about the Will. Or think it in your silence. I have none of those capital letters of yours in me, don't you know that? Only vagrant twitches widening, rippling in the wrong direction, electricity evaporating like water, mazes and tangled wires, small sparks misfiring, all of it covered perfectly, oppressed, by this weight of heavy skin. If I could scrape this putty off my bones would be so light! Skin or no skin, though: I cannot touch with myself. Talk about Will and Real Desire and Hope, suspect what you must about why (what secrets why) some people lie escaped in their apple green buntings while they are probed, lifted and dropped, and I say Young lady. This is no subtle refusal: not the sex of a sad man that will not, will not *lift up to be, afraid to be seized and used.*

I tried to move it, one two-ounce finger, my old friend, twice on that day. That was November.

I need the finger for my life. That and a few more things. I need. I will have to learn to do without, I told myself, simple as that. I was already learning. Grow hands, grow legs inside. But which do you think I miss the more? The lovely swing of my skin and wishbones up and around (in spite of will) or the safety—the old and sweet —of thinking what wishes can do, wishes and princes. What honest wanting sees to. We know, my husband, my children and I, at last, and are relieved, after our fashion: not a goddamn thing.

. . . .

"I don't want to go through this," Laura says finally, blinking her way back as if the light had brightened. "I really don't want to. It's much too intimate to talk about, it doesn't sound real enough when I tell it. It was a month before I could say everything I wanted to because of the way my head got knocked around. And six months before I could get the sleep out of my eye, okay? And then people come along . . . see, everybody *comes along* after that, right, because you can't choose to go to them, so they keep happening to you. Accidents keep happening, idiots you have to talk to who won't go away." She could look hard at the reporter now if she were vindictive; if she were sensitive enough the girl would feel chastened even without the look. "I had a nurse once who said to me, 'Boy, I'm glad I'm not you.'"

Phoebe Landgraf blinks expectantly.

"So you know what I said to her, don't you? I said, 'If there's anybody I'm glad I'm not it's you.'"

The reporter smiles a wan smile of polite disagreement. "But what's really wrong with being honest? What will hypocrisy get you? Or sentimentality? I mean, you *know* people are thinking that. I'm sorry to say it but you have to know they are. If I were in your place—"

"But you're not," Dan snorts, impatient. "Lucky you."

"Have you always defended your wife or did that come with the accident?"

He is going to give this child one more question; then he's going to grab her by the elbow and heave.

"Mrs. Courser, may I ask you, were you doing anything before your accident?"

"You mean working? 'Anything' would mean working? No. Just a housewife. Smelling the flowers, killing flies—your ordinary sort of contemptible housewife."

"So this change isn't actually keeping you from—"

"Well, I haven't killed any flies for a while. I get lots of flowers to smell if I can get somebody to hold them up for me. And I can still yell at my kids. I can scratch my nose now, you saw that, didn't you?"

"All right," Miss Landgraf says, "I am sensitive enough to know where I'm not being tolerated, even if you don't give me that much credit. Thank you for your time." Stiffly she gathers her things and gets ready for flight. Her ankles shake on her high sandals. When she is halfway out the door, cheeks pink again in her flounce of embarrassment, Laura calls out, "Miss Landgraf, I'll give you one hard thing, one quote, for yourself, not for your paper. If there's anything you can do with it. I don't like to be pompous and I don't for a second believe that what happened to me makes me wise or anything like that. But listen, there's one thing you've got to learn about your life, everybody's got to learn, my husband had to learn and my kids, and I have a feeling you don't know it. Maybe you're too young, maybe it's just not the kind of thing you're ready to know yet."

"Oh I love things that begin that way." Miss Landgraf makes that same fastidious face standing in the doorway holding her notebook before her for protection. She looks the way Hallie will one of these days when her passivity turns on them.

"My great pronouncement." Laura is embarrassed at where she's gotten herself. "Is that nothing is promised. Do you know what I mean? Approximately? Nobody ever wrote a contract with you about the way your life is going to be. This isn't the only way it could be turning out, either, you know? Believe it or not, there are worse things. And when you realize that you stop a lot of the fighting against it. It's like when my kids think they've been promised something and they don't get it—fury, you know? But really, the truth is, every second it's up for grabs. Everything is." She smiles a little: this has been a warning issued to a stranger.

There is a long empty silence. Miss Landgraf stands twisting her limber ankle around and around. "And that's the profound truth you've learned? That everything's up for grabs?"

Laura gives her a bitter half-laugh. "As far as I've gotten that's it. Do you want to hear something more Eastern than that? More Freshman-philosophical? You like fancy packages?"

"Well, I guess that just doesn't seem to be much to show for all this. Somehow. Maybe nothing would sound like enough, I don't know."

Dan wants to announce that Laura went to Wellesley. He keeps his teeth clenched.

Laura's lips are pale but she continues to smile; it is her authority that smiles, while her weakness lets the blood run out. "Goodbye, Miss Landgraf. Don't fall into the printing press, it'll shred you up finer than you'd believe."

"Wow," Miss Landgraf says, retreating. She stops, though, and Dan sees she is as drained as Laura. She beats her notebook angrily against her knuckles. "I didn't come over here to hurt anybody's feelings and if I did I'm sorry. But I don't think you people know how you come on—"

"Come on?" asks Laura fiercely. "I didn't know we came on at all, I thought that was the problem." The women regard each other dryly. Phoebe Landgraf shrugs finally, giving up her side as if it didn't matter.

When the sheepbells have tittered against the front door, Dan says gently, "I'm sorry. That was a joke, Lor. I don't think she was real."

Laura stretches again, restless. "I bring out the best in people."

"Well, I think she was scared of you, that can make people say things they're not responsible for, you know. But Jesus, I like that kind of honesty, it's like a howitzer division. Hey, what do you know, we're a kind of people."

"If I let that get to me," Laura says, and lets it rest. When she is exhausted, her eyes sink into a dangerous greyness. "Well, I guess we *are* a kind of people. I guess we've got to think about that a little."

Hope leaps in Dan, one small sharp fragment of it; it is more than she's given him before, that "we." They sit together in a pall like falling evening. This is what it would be like to be old *anyway*, ordinary and old, and sit here rocking, Dan thinks, looking back at all the untouchable memories they share. No one else can do a thing but bruise them; honor them a little, for all that's worth, but mostly step among them handling them, knocking them down. That's what makes a kind of people out of anyone, no matter what they're joined by, love or habit, murder or hatred.

Goddamn, I don't want to say Life is life isn't. I never was ambitious.

But the other thing, after-the-fact, the sometime thing: the side of "specialness" that is no euphemism. That—very hard to say, I tiptoe through the words and won't hear them out loud—I've been saved from the ordinary? There is no one life, standard, parts interchangeable, but it does seem we expect it, the props we dream of pushed into their places. I know I married Dan to jog all that. To pull the rug out. My thorough boy, you did bring the whole house down around the little Oriental!

Now I will not be interrupted every three minutes: I can steep myself in time and feel my colors change. The

dark is an impasto, thick and full of unexpected reds and
purples, did you know that? Laura? Begin there.

Two o'clock: They look at each other through an imagined twilight.

Guilty in the face of Laura's single truth, he still believes
she has been promised him.

Billy Bickford came to take Dan fishing. Go, I didn't say,
I don't want to be hated the way your eyes are. Your
damn fingers drumming.
So I had grilled cheese with the children who burnt
their fingers twice but were afraid to howl, and they did
what I told them and Hallie stared into the urine pool.
"Kadota figs have that exact same color," she told me and
I said we could buy some and compare. She combed my
hair so she could put her green bow in it. "You're sure
you can't comb hair," she said to me squinting. "Because
I see you raise your arms." Malingerer, her mother! "Good,
Halliburton, you hold me to things like that." She needs
approving though no more than ever. I need to approve.
"But it's the brush, holding the brush, and all that raising
and lowering so fast and pushing hard. It doesn't work."
She nodded sadly satisfied and dug the bow on a bobby
pin into my hair but short hair has no catch to it. The bow
fell into the seat behind me and she wriggled her fingers
in to get it and I laughed though there was no tickle. But
there is more to me than ever she thought and it's going
to sit a while and make a knick in my skin, a wrinkle. It's
easier to be alone with her but shame still makes her
timid, she is without energy like someone else's child. She

left the top off the milk and the milk on the counter and the counter under crumbs and I yelled the way I always did and the air broke open a little and out shook a few tears. But she was smiling too, I think, to hear me nattering so she could be mad and safe at the same time and blame me for it. Old times.

Ric Frede turns up into the driveway just before dinner. He is a writer who lives around the corner and he needs to have some bookshelves built. "If it isn't the roof falling in," he says cheerfully to Dan, "it's piles of books. I had a stack so high it fell over the edge of the loft and nearly got my kids down at the bottom. Hardcovers. So I figured I'd better get on it."

"What a way to go," Dan says noncommittally. He is assessing the nature of the request: charity? A little makework at generous prices? He plays poker with Ric in one season, baseball in another. Sometimes they watch the Superbowl together, each a little bit flattered at the other's unlikely company. The man is compact, contained; behind his mustache he may be smiling, but then he may not. Whatever Dan doesn't understand of him he has always assumed to be a function of professional mysteriousness.

"If you're too busy with Laura I can take them someplace else," he is saying now in the kitchen doorway, making a gesture of removal. "I wasn't sure if it was a favor or a—you know, a blight—to bring you work."

Dan makes plans to come to do the measuring. When he walks Ric to his car, Ric stops. "I had a funny experience last night, Danny, I hope this won't seem impertinent. I fell asleep, it was late and I was up working? The stuff puts me out sometimes, it really does. Fifth rewrite. Can you imagine tearing the nails out five times? Anyway, I just put my head down on my arm at the desk for a minute and when I woke up, I don't know how much later, my whole arm was gone. Asleep, I mean. Incredible!"

"Why was it incredible?

Ric is getting into the car. He goes on talking through the open window. "I just mean I had no feeling in the whole arm, shoulder to fingers, and it was terrifying, that's all. I sort of could move it, you know, flop the whole thing around like a —I don't know, it felt like a tree limb or something. And— don't be offended, I hope this isn't awful to say—I just thought, 'Laura Courser, Jesus, poor Laura, is that what she goes around feeling?' I kept looking down at it and there was no damn connection. Like somebody else's except it was there and *I* had to move it. I kept knocking over the stuff on my desk, my coffee cup and stacks of paper, and sort of banging it around at odd angles. I really clipped myself." Ric shows him a scraped knuckle. He shakes his head but doesn't take his eyes off Dan, as if Dan were telling him the story. "I only wanted to tell you, I just thought for a minute I could really feel for her. Petty as it was. That's all."

"That's plenty," Dan says, flushing, leaning on the door of the car. "It's about as close as we're gonna get, isn't it?" The man's effort touches him. Why must a Phoebe Landgraf's fear for herself make Laura into a damn fool when there are so many kinds of curiosity possible—a thousand shades of it like samples of paint in fine gradations—to be given like small gifts that take nothing from the giver?

I'm bleeding. It isn't fair so much goes on so unimpeded. (The doctor said good, good.) Call the neighborwomen, I want to say. Danny, go out and play. Gently he binds

*the wound of my health. If the pad chafes at my thighs
I'll never know. He keeps watch, comes to check, arrange,
ask coolly how I feel. Forgive me, please forgive me. I tell
him, angry, Fine, fine. The blood cakes between my legs
but it keeps coming. Days of it. I want to touch his hand.*

Dan is making things for Laura out of energy and wood.
He has applied for four construction jobs but has heard from
none. Now he is trying to design a frame that will help her
get out of bed herself. Laura complains that it looks like a
gallows. She has taken to reading a book a day; she has asked
him to send for a college catalog: his own flowerless college
with its buildings that feel like airplane hangars. Sometimes
she sits in the small room that has his construction table in it,
turning pages with her wrist, cursing when the book goes over
the edge of her lap table, watching him, moving her head to
the rhythm of his sanding as if it were a primitive music.
There is a fine small breeze that they share; it comes in at the
window behind Dan's head and raises a few of his cowlick
hairs, which makes him look like Jon. He can almost forget
what he is building.

I want a book and a hard one.
    *I don't know anything but myself, my absence, as if I
were a subject. And the less I am the harder to master.
This is a sensory deprivation too. So I want to study untouchable matters: the stone formations of Crete, learn
about Ramadan and Lupercal, get enough Spanish to
dream in.*
    I shove the pages over with my whole hand, a fist like

a bear tipping a honey pot, but when I turn them they stay turned.

Fallen from Dan's pocket. Hallie hands the slip of paper to me, smooths it carefully like a treasure map. (My friend Noreen at the Institute found a note one weekend home that told her why her husband smiled at her so much. Enough to burn holes in her eyeballs, the details, she said, signed with her neighbor's name.)

WHEELCHAIR PUSH-UP BLOCKS *is what it says.*
½" × 3" × 6½" plywood
1⅛" × 3" solid wood, hard
loops: plastic, cloth, elastic, etc.
⅞" × 2½" dowel

Shims may be made to raise the surface of the block as high as needed. If it is raised over ½" the dowel should be longer than the original 2½".

A love letter.

Good God, she has her gentleman callers: Dougie brings a book, just drops it into Jon's hands and vanishes. ("He's weird," Jon says but he can't give reasons. Well, everyone is weird, to kids; imagine what they'd say about their mother if she weren't theirs.) But Dan, not a child, thinks the same and can give reasons. He sees Dougie trailing a black cape, twirling a cane or a whip. Right, a whip. Fwht, fwht: a giant Z flayed in the khaki front lawn, the mark of Zorro MacD, heroic impostor. "Is there a note?" he asks Jon, shaking the book open. All the worse—she's expected to know who it's from and probably why. The book is something called *À Rebours* by A. K. Huysmans, on the cover a debauched-looking young man with a family resemblance to Zorro MacD. Is he sending a code message, from Weird to Weird? Dan sees Dougie stretching a pink towel over the telltale spot in his bed. She has the power to make men as helpless as she is.

And John comes, looking humbler still. Gentle and only a tinge abashed; some kind of smile leaks around the edges of his brusqueness. Making a salad, complaining to himself about his brother's inexplicable presence, Dan cuts his finger on the long tomato knife that has a blade so slender it's nearly invisible. He watches the blood stand in a thick drop on the side of his finger, piled like mercury, unmoving. What do they talk about in there? The pain in his finger is disembodied, it makes him uncomfortable everywhere and nowhere; his chest flutters the way it does when he's played ball too long in noonday sun. He sucks on it, comfort in the moist warm care of mouth against open flesh, self against self. He likes the feeling. One of the other things that is not guaranteed is that you will ever see your wound; that you will ever feel it.

He is sure he could never be secretly injured like Laura. He would bleed and howl, would drip and stain. Hallie has been sent to help with supper. She is setting up a cookie-making operation silently, with a poise that is almost effrontery; she struggles with the ten-pound bag of flour but does not ask for help. Dan keeps his finger in his mouth, teasing the sharp flap of skin while he stirs up meat for the hamburgers. But Hallie is of the internal bleeding school herself nowadays and, though she keeps her eyes on him while she feels around blindly in the closet for the crackling bag of chocolate bits, she doesn't notice him at all.

. . . .

*Why didn't I teach them a thousand things—how to get
the bottle caps off, all about bleach, dry ingredients in one
bowl, wet ones in the other, how you put down wax in a
puddle not a stripe—as if I were going away any minute?
Everyone ought to expect to be gone any minute. But they
are kitchen-illiterate and it is my fault only. I don't care
about the shiny floors any more than I care about anything
but inertia carries you somewhere if not forward, gives the
illusion of movement and now I know how it is for so
many, inertia is what powers everything: the forward
action once begun is all there is   and if you stop*

"High arches," Laura says.

"Sweet voice," says Dan. "Clean uniform."

"Strong hands."

"Independent income."

"Unflappable—when things start flying around here—"

"Not too pretty, huh?"

She makes a face. "Isn't that supposed to be my line?"

"Where in the hell do we find such a creature," Dan
muses, ignoring her.

"Mother told me she knows somebody very good who she
thinks would be willing to come and live here."

"Live here? In the house? Somebody your mother knows?
Why doesn't she just bug the rooms herself the way she's
always wanted to?"

"Listen, I'm not sure you're going to get as much veto
power as you want, you know."

"Because?"

"Because they're paying."

"Thanks for reminding me."

"A fact, that's all. Nothing personal."

"I know, nothing personal. But you know they play it for all it's worth. I'd rather pay interest."

"Oh, be grateful, Dan. Do you know what you'd have to do if it weren't for their help?"

He knows, he knows all too well he'd have to hold a different job with each hand; he'd end up envying her for getting to sit down all day. A little fortune has gone into Laura and barely left a mark. An inheritance. "They ought to call it severance pay."

"Dan."

"What?" It makes him impatient to think the luck of having Laura extends into her parents' safe-deposit vault.

"Do you think they owe you a medal?"

"Shit."

"What does that mean? That expression is so precise."

"I don't know. It means—did you know Hyland raised about three, four thousand dollars for you? *My* family?"

Her face hardens. The smile lines down the sides of her nose tense, the shine rises along their ridges. "What do you mean?"

"I mean what I said. They did everything in the book for you, boy, they called out the heavy equipment. Dances, a penny sale, a magic show. Maestro D and his Disappearing Dog, Binky. Collection boxes. Benefit movies. A benefit *bingo* game, can't you see it? With a big sign somebody painted, I don't remember who, Jay wrote me, in the shape of a bingo card that said L·A·U·R·A instead of B·I·N·G·O. But you couldn't play it, right, because your name has the bad luck to have two A's in it and that would—"

"Will you please."

"What?"

"Stop ranting."

"Am I ranting?"

She closes her eyes. "Sometimes I see myself climbing up into this gigantic lilac bush we had when I was a little girl— I guess it's still there, I haven't really looked for so long—and it had a telephone pole right through the middle of it. And I used to climb all the way up and just sit there looking down on the yard and the roof and my bike and all. But the best part was, from the street nobody could tell how I got up there. Just sat on the lilacs, it looked like. Like a lavender bubble bath." The tears are brimming and then fanning out over her cheeks so fast it seems as if her face is being washed; the more she cries the better she gets, the tear ducts must be a muscle that grows with good exercise. "Facts," she hisses at him. "Nobody's trying to persecute you. My parents are buying me an electric chair, did you know that?"

"An electric chair. Electric chairs are for murderers, they ought to be buying it for me."

"Oh such self-pity, pity, pity. You are shameless."

"You know you can say 'facts' like that to me like some hard-assed businesswoman but underneath you see how sentimental you are with your lilac bush. You think you can con me with your flowers and your little bike lying in the driveway?"

"What am I trying to con you about? I don't understand this argument, what are we doing?"

"We're not doing anything, that's the problem. We're using up energy we used to have better things to do with, if you want to know. We need muzzles, both of us."

She looks away from him. "Would you please bring me some water and my straw, I'm not drinking enough. Maestro D and his Disappearing Dog?"

"Binky."

"Who's Maestro D?"

"Your Broadway friend who sends you the French books with the creeps on the cover. Have you read that thing yet?"

"No. It looks bleak. He must have thought it would cheer me up, somebody else's misery."

"He must have his brains in his back pocket. Hey, do you want to come in and boss me around while I make dinner?"

But "No," she says. "I want a little rest from you. You make me nervous."

He gives her a salute, clicks his heels together. Enough of this fucking minuet. "Okay, you stay here and count your money. I'll see you around sometime."

Because he is afraid of me. He thinks he is living with Lazarus only half returned. Does what he must with me looking away with his inside eyes. Where is your asshole, darling? It's got to be here somewhere. *Does them gently but as a stranger hurrying through, whisking the washcloth like a pro in all the places he knows by heart all eyes closed except the inner. Hums. Talks to me his statue. The VFW monument lies in his bed, wants its shoes off, its neck rubbed. He is like a whore dealing sex without kissing: the job gets done.*

I am the job. If someone else does me, will he talk to me again?

The first woman who came had retired from the hospital though she still wore white stockings and shoes and a snood. A snood! "Put to pasture," Dan said. "Laura could have lifted her."

The second was dismissed by Laura. "Peremptory challenge. You want to know why? She smiled too much. Anybody who sees me and goes on smiling without missing a beat is either blind or brain-damaged."

"That's not fair," John objects when she tells him. He is visiting again on the way home from work. He sits in his grease-dipped longies and lets the day wash off; drinks beer and smiles enigmatically with his mouth closed, which Dan thinks makes him look as if he's suppressing an endless belch.

"Of course it's not fair," says Laura. "What's fair? But it's true."

John shakes his beer to see if it's empty. When he tips to drink the last of it, the back of his head touches the chair. He will go home and tell Donna he caught Big Dan in an apron. Donna will say "It wouldn't do you any harm once in a while—" but John will walk out of the room thinking less of Dan than ever for being used against him. Laura looks at his lean bony neck, all Adam's apple under a day's good growth of beard. He is one of those men who is cloven: different all day among men than he is with women, and proud of it. She is intent on bringing the two together a fraction; on teaching John a thing or two, for her own sake, about the limits of sweetness.

"The fact is, we don't, I don't, need a nurse actually. I need a human being of some sort, I'm not quite sure which, who isn't squeamish, and who'll be decent to have to wake up to every day."

"Sunny face."

"No, not a sunny face, heaven forbid. That's what I'm telling you, I can't stand sunny faces. Smiling through. Those old wartime nurses the soldiers fell in love with. Just somebody with the wit to be—" She shakes her head. "Forget it, John, you've read too many get-well cards."

Dan sees how John lets her hurt him. He likes to be

teased if it's Laura who's doing it, he's like a skinny old bear who thinks he's letting some helpless little animal paw him. Damn fool understands nothing. Or does he go out later and kick stones?

"Anyway, just plain people are cheaper, I imagine," Laura says, to soothe him. "You don't have to go on paying for their training all your life." She likes that; cocks her head, smiling; no one smiles back.

But John looks at her quietly, at how she is like a woman posing a hundred years ago for a glass plate portrait, sitting still for the camera, suppressing her motion. It is her weight-lessness, maybe, the way her feet never move on their metal rests. You could call it repose if you don't like to think of it as helplessness. John's wife never stops twitching—even in her lethargies, which are frequent and which lay her out on the flowered couch, she seems to be vibrating, twanging. She was called a bouncy girl in her day; her day was very recent.

While he is visiting, another woman comes for an inter-view, a practical nurse with an expired license. She is large and highwaisted, a doughy woman from East Hyland, where the women are either fleshy or scrawny, and has a flat face ("sort of Frankenstein-ish," Hallie contributes when her moment for comment has come. "But nice, I guess").

"Well, nice enough. She sort of looks like Julia Child, actually."

"Julia Child doesn't look like Frankenstein."

"You're right," Laura concedes. "How odd." She frowns. "She seems a little timid in spite of her size. And why would somebody let her certificate run out?"

"Well, the stuff you asked if she could do, I'd have been timid." John blurts this and then clearly regrets it. He will always forget how patchy Laura's sweetness is.

"You're not a nurse. What's the matter with the questions?

John—you're looking at a more complicated set of pipes and pumps than the sewerage joints down on Main Street—"

"Oh Laura, bullshit," Dan says. "You've got one damn hose—"

"I'd like to see you with it, my love, the sterilizer, the—"

"You want to lord it over John, you just want him to think he's babysitting a freak."

She looks at him white-faced.

"Your knee's going to go off any minute if you look at me that way."

"Just don't threaten me with my own body if you please, I believe that's my business."

"It's not only your business, damn it—"

"And don't try to make my problems sound like some little hangnail for the sake of your brother's opinion of you."

"Oh Christ now, that's getting complicated."

"Christ yourself, that's what you're doing."

John looks horrified, precisely as he is meant to. Seated in place he looks as if he has backed up a step.

"Let's hire her," Laura says quietly. "What the hell. She's bigger than I am, anyway."

"Bigger than I am," Dan says. "You know, I'll bet she's a dyke. She has a funny look, I can't say just what. What do you think, John?"

John shakes his head, keeping well out of it. "I don't think anything. I don't know."

"Yeah, that's right," Dan murmurs. "Remember that girl you were putting the squeeze on that time, where was it? We were at the beach and she turned around, she had this *voice*, remember? and she said 'Men don't—' "

"Just tell me," Laura says, interrupting. "Why do you think Dan cares if she's a dyke or not. Is that supposed to matter to me?"

. . . .

I move here under the Gro-light awning and study the pots. There are tiny bugs in the coleus, I think, eating its health up, invisibly bloating while the stems soften. I think I see the troop movements, the maggoty pale armies just this side of imaginary. Haven't we given enough here? We've made our contribution to the annual campaign of losses, must they come after us again, bloodsuckers? I sit at my dumb height over the flower pots in their blaze of color, which is terminal. Look, I am spitting into the violet, once twice three times till my mouth goes dry. Not from hate or even anger. A little water. "Why did you do that? Spit," asks Hallie. "Hallie—to touch. To touch. Talk may be good for their souls but does it feed them?"

He has gone out to cut away the sumac trees. Every year they die back and begin again each spring. The wood is still short and spiny, green; the shoots have the moist look of animal babies. Even though he clips them to a stubble with his pruning shears they will grow back, they can't be stopped. (In New York City he met the ailanthus growing in cracks, up walls, over rooftops, out of the dark. Everywhere there is one tree that thrives on neglect.) He is used to paring back trees to make them thrive. Today he wishes he could sow the ground with poison. Some of the branches are so lithe he can't clip them, he holds them with difficulty and mutilates their skin, tears down to the unripe white pith, but they still snap back. Stripping the bark, flaying the little ones, he feels vaguely sick to his stomach. It would take nothing at all— only someone, maybe one of the children watching him from the border of the scruffy grass, saying not a single word—to make him see how he is hurting them, how they must feel their skin being ripped off. He is holding out his own hands with the metal fingers of the clippers going before them, and his fierce dammed anger flows through them gratefully. There is a part of him that expects to hear the torn branches cry out to stop. If there is, that is the part that will refuse.

See him loving his house, this burgher pleasing his mother's hungry memory. His eyes stroke its solid, its vintage, its decent frame. It is his modest woman of good carriage. Some men have pointy cars to make them men.

I loved him first for his refusals I remember for giving the finger to all that, slipping my hand where he did in the same room as my parents with a straight face, so suddenly earnest why didn't they wonder? Laura Jane Shurrock was not much of a good girl ever in spite of, because of, dancing lessons, piano, braces, silk and once a champagne rinse in my endless hair, and thought she was marrying beautifully badly a hood with potential, charm, bad grammar, sweet knees, a kiss that smoked, cool and terror, just who made love to whom was the best question, and he lay down like a docile cat under kindness, more naked of pretense than anyone. His only vanity is body love and I have always taken what I could of that coming on our knees to each other.

I saw him standing among his weedy friends, intense, separated by his intensity, then mine, as he raised his leg and stepped out of the circle.

And now cat's got his cream and he loves the wood-work. August before last (now I remember) he traded me for a set of new gutters, I heard him talk like a lover to the brand-new flashing. He'd rather have reconstructed a lintel or gone on his knees searching for ancient square-head nails. Fell into bed like Jon when he's played too hard. I had to pull his workboots off, sat back on my heels studying the design of mud caked into the tread. That would have been our next fight, I was angry and amused and bored with such—domestication. The house was the other woman taking him away.

And he's still loyal to her. And the house still hates me.

The morning Jenny the nurse is to come Dan awakens depressed. He lies still, prods himself to see what hurts.

They have missed each other, that's all. They have moved all around a tiny room, feeling their way, she with no touch, he with no vision, and between them they have managed to reach right past one another without ever laying a hand on. Now that this other face is going to come to hang there between them like a bare bulb in a socket, there will always be a stranger to keep them half-satisfied, civil and unrelated. Could that be?

He touches her shoulder gently and her arm, touches her hip and her leg, up on the platform of her air mattress; it's time to roll her, in her cage, towards her new keeper. He is feeling her skin as if it were braille, his eyes closed.

"What are you doing? For godsake, Dan—"

"Oh honey," he says, "I'm saying goodbye, that's all. I feel like I'm giving you away to a stranger."

He dares to turn her over, which is done with an effort. She is looking at him wide-eyed. He does surprise her sometimes.

"See, I had my time alone with you but it didn't come to what I expected."

"What do you mean? Whatever did you expect?" Lying down she is stiller than ever. If her arms are raised they will stay where they are forever, looking for gravity, abandoned. If she wanted to put them around him he would never know.

He doesn't answer her. Doesn't she know how he's failed? She looks alarmed. He only pins her eyes with his and holds them. Ten count. One fall.

Then the day begins to come towards them out of the distance, borne forward on the children's voices, and he goes to meet it.

The shattered queen lies on the pantry floor dropped from the highest shelf. Pennies have poured out of her eyes, her broken side, and every porcelain fingertip rolled into a different corner. Who comes to tidy up? Is it the new queen in a skirt round as a barrel, impenetrable, her wrists shining, her shoes pointy, or is that the servant hired by the queen who will put the woman together with the saliva of her own devotion and graft her fingers to the queen's, hold them so tight (the queen feels nothing) that they will grow together, and the queen will have a hand?

But Jenny lasts thirty-six hours.

Laura says, "Oh God, I can see it, it's the old Servant thing."

"What does that mean, 'the old Servant thing'?" Jenny is safely upstairs trying to make the children's beds. Dan is cutting lunch meat for her, he looks like a patient young father assisting his child, so clean-shaven, so spotless and attentive. (He runs the washer a lot to keep his undershirts ice white; he remembers the laundromat he used to drag the family's wash to, the stolid line of Bendixes with their small steamy windows.)

"My mother was always complaining you couldn't find anybody efficient and reliable, both, to clean your house. It was always one without the other, which was just as useless as being neither."

"Your poor mother." Dan's eyelids sink halfway: Robert Mitchum without the butt, giving someone the fish-eye.

Jenny breaks a dish and a glass her first day and manages to unsolder the UHF aerial, but not the way others do, randomly or carelessly: she breaks them because her hands shake; her hands shake, an inch forward, an inch back, because she is terrified. Her terror is surely congenital. Who comes to take care who needs care herself? Dan says, "This is no halfway house, where does she think she *is*?" The woman teeters just outside the grasp of something invisible that she seems to know can squeeze her flat. The children make her jump a foot; when they try to be helpful she jumps even higher. She handles Laura with greased hands. It is instantly apparent that she can't cook, though she swore she could. It feels as if there is a strange dog wandering through the house, huge, light-and-air consuming, everywhere underfoot. Her flat-featured face opens at the mouth in a straight seam which gives her the impassivity of a Japanese mask.

Dan is outraged. But they hired her. They hired her and they didn't check her references: she had dismissed them lightly, said one woman had died (an occupational hazard), another had moved to Florida. In fact, Dan realizes, she had provided twice as many details as she needed. Was he so intimidated by her specialness—nurses lived by their own rituals, after all—that he hadn't recognized that common desperation in her prattle? Still he owes her something; he searches for an honorable solution. She's been out of work for a while, she may be feeling rusty. Yet he finds himself afraid to leave Laura with her and go away. He picks up evidence, like the pieces of another broken dish, that Hallie is afraid of her, goes the other way when she comes near. More furtiveness is not what Hallie needs. Dan is desperate, now, for some kind of work, stopgap, pickup: building something, touching tools and wood, feeding the bank account. Touching ground.

"Laura," he says gently the second morning. He has prepared her for the day, the hard part that he does as tenderly as he can to hide his revulsion. Her two white cheeks, not as smooth as you'd think from a distance, oatmeal-rough, but cool. He dampens a suppository, slips it in, thinking about the girls in *Playboy* and *Hustler* whose asses are as pink as their faces, they probably use powder puffs on them. No scars from sitting forever under the curse of gravity; no dimples from an operation to shave down the tailbone so the spine can stay upright without chafing. The long scar down her back, stitchmarks, pocks from her episodes with stasis. . . .

He settles her sloppily down to do what she can on the plastic pot as Jon comes to the door. He has to hold on to her. "Stay out a second," Dan calls. This is too ignoble a position in which to see his mother. Laura looks away as casually as she can, her mouth tense.

"Hey, that woman's here for Mom."

"Send her up." Laura is not *her* mother.

Jenny comes to the open door in her shoddy plaid spring coat, clutching her leather purse. Irritated, Dan directs her to do an assortment of things, the ones he showed her yesterday, to hang up her coat, to wash her hands. He wants to introduce her to the urinary apparatus, the medication Laura takes to relax her muscles, to prevent infection.

"There's such a lot," the woman mumbles.

"Of medication, you mean? Or hardware?"

She takes a step back from him, saucer-eyed. "No, just—everything. I'm not sure I can remember all of it, my memory isn't—" She touches her hand gently to her low forehead as if it might hurt. It is at that moment—not later when she shrinks from him as they pass at the foot of the stairs; not when she tells Jon she will need him to light the oven because she is afraid to put her arm in; not when she twists Laura's shoulder putting her into a sweater and when Laura shouts out in pain shakes her and tells her harshly to stop—not at those instants but now that Dan knows she can't do it and won't learn, when for ten seconds Jenny lets her head rest mournfully on her fingers as though she is accustomed to being especially gentle with that head, cushioning it, keeping the world's weight off it. Dan is overcome now with a feeling the equivalent of TILT: Disorder. Lightning, thunder. Rumblings inside. Clods of confusion breaking off and floating, jamming all the openings. She has lost half her head somewhere. He wants no responsibility for the other half; nor will he trust her with Laura's or his children's, intact whatever else their little impediments. Did they think they were buying a piece of furniture they could return if it didn't fit in its corner?

Smiling a lot, ignoring her silent tears, without consulting Laura, on the evening of her second day he lets Jenny go. "I think you'll be happier," he says gently, gesturing towards Laura on the sunporch. "She's—it takes a lot, Jenny."

"She makes things hard for me, not moving even a little bit," Jenny says, her face still unmoving, only its slit of mouth working. Her eyes are aghast behind her plaster mask.

"Well, look now, you make it sound like she's doing that on purpose."

"I know I never said this but I don't believe in paralysis, actually," Jenny says weakly but defiantly and looks at a strand of her grey-brown hair. "Actually I'm a believer in will, healing by faith, charity and diet."

Dan smiles bleakly. "I'm a believer in Girl Scout cookies, myself, and a shot of brandy when you've got the chills. Thank you, Jenny, really." He hands her a check scrupulously pro-rated, and her shopping bag full of mysterious weights and shifting shapes which he hopes did not originate in this house, and opens the front door for her.

I thought it was a woman come to rescue me but it was no one.
    Poor Jenny.

"At this point," Laura says, holding up a piece of potato in her clip-on fork, "I begin to feel unreal. Like some package you're trying to fit in a locker at the train station and I won't go."

Laura is in a bad mood. Dougie comes. He brings a potted plant, a cyclamen with blotched leaves and cold white flowers that is said to be very beautiful.

"Those flowers are like lilies," Laura says, objecting.

"Perfect as lilies, yes," Doug agrees, sitting himself in a chair next to her.

"I suppose I should thank you anyway. Thank you."

"How about I take you out for a walk, Laura. It's nice out."

"It is. Why aren't you working on a day like this?"

"Oh, the store's closed for inventory and I don't have to be there every minute. We're breaking in somebody new anyway. Another sucker bites."

" 'How about I take you'—there's no such construction, you know."

Doug smiles, a little sheepish. "Will you come?"

"You know, if you start pushing this chair I'll have to come. I assume you realize that."

"But I asked you if you want to." Dougie's cheeks are becoming the color of an extravagant midsummer sunset.

"Did you ever think you could be an understudy for Danny Kaye?"

He laughs. "Well, he's got about thirty years on me. Maybe his son."

"You mean you've got thirty years on him."

"I don't know which I mean. You're stalling. The sun's going to go down before you decide. Just out on the side of the road, we'll walk up towards Moody's house, get some fresh air. You're very pale."

"I'm supposed to be pale, I'm an invalid. I don't want to get a chill."

"You won't get a chill. I'll be careful."

"Were you Maestro D, with a disappearing dog?"

"Jeezo, you found me out. I'm a hell of a magician, didn't you know that? I'll do some for you sometime. Pull a frog out of your ear, or a rabbit."

Unsmiling, she appears to be gazing down the long well of her sadness. "A frog's more like it. Maybe you can make me disappear."

Dougie cocks his head in his disarmed way that says I'm cute and gentle and my ears come to a point: spare me. He is listening to the strange rough quality of Laura's conversation, the stops and starts and changed directions. The action of a bump'em car, off balance all the time, veering off wildly before the last arc is complete. It's a prerogative she's taken, aggressive and a little disrespectful. She is looking for a way to scratch, to make her mark, assert some power. Nonetheless, frowning, Dougie walks her chair to the kitchen door and stops, uncertain how to get her past it.

"You call my husband is what you do. Indispensable Dan, the built-in man. He's hovering somewhere anyway, he's probably crouching at the keyhole, he thinks I need a chaperone."

But Dan is flat out in the big blue chair in the living room, sagging in angry midafternoon sleep. He wakes spiteful and shivering but he carries Laura out obediently without a word, puts a belt around her, hard, straightens her into her seat, then, empty-eyed, watches the two of them head shakily over the rutted driveway.

Dougie caresses my shoulder, seeing a breast there. Brother John comes just to spend hours not mentioning his wife: cheap cheating. He stares into my lap which he calls immaculate, I'll bet he sees white blossoms gathering there. I'm worth about half a genuine virgin in his sleep.

I miss my friends who woke and moved with me swimming out of traction like fish in our tank, between one dead piece of hardware and the next. We had to make living parts of such dead stuff. We never touched each other and just as well: imagine the plastic, metal, rubber grip of pseudo hand in hand, although we'd never feel it. I didn't talk much but we soothed each other lying becalmed in the same waters. Numbness. Misplaced pain, movement rippling unexpected through some part that looked like it must belong to us. Seeing ourselves bring tears to the eyes of the outside; shrugging. Sometimes the fate they pity is as unattached to us as the leg kicking up against our will.

Ellen came back from a weekend home smelling fine of sex. Fiona went home with the man who clubbed her legs dead and he clubbed her again to show her he meant it. No tears in those eyes. Jones went home and decided it was none, and he never came back: he rode neatly off the Twelfth Street pier in his Everest & Jennings fancy number. They found his railroadman's cap scudding like a gull. Then they found him strapped in tight, head to knees like a diver in midsomersault. The pamphlet says it never would have rusted, not that model. A bunch of cripples mourning Davy Jones. He would have called us sentimental assholes, that was Jones's best sentimental all-around word for the people he liked.

I have my place on the scale, I wish everyone could see that. Some are luckier than others, some haven't much head left. Some were unbearably sad before their legs gave out. But we all laughed in unison more often than anything was funny, our community of exiles patched and plastered, big as a city. Together we judged and were tough on anyone who suffered insufficiently. Guilty, we said, of creeping ease. (Or ease creeping.) Toughened our nerveless hides to keep from softening and decomposing. We read the papers (shoulder adductor muscles pushing the hand to turn the page) and there was a young man who asked to be killed (and was, and was) because his legs were done by his own motorcycle. His brother obediently shot him and got a suspended sentence (though he has the rest of his life to live and nobody'd envy him that).

Well, did we jump. What parts of us could rise to it. Aw gee, said Jones, poor bugger, and we're supposed to cry. His legs, for lizard's sake—his legs? Visions of all the sugar plums we could pluck if our hands could take short messages. Why didn't he shoot himself? Jones asked out loud. (Paras are more our friends than the rest of the world but they don't impress us much, is what he meant.) His face would redden like a hardworking man's, a man planting fence posts, ditch-digging. Ah, to be able to do yourself in like a man! You bloody well wouldn't have to if you could, said Jones.

And had to roll to his own death, but he did it to himself. We were proud of him though it brought us down a bit, the judgment his death seemed to make on all of us. All I could do was turn away from it. Jones had two families to support, teeming numbers, and half a face. He had a voice to frighten his own children, that came out of his trake tube; permanent hole in the throat, blood spurting like a water fountain when anything slipped. His own ghosts he had—there is no mutual, central Soul of Cripple, however much we hung together on the sixteenth floor, pooling our small resources, tugging on weights, sanding and sorting and cheering each other's infinitesimal gains.

His own death, then. And I turned again and wished him peace: an eternity of sweat, real hard work, not O.T., and realer booze. Miss Toko opening his mouth and pouring Johnnie Walker down. No—not having to do it for him. Jones himself hitching and scratching and chasing her down the hall on his own heavenly legs.

Friends step forward with acquaintances and relatives for hire but Laura insists on a stranger. Somebody passing through. If they had a train station she'd go sit on the platform and hail the first kind face. The bus comes through town once a day and drops people in the Hyway Motel parking lot, but she insists that isn't the same, anyone who knows anything ought to know that. Dan doesn't argue.

They hire an older woman with the references of Florence Nightingale. Although she is slender and straight as a birch she is so solid the old floorboards whine and snap under her aimed white shoes. It is clear she can do anything, and she demands commensurate respect. Her name is Mrs. Archambault and she reminds Dan of Mrs. Hurley, his nemesis from fifth through eighth grade. Under her firm white curls her smile is a cold ray of light, dry and chilling.

"You know what that lady makes me see whenever she smiles?" Jon asks. "When we go see the computers at the science museum, if you push the right answer and it says YES GO ON TO THE NEXT QUESTION, those little green letters."

"You're crazy," Hallie says. "I like her. She already showed me how to make a pomander."

"What's a pomanda?"

"It's a thing with cloves, like if you take an orange or an apple and stick them in all over."

"Yuk, that's old granny work. What are you going to do with a clovy apple anyway?"

"It'll never go *bad*, dummy."

"So it'll never go bad. What do you *do* with an apple that doesn't ever go bad? Put it in the museum along with the mummies or what?"

"Oooooh." Her answer has an echo. Oooooooooh, irritation like impatience like real pain. Dan tries to account for Hallie's attraction to this fish. No, steadier than a fish, that's the secret: a ship with a hull that doesn't even shimmy in the tide. Someone to grapple on to. Some children scream and others only fester. Hallie holds on. That "ooooooh" is prickled; it means, he supposes, "Back off, brother, this one's mine."

Mrs. Archambault, however, develops her own qualms. "Your wife," she informs Dan on her third morning, "has a number of ideas of her own."

Dan is sanding the edge of a lap board he is making for Laura, doing it by hand to enjoy the rhythm of it, the rasp like steady breathing. "Yes she does," he answers innocently. "It's a good thing too."

But this charm irritates the nurse into a greater precision. "She has a few too many, Mr. Courser, under the circumstances." She stands in the doorway of his workshop empty-handed as though she expects him to hand her some tool she can apply to the situation.

He puts down his sandpaper obediently. "Too many for what?"

"I cannot work with her if she tells me how to go about my business," the nurse says. "Patients are notoriously sure they know what is best for themselves when they are in fact often the very last ones to know."

"Well, what kind of problems are you having? As far as I can see, your business is her comfort. Isn't it?" (He asks himself; double-checks. Surely it isn't the nurse's comfort that's at stake. He wishes they had hired a friend.)

"Then I think you'll understand if I say this is a situation that is not—is *not*—going to work out to my satisfaction. As a professional, this is. Your wife is a perfectly nice young woman but she is going to make no progress with her infirmity if she doesn't take herself in hand. Certain things are clear as glass and this is one of them."

Dan stands before this woman empty of opinion, fingering the rough paper in his hand. It licks back like a cat's tongue. He must have a silly grin on his face, he thinks, and puts his hand over his mouth, his lifelong expression of confusion. ("Right," Laura has been known to say, "and keep it covered before you say another word you'll regret.") He has had moments like this, not one of them clear as glass, when Jon or Hallie have had fights with their friends; when all the parents have stood, locked, over the blameless heads of their children, wondering whose story to believe.

He goes to Laura and finds her in hot tears, unapproachable. "I want her out of here," she tells him very quietly, shaking her head as if to get water out of her ears. But the quiet is charged, the low throat-snarl of a threatened dog.

"What did she do, hon? She said—"

"I don't care what she said and I don't want to work it out. I am not going to negotiate anything, just pay her her goddamn two days and get her out of my sight."

He is assaulted again: she can't even slump to cry. "Laura."

"She *hurt* me. Okay? I'm not supposed to have any opinion about that."

"What do you mean she hurt you?" *You're unhurtable. You're stone, my beauty, you're wood, you can be chipped or cracked but not hurt.*

"I mean she moved me around during my range-of-motion and snapped my neck and thumped my head and all these— sadistic things—I mean violently, I don't mean firmly—and when I pleaded with her to stop she said to me"—Laura pushes her voice towards baritone—" 'Young woman, you need to feel everything you can, sensation is what is necessary to your poor deprived system, you must experience pain like the rest of us.' "

"What, to keep you humble? Is this religious?"

"No, it's therapeutic. Apparently. I don't *believe* this!"

Laura, when she is angry, is as focussed as an arrow. She sits now, drawn up, concentrated, narrowed to a point. She is entirely familiar to him in these moments: Dan can remember the first time he saw her close around an opinion, defending it with her entire body as if it were a small protectable object, a jar with a turtle in it.

"First we get hope, charity and diet—she didn't believe in paralysis—and now we get a righteous flame thrower? Laura—"

"Don't 'Laura' me, Dan, I'm only sitting here."

"Jesus, honey, I thought California and New York were where all the nuts hung out. Aren't nurses supposed to be all kind and sort of cozy and dull? My mother had one that was a real whoopie-pie, you know? Soft sugar on the inside, warm fingers. They used to watch soap operas and cry together. What *is* this?"

Because he is terrified suddenly, stripped and terrified at their joint defenselessness—that they have had to open their doors and invite such strangers in. His mother knew: she was always afraid to leave the door open. *Animals walk in*, she said, *and they won't walk out on their own.* Laura, modest Laura, being turned bottom up, all her intimate places fluttered over by women she's never seen before. ("But every part of me is public property now," she'd told him once, it's nothing new. "You gave your monopoly away, my friend. The doctors have me and I don't. You don't.") But that was a hospital, he thinks, making the distinction to save himself a shred of hope. This is her house, her bedroom, her bed. Can anyone come in for hire, talk about fringe benefits and social security and make her cry like this? Is that what you pay for asking someone, even for a price, to cart away your shit, your piss in a big yellow jug? For sponging you all over? Do these women want to punish her somehow, for her soft bright-eyed breasts, her lovely ruined body? What's her beauty to them? Do they need her helpless? Available? Is she their cadaver, to be teased and practiced on?

Laura sits in her gleaming chair, staring straight ahead like a woman alone on a promontory. (Remember Laura at the lake in denim shorts staring into her future, twisting her long reddish hair nervously around her finger, squinting, trying to make it out as it disentangled itself from the trees and the blueberry bushes and came towards her, slow and indistinct.) "Dan, please," she says quietly, "tell her to leave. Why do you have to think about it?"

He breathes out, vigorously, as if clearing his nose of stale air will clear his head. "Why don't we let her stay till suppertime, Lor, and just see. Maybe this was a misunderstanding. Maybe the rest of the day—"

"Dan, she hurt me. I mean, she *already* hurt me." Fight for me, her eyes say. No more challenges between men, this is the kind of violation she needs protection from: the habits of strong women who do not love her. Arbitrary pain.

"I'll talk to her," Dan says. Leaving, he hears a little moan from Laura that crawls in his chest like an infinitesimal worm, itchy, guilt-provoking, ineradicable.

Downstairs Mrs. Archambault is rearranging the kitchen cabinets. It will be a week before he can find everything he needs.

Running. Walking fast. Banging the pots, letting them tip and clatter down. Elbows against the wall. Fists. Knocking for escape, stamping till the floor kicked back. Oh, I do remember.

When I feel myself rising inside that way—rising from my chair, boiling over the rim of my body, brimming

*out, flowing onto the woods path where I used to run it
off, get past it, saying* NO *with my whole body going—
what do I do with it now? They forgot to tell me. Sleep?
Scream? Eat myself alive? Those terrible mystery sores are
simple: only anger. A slow burn. My dumb self trying to
curse, eating from the inside out, trapped animal with
teeth. Trying to get some light, some air. Looking for
action.*

*One of these days I'll find it, whatever it's called. A
place to go inside that won't brew poison in a stagnant pit.*

"A couple of perverts," he tells Jay Hatfield. "What in
the hell am I going to do? Imagine cracking her neck—see,
she told me she studied chiropract—y?"

"Ic," Jay says. "Chiropractic. Marian went once for a
pinched nerve."

"Okay, whatever it is. But they're only half right, is what
she thinks. Where there's been deprivation of feeling you've
got to stimulate the nerves—sort of make them hop to, you
know, like foot soldiers or something."

"Why? What's supposed to happen?"

Dan shrugs. "God knows. Great God in his heaven only
knows what she thinks will happen. What's so strange is, you
know, you'd think somehow these people would be the most
realistic, they'd be trying to help her adjust to what she can
and can't do instead of—I don't know, I got the feeling this
woman was desperate for some kind of power. Maybe she's
a frustrated doctor or something. The other one was just desperate period. Bonkers."

"So what did you do?"

"Canned her. What else could I do? I tried to call Laura's
doctor in New York and ask him, but I couldn't get him,

so . . . I don't know, Laura was so mad that I didn't just believe her, I decided kindness, goddamn it. Common sense. I can't believe there's anything therapeutic in making somebody hysterical." Jay nods avidly; he is a commonsense man himself, his flourishes of paternal authority come from his ability to reduce all situations to the visibility of a good classic board game. A round of Monopoly that takes a lifetime to play out.

"But her nerves did hop, boy. She went to sleep crying last night, and crying and crying, she said I couldn't begin to imagine what it was like to have all that pain sort of compressed into one part of her body, her neck and head and shoulders, all of it there. But I think I can imagine. Enough." Dan closes his eyes and takes a deep breath. "She must have cried for two hours, like she was stuck in a rut, and I finally gave her some Valium to get her quiet, but she kept quivering in her sleep, half the night. Legs kicking and arms knocking up against me. Overload."

"No wonder you look like something they dug out of a swamp, I was wondering." Jay leans across his counter on his long elbows. His rolled-up shirtsleeves flap.

"Thanks, Jay. You do wonders for my soul."

"Look, hang in there, Dan, is all. You'll find somebody decent, there's got to be. I never heard stories like this before, I didn't know nursing attracted so many odd lots and broken sizes."

"Maybe it doesn't." Dan bends down to pick up a paper. "Maybe it takes perfectly decent people and drives them over the edge, and we just never happened to notice before. Emotional basket cases."

"I don't believe it," Jay says, standing to take his quarter. "Don't forget, my mother-in-law was a nurse." He flips the coin once, catches it and closes his hand. At least he'll let Dan buy his own newspaper again. "Maybe you're just jumping

too soon. Hang on and wait. Wait and see what comes that
you feel you can trust."

"Yeah, something'll wash up in a bottle. Wait for the
tide to change. Look for the silver lining." He shrugs. Time,
time. It's Laura who's got the time. He goes out to his car
hearing the insistent thump of the old cheerleaders' hymn, the
one about who had what. Miralee used to do it, all of her
heaving and lurching in her navy sweater with the innocent
white collar. *Boys got the muscles! Teachers got the brains!
Girls got the sexy legs and We Won The Game!*

The tide does not change.

There is a gross good-natured woman whose voice would
drive Dan wild in a week, who slaps him on the back, staggers
him with her uncalculated force. But she is really a baby
nurse. She looks at Laura with dismay. "It's a shame you're
not about to deliver, dear," she says. "I'd come to work for
you in a minute. But—"

"But," says Laura, smiling at the idea. "I'll see what I can
do about it."

"Listen," the woman begins, "you wouldn't be the first,"
and Dan dares to take her lightly by the shoulders and move
her towards the door.

There is an overpriced charmer who looks like an airline
stewardess; Laura vetoes her on financial grounds. Dan is
relieved.

There is a male nurse Dan dismisses on the doorstep.

*My ears are open as a bird's throat, hungry. What the day
drops in—inchworm, blindworm, stunted snake, walking-*

flying-fish, four bugs caught by the wings by Jon—depends on the state of the cripple's market. The Exchange is glutted with a great many friends sometimes coming to visit between obligations: get the dog-tag, go to the cleaner's, visit Laura, don't forget the chicken livers and the thin-sliced cheese. Wouldn't I do the same? I'm on the duty roster. They rotate me. Often they come in pointed the other way, already, and have sharp edges and the inclinations of bondsmen. Hello I say   Hello goodbye   I say sounding invisible.

Jon hands him the mail and goes off on his bike. Dan leans on the front of his car to open the envelopes. There is a schedule from the Round Hill Children's Rehabilitation Center to which Laura is going to go once a week to dabble as best she can with the childsized weights and springs; an ad for bubble-plastic carseat upholstery that stays cool in summer; a note to Laura from an old college classmate who has "just heard," which he opens for her and places on her lap tray. It will be obsessed with survivor guilt; they always are. There is one more envelope, a large brown one with no return address. He pulls out a grey sheet of advertising torn from one of the hot young Boston papers, the kind they hawk in Harvard Square. Red crayon lines circle half a dozen ads and across the top with that same red crayon someone has traced through a stencil so that the words look anonymous and official:

NEXT TIME YOUR IN BOSTON TRY THESE
SLAVE AVBLE. Young gdlkg M slave wants to be dominated by females/couples/horny men who are really into the scene any desire fulfilled. Send phone or place to meet. I'm perf for household duties. Box 1103.

MENAGE A TROIS. Wake up to new possib. for stale marriages. New thrills in 3some. Clean safe educ. Days best. Photo helpful. Can you stand unblievble heavy sex. If not don't answer. Box 38.

↙FOR YOUR WIFE

ADULT BABY PANTS. Handsome kind prof single wht. M 30 seeks permanent relation with a naughty female who would love to wear rubber pants and diapers. And return to the happier days of being a baby again. Box 642.

The hood of the car he is leaning on is very hot, it reflects the sun up into Dan's face. The hair on the back of his neck rises, though, as if he is standing in a draft.

GD. LOOKING WELL EDUC. MALE would like to explore bondage and other sensuous fantasies with alive, bright, innovative and fun loving female. Pleasure and excitement together but always with gentleness and mutual respect. Box 809.

He has never come near this feeling before: he would like to take his rifle and go downtown, hide behind a car and pepper the street with bullets till they all fall down. Easy. Then he would walk Laura in her chair, down the aisle in the middle, between their shoes, their dropped handbags, their crewcuts and sideburns lying like flung hair on the barber's floor. "Bondage!" he would shout. "Gentle respectful bondage anyone?" There would be no takers. He and Laura would survive, would even forgive, and the ones left standing would damn well know it.

"Sandy, I want to see some houses." Dan sounds as if he's come for something illicit. Sandy Mead, before he's even spoken, is rising from his desk, rubbing his hands together. Surely he doesn't intend to look like a predator into whose lair fresh food has just walked on its own two feet; he intends only to look ready: realty is a service profession.

Sandy spreads his hands wide. "You're putting the house up!"

"Look, hey, that's the last part, I don't even want to think about that till I have to. First I'm looking for something we can both live with. All, I should say."

Sandy nods gravely, humbly, attentively. He is a stranger doing the darky shuffle. Smooth-faced, blond-faced, he plays this game so perfectly he seems to be asking not to be taken seriously. "Striped tie, Sandy, wow," Dan says, hoping to jolt him out of his role. "You look like a banker."

"Wish I was, Dan, wish I was. It hasn't been much of a season. But look, you'll want to get rid of the big house, Dan'l, the equity is something I suspect you're gonna need, you know."

"Hey. What can you show me, sport?" His patience comes already curdled.

"Okay. Let's look on the optimistic side."

Dan is instantly pessimistic.

They go and look. Sandy insists that he knows what Laura will need. The inner walls of the brand-new house which he predicts Dan will love for its "flexibility" feel like the inside of an airplane cabin. "What *is* this stuff?" Dan asks, pounding the repellent figured cardboard with his fist, fully expecting to crash through. "Sandy—Jesus. Is it that soy protein they make hamburgers out of?"

"Dan." Sandy laughs.

"Okay. What else do you have? Something with walls, maybe, I have a kind of an old attachment, childhood sentiment or something, to a real wall." Dan knows he makes his friend nervous, makes him want to be busy elsewhere, even with easy browsers who are wasting his time.

Back in the office, in the spray of the Muzak speaker, Sandy says, "Look, I haven't forgotten I'm talking to a construction man." He turns the pages of his big book, humming no melody, stopping to consider photographs under plastic, descriptions that list their characteristics with X's in the proper column: Fireplaces XX   Town water X   Oil heat   Forced air   Electric baseboard X. The X's sap the houses' uniqueness: it is all a matter of categories. Like Laura's rehab chart: Maneuvers curbs   Sensation left fourth finger X   Lifts glass X (unreliable).

Although it is clear this is not the way to do it, Dan consents to see another house, for Sandy's sake, so as not to appear as sick as he feels. There are still people in this one; he keeps his mouth tight shut. The wife of the house, a young aproned woman with Jane Wyman bangs who would be comfortable on a television ad for floor wax, circles anxiously, answering questions no one has asked. Her nervousness, in a seller's market, makes Dan wonder if the problem is the heating bills, the unstanchable roof leaks, the thinness of the walls, the neighbors. You buy a house like this, he thinks, you get what you deserve.

The furniture that springs into view like a virulent growth as they cross each threshold speaks to a different dream, though. He is fascinated. Even Dougie would never peddle a roomful of such dirty fantasies. Why does he think that, he wonders; it's only furniture. Some kind of lurid sensuality floats on the darkened bedroom air. Why would anyone need such an odd chair, for example, that invertebrate crushed velvet slither? Is it supposed to remind you of a woman on her back? He imagines Laura on it, bent to fit, in all her unbendable places. Everything is massive, the lamps like swollen pillars, the couch striped emphatically, an eight-foot beach towel. What a fine one-family repudiation of the Sears colonial in whose veneered wooden grip most of Hyland lies docile.

"Sandy, no. I don't think so, no."

Sandy is opening closets frenetically, pushing him into bathrooms, reciting a litany of hampers and concealed lighting, leading him into the basement where gusts of steam belch from the dryer like a New York manhole in January. If all his friends understand as well as Sandy what he needs to survive, then his first terror was the right one: he is alone with his pride and his broken wife and they might as well take their business to Arizona where the flat-out houses grow.

Sandy's fair face is a wonderful broad globe, skin stretched taut over small features, shiny forehead beginning to dominate. There is a little haze of sweat across that brow. Dan has always thought he looked like a smart young doctor: healthy, snappy, keen, self-satisfied. He is being sold out by a pro.

Sandy pats the woman's shoulder for comfort as if he were that doctor, watching her sink back on her heels in weary disappointment. He blames the doorways and the kitchen layout, talks in a lowered voice about Laura's needs as if they were the unreasonable demands of a crank.

But back in the car, loosening his tie by thrusting a finger into the knot and swivelling his neck around, he says, "Danny, don't look at me that way, do me a favor. Don't you think I know what you'd like? I also know what it costs these days. I'm trying to find something realistic for you. We've got this bullshit motto, you've seen it in the window: IT DOESN'T COST ANY MORE TO HAVE YOUR DREAM HOUSE COME TRUE? Huh! When the hell are we going to be honest with people? A really well-built contemporary—I don't understand, Danny. Why aren't you thinking about building your own? Nobody around here's going to meet your standards, no way. You ever take a good look at what gets hidden behind the moldings? You're off two inches where the ceiling meets the wall? What the hell, you slap a little plywood crap on there, a little edge, it looks like what you put on kitchen shelving, so what? So does the next guy, I don't have to tell you. That's not something I go around putting out to buyers, I mean—but why in the hell don't you get some land and just sit down with Laura, plan out exactly what you need? You could bring it in much cheaper and you'd have what you want. No stripping to cover the mess."

"I should," Dan says very quietly, floating somewhere absently. "No real good reason I can't, I always wanted to build a house." God, he is tired. Confusion, indirection; anger isn't the only exhausting emotion. "It's hard to say what's wrong right now. I ought to have the time, God knows I've got time right now with no job, but it's the energy, somehow. Nothing ever happens the way you plan it, I found that out. I never thought about it much, how you don't only need the right lot and the good wood and all that, you need the right time in your life." He is looking out the windshield seeing nothing. "I don't want to start something and then regret it, that's all. And I love my own house like you'll never know. Nobody knows what that house gives me." He shakes his head, whispers. "Nobody knows." All the losses that don't go on the bill to the insurance company, the diminishings.

"Danny, you're discouraged." Sandy puts his arm across the back of the seat, ready to hear a confidence.

"No, no, we'll make it. I mean, Laura and I are okay. She's got more drive than this baby here." He slaps the dashboard. "But the rest of us . . . I just get tired, is all. I have trouble concentrating. It's hard to explain." He feels like an exhausted housewife making her morning complaint.

"Well, you're not *doing* anything." Sandy starts the car, easing across the shoulder. It sounds as if someone is throwing pebbles at their windows. "Jeez, you know, there's some things, my wife used to say, work is like nursing the baby. You stop doing it there's nothing there. People go around thinking they want a lifelong vacation, Danny, but I don't know. Some makes more, more makes enough, but if you keep it you just go dry. Just like that old udder. Magic."

Dan nods. He sees two different painting jobs on one block. Up on a scaffold someone in a white suit like a baker's is turning a scuffed white house robin's egg blue. It's the season for perfecting your holdings. Is it losing his sleep, the regular kick in the gut by the alarm clock, that has him unstrung like this? His eyes burn as the car heads down the Main Street hill; he has the feeling he gets when his car is not quite in control: about to career off to one side and welcome the instant of rest when something stops it, hard. Sandy is too intent on waving to friends and satisfied customers to notice. Who sent the classified, which of these friends and neighbors?

Laura said it: happy endings are what strangers see just at the moment when they want to turn away. There's always another Technicolor sunset somewhere, pal, she said. And then the dark comes down.

There will be a door in the middle of the sunporch. Or not the middle, off-center, so she won't have so far to go to get into the house. There will be a long smooth path, concrete, from the driveway to Laura's door and then a short ramp to get in. "What will the sign say?" he asks Hallie. "We'll put up a sign that says 'Laura's daur.' Or maybe 'Loora's door,' what do you think?" Her giggle is back to normal, abandoned, silly. Her logic in his hands.

The room will be reoriented—it will be their bedroom, not haphazard, camped in. All the furniture, their clothes, the little ashtray with its collar buttons and pins and pennies.

She will go upstairs on special occasions only, they'll take her up for her birthday; otherwise it will not be necessary.

"Am I going to trust you to clean a whole floor without supervision? Oh, the ceiling's going to cave in under the load."

"You're free, woman! There are millions who would slay to have the housework torn from their grip."

"Poor Molly Bolt, beloved consort, whatever would she think of me?"

Dan, excited by his renovation plans, stands empty-handed with his legs apart, the way men in shirt ads stand holding blueprints, pointing here and here, no wrinkles in their shirts. "Nothing compared to what her husband would think of me for mutilating his house. But Molly Bolt of all people would understand, love. You can bet your little finger *she* was on speaking terms with catastrophe. I wonder how many kids she lost to diarrhea, for Christ's sake, and mange and fever and all those other insignificant little murders."

He leaves Laura sitting with a book half in sun, half in shade. He and Jon try some slam-dunk fancy stuff under the blue hoop on the garage.

I hang in the tree and watch the house. Dashing of swallows in the door and out, flipping, banking, holding in midair. Children taking five steps where they might take one. Jon's ball lofts, hits the basket rim with a flat twang. Dan's whistles on through. When Hallie runs her hair flies out behind like a brown silk scarf, and there's more symmetry in this than I ever knew. The long day has a shape to it: round in the morning, bulbous I suppose with expectations. Narrow in the middle (I shout "Lunchtime!" reeling them home with my voice and they do come at a

*run). The yellow-white part of afternoon is shapeless,
stretched full of the heavy-work of play, everything stuffed
in. The children have time to grow up, if ever, after lunch.
And all of it narrows in late afternoon to a little plank
to be stepped across into evening. I come down from the
tree and meet them on the other side. Courteously we all
go in to dinner.*

From a distance, coming around the side of the house, he
sees her moving peculiarly in her chair. (Half of everything
she does still seizes him by his heels and flings him upside
down with surprise; she is still a stranger to him every other
minute of her movement.) Now, for example, she is slapping
at herself wildly, inaccurately, with the back of her hand,
whimpering like a small child caught in something sticky.

"Jesus," he shouts when he sees her eaten everywhere by
the black flies. They hang like a lacy veil across her eyes. He
sees old unbearable elementary school movies of African
children in a caul of flies, suffering their trachoma, ignoring
them because they are thicker than air.

They have drawn their own peculiar kind of syrupy blood,
nothing like a mosquito's. It lies on the skin of her arms and
neck and hardens there. Hallie and Jon used to sleep helpless
like that as new babies before they could protect themselves.
Laura bought mosquito netting but the damn things were
so small they got in anyway, like fleas. He remembers once,
later, calling to Hallie at the lake to come out of the sun, but
she stood her ground, stubborn as she's always been, and
before he went and seized her in spite of her howling, he
watched the thick blood pop out on her skin like infinitesimal
buckshot holes.

"Bastards," Dan murmurs and wipes what he can of the blood, which instantly springs back to the surface.

"You look like a hundred needles came and sewed you!" Hallie cries, half attracted, half repelled. "Oh Mama!"

"Keep me in the cellar next black-fly season," Laura says, trying to laugh. They drag their bodies, like shiny black rice, through the perspiration on her upper lip. Dan thinks of flies on a camera lens—but she *does* feel them, not the ones on her arms but surely the dozen on her cheeks and forehead.

"Watch out," he says, "I'm going to belt you!" He swipes his hand, cutting with the pinky, across her mouth, then rests his fingers on her cheek. "Which are the worst, hon, the ones you feel or the ones you don't feel?"

She closes her eyes, which have reddening welts under the brows on both lids. "Sadistic question. Do I really have to choose? I feel like—which was the god who got chained to a rock and the vulture came every day and took another bite out of his liver?"

"You're asking the wrong man," he says, and wipes her face, slowly, with his half-clean handkerchief, pushing her hair back from her forehead. It's growing back, he will be able to hide in it again soon.

"Why was he chained?" Jon asks, collapsed in the grass at her feet.

"Oh, he brought fire to the earth, he robbed the heavens, I think, and he gave it to mankind. They never had fire before that. And Zeus got mad—"

"Like stealing the bomb and giving it away to the Russians?"

"They never had *fire*?" Hallie asks. She looks up like a disciple.

Dan doesn't much care about gods and their livers. He

leaves them there looking like story hour and goes into the kitchen to get cool water for Laura's face.

The still point of the turning world—what was the rest of it? I've read so little since my freshman year, grown up into a Yahoo. . . . Neither flesh nor fleshless? A grace of sense, a white light still and moving. Now I think I know that poem from the inside out, I can come up through the stem or the bole or the core—whatever it would be. Something about roses with the look of flowers that are looked at. All the details of my life are lying around me like petals, casually plucked out and powdered between the fingers. But there in the center the nub that had no dimension to start with, and no movement. None to lose. Sitting composed, I feel how my center of gravity has only shifted upward. Still point on which the whole of me is written, all my angels on the head of a pin!

In the middle of the night when she awakens shaking, Laura tells Dan her dream. Someone has raped her. "This girl at the Institute told me everybody has a rape dream eventually, it's inescapable, the quads' communal dream. Like a punishment, for all the things we don't want anymore. We pass it around. Even the men do."

"Inescapable?" Dan asks in an awed whisper. It is the first time he has held her unselfconsciously. He rocks her body and smooths her hair, tenses his angry fingers in its warmth. She doesn't know who the rapist was, he was backwards on her, anonymous back and shoulders, all of it finished already, a fact somehow, as if it had happened a long time ago, or maybe many times, distant. But then she heard the emergency whistle and the firemen came running, they told her she had pulled the alarm. The rapist stood up on a painters' scaffold and confessed what he'd done and the men in their rubber coats laughed and retched and pointed their fingers. "Sick," they said, and "G-ross," the way the children say it. What kind of freak is he? they asked, and at last the man backed down, she saw him walk away with his head lowered, saying "You're right, I didn't, I never did. Who'd want to do a crazy thing like that?"

"Don't, Laura, you're only saying that," Dan tells her, pleading.

"No, that's what happened. But then, together, see, the firemen took the fire hose and they pushed it in me with the nozzle . . ."

"*Laura.*" He is going to be sick, she is doing this to hurt him.

But, she says, it leaped and jerked, she on the end of it, impaled. "It has to hurt or it's no good," the firechief yelled.

"Was it Jay?" Dan asks, shocked, as if she is reporting a real crime, for which he can exact punishment.

"How should I know? No, it was nobody I knew, just some man, shouting. But the hose looked just like the catheter."

"Sure," he murmurs, relieved. "Of course. That's all it was."

They were all down on Spring Street in front of the firehouse, dancing and laughing. A block party, a party for Laura. The water in the street was turning to ice, and the hose was icing, stiff, sticking to her, icicles hung down between her thighs, grey beard. Only then she was standing on the subway in New York and she was trying to get her fingers off the bar and they were stuck, iced on, she was tearing flesh to get free. It was her stop and she was calling out to stay in the station, pull the cord, stay till she could get her hand back. "Danny," she says, and he warms her in his arms, angry, seeing the faces of his friends the volunteer firemen. "I want to go to sleep and never wake up. Please."

He tightens his grip on her. "Never."

"*Please?* I'm a ghost."

He wants to kiss her. Someone wants to kiss her, if only she'd believe it. He touches her lips, which are cold (of course, of course), and all the rest of him, chest on down, falls. Moves sadly, turning over.

"Ghost," she murmurs. "See, your hands go right through me." She lets him into her mouth at least. He may not survive her helplessness; it is far more powerful against him than resistance.

When the Shurrocks arrive, Dan is happy, happy. He has always found it impossible to present less than a smooth glass surface over his marriage to their daughter: He and Laura are under the obligation that dogs all the mildly rebellious to live perfectly, to justify themselves without end. He smiles untouchably behind the pane, and the smile is two-dimensional, even, untroubled; all the more so now. They had only recently left off dealing with him as if there had been a shotgun over his head at the wedding—how else to explain Laura's dereliction from sanity? Now that strained delicacy and sarcasm are back in place again, almost comfortably familiar, to remind him that they think of him and will, no matter what the evidence, as the man who tried to murder their daughter.

He is tearing down kitchen cabinets when they come, so that he can widen the doorway for Laura. He has, in fact, begun the work that very morning, which Laura tells him is insane. He knows that. She makes him try on half a dozen valid explanations for his need to present his parents-in-law with a kitchen doorway strewn with shavings and wood chips. They range from hostility to the need to impress them with his industry and optimism, exactly, she says, the way he carries on when his brother John is around. "Yeah," he agrees mildly, bored. "Yeah, I suppose that's right. You should have been a psychologist."

But none of them touches the real point of pain. It is too simple and too complex for him to be able to say it. That he wants to be happy. No, just to *do* something that will make him, for a few hours at least, or a day or three or five, happy the one way he knows how to be, lost in something not himself. And *he* wants to be happy, put the stress there, he thinks. Not she, not they. He. Me. Bad enough to do without sex, to do without so much of the grace Laura brought once to his life, the kind he gave no thought to. But to go literally empty-handed this long. . . . He wants to shore himself up against the weekend visit of DeWitt and Eva Shurrock with a fistful of halfpenny nails and a saw with real teeth.

They stand in the doorway that opens to the mudroom and watch him. They have missed by a few hours the spectacle of Dan's approach to the cabinets, which is violent and satisfying. There are many ways to detach a cabinet from a wall and most of them leave the cabinet intact. Dan's, today, is to attack it as if it were the roof of a burning building. "Stand back!" he calls to Jon and Hallie who are watching from across the room. "The chips are going to fly!" And they do. The axe sinks into the pine and crazes it into feathery lines like Laura's good china cups after a splash of hot coffee, and he hacks and wallops in a noisy crescendo. The wood whines, recoiling. The last few weeks would have been better if he'd had some wood to chop and split. He wishes the cabinets were logs.

The Shurrocks are standing, watching him tear and curse and tear some more. By now he is using a crowbar, trying to free the back of the cabinet from the wall. He is pink-cheeked and sweating and, though he is wearing his contemptible work clothes and doing a laborer's duty, still—without romanticizing, DeWitt Shurrock will say to his wife later, or not dare to say to his wife but will silently think, as will she to herself —he is someone to reckon with, or almost so, when he is doing what he is good at. (That he is doing it badly is not for them to know.) He has a certain attractive vigor—aimed, somehow—the way a man might shoe a horse or deliver a calf. Not to exaggerate: no one would mistake the stance for grandeur. But he is a self-sufficient young man in his way, whose muscles gleam picturesquely when he perspires. "You appear these days," Eva Shurrock tells Dan from the doorway, forced to raise her voice above the racket, "to have the whole ration of health in your family to yourself."

She sees him put down his hammer and force himself to smile minimally from behind his safety glass, whose faults have been repaired since their last visit.

Laura's younger sister, Carol, has come with them. Dan sees her shadowed in the doorway behind her mother and does a classic double-take: begins to look elsewhere and then swings back to stare at her, astonished. She has been in Paris for a few years studying the cello, and though she phoned once after the accident and spoke to Dan very quietly, her voice disappearing into the transatlantic rumble, he has no memory of her shocking resemblance to Laura. He keeps his eyes on her so long she becomes self-conscious and walks into the kitchen nervously, casting around for a place to put her suitcase down.

They settle themselves into the house, filling it, lowering the ceilings, pulling in the walls, suddenly everywhere (though Carol and her father are quiet, serene). Hallie and Jon are dispatched on errands, they run here and there with great urgency, flattered, always, by the ragged unpredictable attention of their grandparents.

Dan's resolution not to witness first meetings with Laura turns out to be impractical. Laura and Carol are in tears together on the sunporch. Their shapes are sculpted in light, curved masses heaped one on the other: Carol's head in Laura's lap, Laura's head bent to her sister's as though to comfort her. DeWitt Shurrock visits the begonias that are washed with the Gro-light, he wanders to the kitchen and back again; then he settles in with his newspaper, legs crossed with an indolence Dan recognizes from Laura's *New Yorker* cartoons of men at their clubs, nearly invisible in huge leather armchairs; he needs stuffed elks' heads on the wall, and a plaque that says VERITAS. Eva Shurrock is remaking the confusion Mrs. Archambault left in the kitchen. Every now and then she shakes her head to indicate her revulsion at Dan's sense of order which, she would say if asked, bears the same relation to Laura's as the received message bears to the original that is passed along a wavering line of children playing Telephone. Dan goes back to his cabinet, whistling faintly under his breath. He hopes he is offending them.

Carol watches him. Her head moves in tiny nods and her eyes follow him, as though her neck is fixed. Laura does that. He wants to ask her what she's thinking but he is afraid she will tell him. He puts his plane down for a minute, aware that he is sucking in his stomach muscles, and he turns to her with a neutral half-smile of invitation. But Carol, out in the open studying the hulk of his body gravely, as though sent to observe him, does not smile.

. . . .

Laura doesn't bother to talk to Dan when her family is with her. She refers practical matters to him as if he were the handyman whose business it is to keep track. After he has told her what she needs to know, or done something to accommodate her, her eyes dismiss him.

Eva Shurrock, the one functioning parent, is taking a hard line. She has resolved, with or without advice, not to baby Laura, or pity her, or appear, even, to give her special consideration. Dan sees a self-satisfied determination come up like a light behind her eyes every time she orders her daughter to come here or let her see this or that. Her tanned face with its extraordinary creases, like a windswept desert viewed from above, is bent on rigor now and not sentiment, as though Laura were one of her English students who is going to be dragged to a Pass and made to graduate come hell or high water. It keeps her busy. She too, engrossed in her unsubtle plan, ignores Dan.

Dan finds Carol fiddling with Laura's recorder.

"Do you play it?"

"A little." But her delicate fingers unbend. She puts it down.

"Don't let me scare you."

She takes him in from head to belt. "Why should you scare me?"

He shrugs, embarrassed. She is profoundly disturbing to him, he feels himself angry at her for resembling Laura.

She makes her sister—unoriginal. She makes her less real, somehow. Less absolutely herself. He doesn't understand it, his half-formed anger itches at him and he can't get to it. "Do you know how much you've begun to look like Laura?" he asks finally. His irritation seeps through his question.

She makes a little gesture of dismissal. She has darker hair, which is not drawn back as Laura's used to be, but hangs straight like open curtains; her face is rounder and her eyes appear to be blue, though she never looks at him so it isn't easy to tell. She conducts herself like someone who is guilty. "A little family resemblance, I suppose. We're so different I can't see how we could ever look—essentially—alike."

He wants to ask, how are you different? What does "essentially" mean? She is hurting him with her presence, the ghost of Laura, an old shadow, in her movements. How far would such a likeness go? Would she feel like Laura if he touched her? Does she sound like Laura when she laughs? (She almost never laughs, how will he know?) Her grimness seems to him to be studied, a beautiful woman cellist's gravity, cultivated for the stage, like the calf-long dark skirt she is wearing that looks like a dancer's. He wishes he knew her better, as though she could throw some useful necessary light on Laura, tell old secrets, bring her back to him as she once was. What light does he need, though? What light would he be able to bear? Laura stands still—sits still—while her sister moves. She is an echo, a reverberation. Muffled, underwater. "You're staring at me," Carol says.

Dan shakes his head slowly. He is vaguely queasy from his peculiar concentration, this mirror-play inside his chest, the sisters' images shining back and forth, one off the other, neither of them solid, both of them real. Again the unspeakable frustration, weariness, finality of his mother's dying. Is there a world of shadows, of memory's survivors, that floats parallel to this one? An irrecoverable world?

"Not you, really," he answers. "You have Laura's—eyebrows." Absurd, desperate, although she surely does: tenderly shaped, precise, feathery at their highest point above the eyes.

Carol touches her face defensively. "I have my own eye-brows," she says firmly, as if he has accused her of stealing. What a sense of humor. Has he done anything to deserve the anger with which she turns and walks away?

At dinner he studies the sisters who sit side by side, Laura unmoving, Carol unspeaking. One more and they could be the monkeys, Hear No, Speak No, See No Evil. Laura has the sharper tongue, her sister the mystery, the bottomlessness. There is surprisingly little conversation at the table. Hallie is telling her grandparents how she makes paper with flower petals in it, and three kinds of texture, depending. . . .

DeWitt Shurrock, without a word, consumes many times more food than anyone else, neither asking for it nor accounting for it, simply filling his plate himself, silently, again and again. Dan, watching him, suddenly knows with a certainty that his father-in-law has lived a life of his own. He has had one woman or a hundred women far from home, and who knows what else; who knows what kind of a voraciousness at work. The mildness and indifference he must pull around himself on the way home, the way some men take showers after a rendezvous. His body, which is larger and thicker than it seems when he is wrapped up in that laughable preppie bowtie and blazer (Dan remembers it from the summer on Pottery Lake), has not cowered behind the *Wall Street Journal* all these years, it is a stronger and more vigorous body than he lets anyone believe. Laura's robustness and Carol's secrecy. No wonder Eva Shurrock has that avid woodpecker's concentration on the thing right before her eyes; that desperate insistence that she can hold anything there, keep it. (Will he have to find some sympathy for the woman?)

Idiot, Dan tells himself, for never noticing how subtle and hidden a man's power could be.

After dessert, after a reasonable amount of time spent on reassembling after dinner, Dan announces that he's going out for cigarettes. There are no objections.

In fact he is going out to try to stop sulking. His nervousness, suppressed energy, lies all around him like the wood shavings he has swept into the dustpan; everywhere he walks in his idleness, he kicks it up. Those cabinets left hanging suspended like an eroding cliff, Jon and Hallie twirling busily in their grandparents' company, the Shurrocks too anxious to let them stop spinning, stop bringing things down from their room to show and show, to be absently admired. And Laura is disloyal. Whatever her arguments with him, she has no right to give him that vacant spoiled daughter's eye and cast him on her parents' frozen mercy.

He takes his cigarettes from Joe Mack at the counter (Joe the best pitcher in the league, possessor of a brutal sidearm that must warm his shirtsleeve out of season!) and lights one before he leaves the store. Then he goes back and buys a six-pack, counting out change nickel by penny.

"How you doing, Danny?"

"Okay. Not too bad." He notices, now, when someone deals to him straight: no careful concern about Laura, no extra hint of gentleness to him. He doesn't know whether he misses it or not.

He feels angry and self-indulgent, wants to go somewhere and chug-a-lug the beer, piss in a huge arc, maybe make a circle like a dog marking his turf. He listens to himself cursing vehemently in one of the back rooms of his brain. (He can open and shut the door on it; the voice goes on whether he hears it or not. There seems to be a crowd in there, listening.)

As he reaches for it the door rattles. A girl is pushing where the sign says PULL. That reporter, whatever her name was, who wrinkled up her nose at Laura's pain. Phoebe. Imagine a girl named Phoebe, what a history of lacy drawers and velvet ribbons. Worse than Laura's tedious past. Dancing schools and teas. Miss Porter's perambulating chastity belt, the key dangling within such easy reach.

"Hello," the girl says to him with remarkable timidity.

"Do you always pull when the sign says push?" He sounds like a man who's already had his six-pack.

"I don't feel too comfortable in here, actually. This place always makes me feel like I'm in"—she puts her arms around herself to indicate chill and the need for protection—"I don't know, a gas station."

Dan laughs. "My kids come in here to buy Devil Dogs," he says. "Pretty dangerous. Hey, you look better without your pad and pencil."

"Oh—"

"Less ferocious. I thought the day you came to see us you'd make a hell of a left tackle."

"Look." And she begins to apologize. Oh Christ, cut it, Dan thinks. Leave it alone, it's not something you can be forgiven for: stupidity. Immaturity. Better to look away and hope you get riper with age.

As to the rest of it: he wishes she'd be quiet so he could get on with it. He has his six-pack and his cigarettes, Laura and the kids have their all-night babysitters, and he has his feeling of reckless mutilating anger. By the time he recognizes he is flirting he is already bored with it. But he's started, he's in the middle even before he's started, and he knows the harsher he is with this girl, the more he smashes his brittle hunger against her, the more she'll be grateful. It will be

Experience; it will not be reported in the marshmallow Scenes Around the Village column; and she'll get her own back on Laura, no? And if none of this is true, he thinks, pushing open the door from behind her, over her shoulder (pushing where it says PUSH), then she ought to be more careful who she takes home with her.

He doesn't want to talk to her or see her Indian lamp-shades that look to him like stretched skin. She burns incense, which makes him sick. She believes in indirect lighting as well as the New Journalism, and she wants to have music, one of those noisy groups turned down, their motor cut back to a throb; it beats like a headache. She sits on her studio couch with her long jean-legs straight in front of her, feet flat on the floor, and shows off her technique with cigarette paper. "Want some?"

Dan can't stand grass, he doesn't want the edge off. (He is the right man for the Drug and Alcohol Committee at school.) "I'll drink this," he says, raising his beer can in a salute. Laura's rape dream plays in his head like a tape. STOP. Strange to see somebody else's dream. SLOW FORWARD, scanning. If things were normal he'd have been one of the firemen. He looks for his face in the crowd. He squats, stares from under his rubber hat at the little icicles hanging between her thighs like a grey beard, she said (who dreams such details?), like her hair gone white with shock. In her dream she was trying to run up Spring Street towards the Chicken Fry place. STOP, REVERSE. He is afraid he will mutilate this girl, this nosy child, trying to get to Laura locked somewhere in the ice of her dream.

This Phoebe, rapt, intent on his eyes as if he can see her, thinks it is emotion that makes his hands shake. What would she do if she knew the desperation with which he is holding it all back? He is afraid he will kill her without knowing it. He is a weapon and he is aimed and when he goes off he does not cry out *Yes*, he cries out *No* and *No* again.

Her knee socks, a smooth salmon-orange, have all the Marx Brothers' faces on them. She keeps them on because he isn't noticing, he never bends to pull them off. It makes her feel like a pervert. "You bastard," she says. "What the hell was that."

He could be convinced he has no voice left. His throat is strafed. "It's what you get from a country creep you meet in an all-night beer store that feels like a gas station."

"That's what I figured. Jesus, you could have done that alone. You could have humped a hollow log."

I did, I did. He says nothing. He would like to thank her nonetheless, but he can't imagine how. It was slightly better than a hollow log, a little more consoling. Like his axe as it hit the wood in his kitchen—gigantic ripping impact and a wild release. But the pain, some kind of pain, has left him winded. He has used the kind of effort that makes his heart feel endangered, not fortified. Like picking up some heavy object at the wrong angle. He has torn something that doesn't show up on anatomy charts.

"Well," she says coldly, pulling herself out from under him as if from some kind of wreckage, "I don't suppose your wife is going to suffer much from losing *that*." She is wrapping her long thin body in a robe that goes with the socks: flat, stamped all over with some kind of face. Ah, the Maharaj-ji. That smile, creased across her breasts, under her arms. His chin on her elbow. She knots the belt with a tug. When she begins to say something more, something about wanting to

write an article about men who think all women are small-
town whores, he raises a hand. Surrender. "All right," he says.
Her only attraction is that she doesn't look like Laura. "All
right."

At the door, clammy in his shirt and chinos, he summons
a huge effort for gratitude alone, for duty, and bends to kiss
her breast—approximately her breast, behind the slithery
cheek of the smiling guru. She is startled; clearly will re-
consider the kind of bastard he is if only he gives evidence of
knowing she is there. She cradles his dark head in the crook
of her arm. He pretends to search for her nipple in the dark,
pushing the cloth open with his mouth. He feels like a very
small child, eyes closed, nuzzling his mother. Monkey child
with a terrycloth mother, recording of a beating heart. If she
wants the expectable signs of excitement in him she will get
them, but he is the chisel and the ice and it is still himself
he goes searching for. It is worse than failure, this battering
strength he uses on her.

Twice, then, and the second time just as harsh and his
eyes rapacious.
"You are doing—" she tries to shift under him—"damage!
Please. I've never—"
He runs his hand over his face, covers his mouth to push
self-pity back. Finally he covers his eyes and, blindly reaching
out, takes her hand, pulls her up. She is much lighter than
Laura, bone straightening against bone like a folding chair
snapping closed. She tilts towards him, away.
"Nine, almost ten months," he says quietly, not looking
at her, studying the chain lock on the door, wondering if she

bothers to use it. "Nine months and you begin to turn to stone. That's what happens. I'm sorry if I hurt you."

He lets himself out the door with calculated modesty before she can say a word and moves down the hall flushed with a shame he never felt in all those years when he leapt on every girl who moved. She will be touched by his helplessness. She will be sorry for him now and forgive him for holding her hostage. All the worse that he deserves forgiveness.

How many layers must he drop through, must he renounce, to come back to feeling? "Your hands go right through me," Laura had said to him, stifled, the night the firemen had their way with her. "Ghost," she had murmured. "Ghost," he whispers, himself to himself. "You fucking ghost." What she has lost he has lost too.

The house is dark when he comes home, although it isn't ten o'clock. Carol is sitting at the kitchen table.

"Where the hell is everybody?" He takes the car keys out of his pocket, drops them on the counter noisily. Home for good.

"They're all in there watching *Upstairs, Downstairs.* Laura's half asleep."

She looks at him coldly and sees every move he's made in the last two hours. He hangs on a wire upside-down between Phoebe Landgraf and this vengeful sister.

"You must have had to go a long way for the cigarettes."

"Jesus, you sound like somebody's wife." The cigarettes are at Phoebe's, on the table beside his empty beer cans. He will not lie, though. "Not too far." He sits down at the empty table, looks hard at Carol, waits.

Waits.

Her breathing is invisible; her eyes never flicker.

"Do you want to say something to me?"

She has her own unhurried rhythm; maybe music teaches it. She waits, now, a beat longer than he expects.

"You do think you're the center of the universe, don't you."

He shrugs. He doesn't think in those terms. "I'm my own, I suppose. Isn't everybody? If they're honest? Aren't you?"

"What about Laura?"

"What about her? She's got herself in the middle of my universe, as you call it, without having to move her little finger. But whatever it looks like to you, coming in here like this, I've got to breathe once in a while too."

Carol shifts. Her skirt makes a zipping sound like nylon stockings crossed at the knee, a sound he made himself a connoisseur of, years ago. "She's got herself? That's an interesting way to pin the blame."

Dan wishes he had his cigarettes. "Listen. Try to listen to this, okay? You're talking blame—blame was the first part of this thing, when this first happened to Laura I couldn't get my mind off blame. And then again when we first came back here, it was all guilt, sackcloth and ashes, the whole thing. That much I accepted. But look—"

She is in fact looking hard at him, but she seems only to be waiting him out. She has no sense of humor and she has no accessible, listening ear. Essentially unlike her sister, as she told him; she is a wall.

"It begins to seep away, you could say . . . because . . ." He taps his fingers and looks around the kitchen. Looks for the words. He hadn't realized how far he's come.

Carol waits, impatient.

"There's no way to get through the day, do the things you have to do, deal with the kids, anything, if you're on your knees. That's all—it turns out to be simple. You just can't crawl the whole rest of the way."

"But if you deserve to."

He looks back at her. "What?"

"I said, what if you deserve to? Crawl. Don't you get off easy?"

"Oh yeah, it's a cinch." But he regrets that. He straightens himself at the table and leans earnestly towards her. "Carol. Does my crawling put her at the center anyway? If that's really what's on your mind. If I'm crawling, those are my knees that are going to hurt and that's my blood all over the linoleum and who in the hell is going to clean it up?"

She continues to watch him silently, not warily but aggressively, eyes dark with her first anger.

"Look, you're her sister, you've got plenty of reason to be mad, how could you not be? I mean, it's normal. I don't have any argument with that."

"*Thank* you."

"But Jesus, don't forget she's my wife—"

"More's the pity." She looks at the ceiling.

"Oh shit." He slams the table with his open hand. "You're doing your parents' dirty work, I see it. Screw this Neanderthal Laura married, he can't have any worthwhile feelings or ideas about this. He's a two-bit carpenter, right, who picks up women and breaks them in half for the hell of it—"

"You're very defensive about all that."

" 'All that' is my life, babe—it's my fucking life."

"Don't 'babe' me, please. And lower your voice."

"And all the rest of this 'character' business. Is he responsible, did he make this happen for this reason or maybe it was that reason—those are all *luxuries*. Let some psychiatrist play with all that stuff if he wants, don't you know what's beside the point when you see it? Vengeance is what they are. Punishment. And it doesn't get anybody anywhere."

She lets out a long breath. "You believe that."

He covers his mouth with his fingers to consider her challenge. He has broken another woman in half for the hell of it tonight—well, bent if not broken. She'll heal. "Sometimes I believe it," he says. "But I've got to figure out how to believe it all the time, because all the blame in the world isn't going to put Laura back together again. And having me out of action dumping ashes on my head isn't going to get dinner cooked or Laura's wheelchair oiled. Right?"

"You know, you're the one who likes to consider yourself a Neanderthal, I wonder if you've ever noticed that. You seem to find it so convenient to take a pragmatic view of everything. But what about at three o'clock in the morning, what do you have to say to yourself then about what matters and what doesn't?"

He laughs. "I'm turning her over at three in the morning to keep her from getting sores, my friend. The bed is like a goddamn spit and I've got to rotate her so she won't get burned. I'm sorry to tell you this 'pragmatic' view you can manage to look down on, this poor unintellectual minute by minute *slog*—if you don't have that, you don't have any sister. It's about as simple as that." He looks at his fingers, nicked from the violence of his attack on the kitchen wood-work. "I get the feeling you don't know what it means to be altogether helpless. Who does? But listen: she needs either people or machines just to get up in the morning. She needs so much equipment she might as well be a bloody astronaut. It sure as hell doesn't leave much room for the cello."

"May I have a cigarette?" She gives him a clear blue look.

He studies her for clues. Only her sudden sunniness gives her away; it is like a wink.

"Smoking is lousy for your health," he tells her and pushes himself back from the table. Stands. "It's a good thing your sister stopped."

For which he has his satisfaction: Carol's face cracks open with revulsion, she has confirmed his vileness. He sees inside for just an instant, where she is alone with her terror. They've all moved on a step or two ahead of her and she, hauling this fresh weight of anger, is lagging.

The Shurrocks have brought Laura the electric wheelchair. It is custom-made, to very precise measurements. There is some camaraderie while they get the kinks out of its operation, they stand around like children watching a set of electric trains take shape under the Christmas tree.

All that day Jon and Hallie plead for a chance to ride in it. "Honey, I'm afraid you'll break it," Laura says gently to Jon. "It's not a toy." She has the look of a woman who is stroking her son's hair.

She will have to practice the necessary shove to get the mechanism going. The one in the hospital had its own idiosyncrasies; they are nearly as different as—"Sisters," says Dan. (He likes that.) "Multiplication of power," he mutters, sitting beside the back wheel, which has taken some adjusting. "That's better than the rubber-band hookup." (The in-house genius at the Institute had strung up her arms with springs and pulleys and rubber bands, which he had promised to duplicate expensively in presentable materials. Her hands had dangled so efficiently she could type one "and" or "the" a minute. Dan had unhooked her and her arms had floated slowly, gratefully, back down. "Dictation," she said. "Dictation," he agreed. "I'll learn to type for you, me love, to keep you out of harness.")

"Well, it costs more than rubber bands," they all assure him in their separate ways. She pushes the lever and the chair springs forward. She needs to be rearranged, maybe belted till she learns new balance at these speeds. Jon watches it lovingly: as good as a snowmobile out of season. Now that he can see her as the driver of a bona fide machine his respect for his mother has vastly increased. But there's no place to open it up, see what the motor will do.

"It will get me everywhere, Jonny," Laura insists. "The kitchen, the sunporch." Her compass points. She deflates visibly.

"You need to take it out to the playground," he says, still hopeful. "The way we taught Hallie how to ride. Zzooo-oom, zoom," and he's off, with his hands clenched in front of him as if there were a steering wheel in the air.

Hallie stands beside her mother. "We'll see your name in the paper, Mommy. Fined for speeding, Mrs. Courser, ten dollars!"

Everybody laughs. They look like a family, Dan thinks. Almost like one. To have come to the point where that's a virtue!

Virtue or not, Eva Shurrock shakes the kaleidoscope. "But surely you're going to get rid of the house, Dan. How will she ever get outside in it? And all she comes upon is walls here. I'd like to see this chair do her some good."

"News to me," he says. "Are we?" He gives them his most innocent look.

"Dan, really." That is Laura. "Don't be disingenuous."

"Really what? Has something been agreed on that I don't know?" If they would only leave her alone.

Even DeWitt Shurrock has an opinion on the subject, coincidentally in line with the others'. "You could build one of those—uh—"(he snaps his fingers, summoning the word as if it were a servant) "—solar! Solar houses. With ramps and all the rooms on the single floor. Surely you're clever enough to figure out how to do just about anything along those lines."

"Surely," says Dan and scowls. "Very surely."

"Don't speak to my father that way." Laura has moved her chair, perhaps unwittingly, across a line that separates them all from him. Carol, her shadow, sitting, looks on with grim delight.

"Laura, would you like to go home with your parents for a while? Or have them stay here and let me go someplace else?" His lips are so tense they snap out a hard smile at the end of this and then, mechanical, snap it back. "Because there is no way I'm going to take what's going on here."

"Goodness, are you fighting over her?" Carol asks gaily, as if she has just that moment come in from Paris.

"I'll show you the diaper change and a couple of other quick tricks," Dan says, "and I'll give her back to you with my compliments. All right? Is that what you want, you want your little girl back?"

"Hallie, please go in the other room," Laura says when she begins to see he is serious. "Go. Go on, leave us."

Looking over her shoulder, the child leaves. She makes sure they all realize she wants to protect her mother; she tries, with her frightened eyes, to bind them to her protection.

"Because not only would I like some peace before I crack up, frankly I'd like to be somewhere people don't look at me like I'm a murderer."

Laura's eyes are damp. Who can tell her anger from her repentance from her fear?

"I'll take the children or leave them, whichever way you want, but you'd better tell me now."

Laura's knee has begun to quiver.

Dan stares at it as though he has never seen such a performance. She is trying to get him in worse trouble.

"What's the matter with you now? I'm telling you what you want to hear but it makes you feel guilty, that's all."

Still no one makes a move. He could be going out for cigarettes again. "All right. With or without the children?"

"You are decisive, aren't you?" says Carol. "What a man."

Laura does not defend him. "Dan, this is foolish."

"If I take them—"

"Dan."

"The only thing wrong with this," he says to them, beginning to warm to the role of injured party, beginning not to want to be called back, "is that it makes you happy. All of you and that harpy who just got into the act."

He takes the stairs noisily, by twos, and begins to pack.

He gives them a recitation from the doorway that will make no sense when they come to the necessary moment. Let them puzzle it out; they think they know what's good for her. May her bladder not betray him for a dangerous fool.

Saying goodbye to the children he nearly throws it over. He explains nothing, only instructs them to be patient with Laura and obedient with their grandparents. To Hallie he says the hardest thing: "Remember the little escape you made, honey?" Her eyes flare up at him. He gives her time. Slowly, laboriously, she damps them down. "A little breathing room?" But he doesn't know what she sees when she remembers. This is a strong, maybe a dangerous, drug of mysterious potency. "Honey, but you have to know, it isn't you and Jon I want to leave. It isn't even your mother." They understand none of it, he supposes, except by elimination. "And I guess I can leave you with them because they're your grandparents, they love you, right? But they're nothing to me. See? No relation. If Mommy needs *her* parents right now . . ." Their confusion warms and chills him. He flees from it at a run.

He drives around the Shurrocks' car that gleams even in the pale light of a fingernail of moon, out over the pebbles, raising dust, and down the road faster than a chased man. He has no place to go except away.

The drive home from Boston is through a corridor of con-
dominiums with mod angled roofs, succeeded by truck farm
fields and the thickening trees of old good towns with prep
schools in them, inns and white houses behind discreet signs:
1799. ANTIQUES. RESTORATIONS. Dan drives back through
most of it oblivious; it has always been Laura who has
prickled with opinions on the relative callowness of the
Groton to Lawrence to Andover to Exeter boys who camp in
towns like these, or on the egg carton architecture of the
housing developments called "Eden North" and "Summer-
spring."

("This was the stagecoach road once, oh God, oh God!"

She likes to parody the possessions of the suburban Bostonians in their high-ceilinged hutches. "Now listen, Hallie, what you need to qualify to live in one of those places is—I'll bet they hand out lists when you give them your downpayment, like the lists of underwear I used to get for camp—let's see: You need one set of le Creuset pots and pans, blue or orange, but they call it 'cookware,' that's sleeker. Like 'aircraft.' Pots and pans is too workaday, you don't need taste to own a *pot*. One Chemex coffee pot. Excuse me, coffee *maker*. One wine rack in some kind of blond wood. One Rya rug. A minimum of one asparagus fern, preferably hanging. One—"

"For somebody who hates that stuff you sure have got the brand names down," Dan says and pokes her. She grabs his hand and pinions it. The car swerves a little but the road, after Groton, is always empty.)

It is only the fields he notices today. The signs are beginning to sprout like a spring crop. PEAS. LETTUCE. RHUBARB. There are flats of pansies and marigolds stacked in tiers, little forks of tomato plants, a few of them already bearing fruit big enough to be seen from the road—for cheaters, the kids would say in their mother's tone of moral outrage.

The Nashoba Valley is a gentle rolling sea, the only ocean Dan knows. Rises swell to left and right with a calm and undramatic sweetness, horses stand like props attesting to the perfect unreality of the hillsides. It is so green, so newly green, and, an hour from home, he is coming to the one dark ancient house and its barn with arched doorways, huge, rough, authentic, set in a pasture of uncropped brake and bush, that always makes him want to park the car and stare. He lusts to see what's been done to it, what hasn't, what sharp musty smell of the last two hundred years remains between the floorboards. It is the only house he knows that makes his own look small and tacky.

He lets the car head home itself. It can do that, go for the stable.

A spring without a garden. Billy has his in, and Jay, and everyone else (except for Sandy Mead who's thrown in the towel and given it all to the woodchucks to save himself an ulcer). In Boston, a month spent moving along the sidewalks looking for what might please him, usually managing to get it, for lack of imagination most of it flesh and hair, eye-liner and this or that unforgettable fragrance instantly forgotten, he didn't remember garden season. Wouldn't he have laughed at this vision of his Rototiller conjured up like that of an old lover: his favorite toy closed in the toolshed drained of gas, wintering under its tarp, a little cocoa-colored mud still caked between the blades? Seeing the fields now, some brown, some already green as soda pop, laboratory lime-green before three months of sun can fade them, he discovers that he is in pain.

Three clutches in, the Rototiller—eating up grass and corn husks, spitting them back—bucks in the hands like nothing in the world. It advances on last year's outworn garden like a movie monster, flings out string and the thousand stones that try to stop it. Its inexorable patient roll and its noise that kills all distraction—they are the householder's tank, his compromise DC-10, his personal smalltime caterpillar. Adequate. Adequate as a beautiful wife and two good kids and a house you've got to drive this far, to that big old farm, to improve on. It *is* enough, isn't it? Wasn't it? Sweating into the straight rows, slapping at the goddamn black flies that come out to feast on that sweat, earning his part of Captain Bolt's acres by using them, laying on a cover of leaves in November, in April feeding them manure swamped with sawdust, piling spoiled mulch hay between the green shoots in July, washing down the carrots and parsnips out on the backyard table in September, hosing their thick mud onto the grass before he plunges them blind into their box of sawdust, eating them all winter—the specificity of his love for the garden is a blight, another loss he can finger and smell and lay his face down in. The details are as intimate and close to his body as anyone could ever be. This year, when other people have had wives and houses, other people have had gardens too.

The car takes the sharp turn from Massachusetts towards New Hampshire with no attention from the driver; climbs, charges down the long hills truckers take in low. Dan sits with an elbow out the window, frowning. It's easier to lose a year than to lose a season.

There is no car in front of the house.

Someone has planted pansies along the border of the path. They look like a flounce of ruffle on a large sober coat. The children's bikes lean against the house in an antler-tangle of handlebars. Hallie has a new basket stuck with purple plastic flowers; her jump rope dangles over the side. It hurts him that he knows a new basket when he sees one: that he still has so much of her life in the palm of his hand, and yet could have gone away from her.

He stands on the granite step of his own house hesitating. Is it possible that he can feel himself growing? That's the kind of question Jon used to ask him when he'd stand still against the doorjamb where they kept the children's pencilled measurements, with dates alongside (beginning with the cat at a little less than a foot and terminating, at least for now, with his second cousin Bumpo Shea at six foot seven). The growth he wonders about now is not so visible as Jon's; is more what he would dryly call, in others, "wising up." There have been times since the accident when he's felt complications and new perceptions multiplying in his brain, moving, increasing as if they were numbers on a meter. He can practically hear the metallic click as each unseen dimension reveals itself—the old taxi meter click he lived with this year, dull, irrevocable, costly. No one who appeals the meter wins.

Should he, for example, knock on the door of his own house?

He had expected the kids to be out tumbling on the lawn, Laura sitting tall among them. The whole family was what he wanted, set like the scene inside a perfect remembered Easter egg in a box of bright grass-green confetti. They would be so relieved, so grateful to see him. He had allowed some necessary anger into his imagining but they would exercise it briefly, then proceed with delight, with welcome. (This was half his expectation; the other half was invisible, cowering behind: the one in which Laura called the cops.)

He knocks, assuring himself that he can surprise them more thoroughly if they're expecting to hear "I'm selling lightbulbs for the Lions Club." But they aren't home to be surprised.

So, reprieved, he enters his kitchen, looks with hungry curiosity on all the countertops, in the living room, on the sunporch for a clue. Who has had her, has kept her alive, has coped? He's afraid to ask himself if she's all right. Would there be pansies out front if she weren't? The borders are newly weeded.

They've been here. He had been afraid they'd all removed to Boston. Every time he walked down a street there he was sure he would meet Eva Shurrock hurrying from her classes, or DeWitt Shurrock with a briefcase; maybe all of them sunning Laura like a baby in the Public Gardens. But look, there are wet dishes in the drainer; the stuck floater in the toilet tank makes a distant ghostly roar in the downstairs bathroom, the sound heard inside a seashell.

There are two clues, solid: opened mail in the copper kitchen bowl for Ms. Carol Shurrock, c/o Courser (a bill from G. Schirmer, music publishers; an advertisement for the new thorough improved services of the Women's Center in Cambridge: abortion and pregnancy counselling, career decisions, psychological referrals). What have they done with his mail? Burned it?

Beside the bowl, face down, a magazine is turned open to a page of wheelchair maintenance hints: Thou shalt check for side play in bearings, for tightness of locking nuts. He flips through, stops at a cartoon that shows a wheelchair cowboy holding up a stagecoach. The magazine hefts like a thin issue of *Playboy* in his hand; it is for people with half a spinal cord, he thinks. Company, company. Pretty smiling women sit halfway between sidewalk and open van door suggesting, in universal hard-sell, conversion to this easy automatic lift, that safe manual ramp. The index makes it seem desirable to be part of this company, to become expert. Laura's *Track and Field*, her *Mechanix Illustrated*. On the back of the cover is a full-page announcement for a Paraplegics' Convention: Talks. Demonstrations of new equipment. Social hours. What hostility he would feel if he walked across the floor there, swinging his arms. How comfortable Laura would be.

And in the living room there is Ms. Carol Shurrock's cello. He stands in front of it and stares, in her absence, the way one can stare at the blind. It is as forceful a presence as a live woman, leaning, not carelessly, against the far wall. The brown of its blunt side is the complex color of her own dark hair.

He wants to investigate upstairs but it's suddenly unnecessary. He knows what it's been like, the cabal of sisters, Carol's sympathy for the wife of this joker who isn't even sure which sound the cello makes. It is going to be brutal and as messy as they come. He would rather have a fight to the kill with a man and his fists than the leeching, the bloodletting that he's going to be pushed to if he's going to get her back.

He realizes he is unbearably tired, as though he'd never left at all. Waking every two hours is not the only way to turn up exhausted. Probably he ought to do something decisive to reclaim the house: make himself a sandwich, unpack, straighten up his tools. But instead he stretches out on the couch, ankles crossed as if casually, and orders himself to sleep, for strength and for the sure obliteration of this time till they come home.

No one comes. He wakes with a jerk, his mouth full of the spittle of a daytime nap, and strains to hear: once in a while the floors expand, contract, give out a small cracking sound as if someone were moving invisibly across them. (That must happen all day every day, only he never sits still to listen.) Having tried to turn from them for a month and wonder nothing, he is ashamed to dare wonder where they are at this particular moment. He keeps an ear to the road, waiting for a car to grind up to a stop on the pebbles, familiar sound like a sudden rainshower.

There's no beer in the refrigerator and nothing else either. Half a black banana (who puts bananas in the refrigerator?), hamburger rolls, maraschino cherries afloat in their objectionable pink. At this rate his kids will weigh in at twenty pounds apiece.

The anticlimax is unbearable; he has not allowed for it. The dozen things he wants to do—walk in the woods, rearrange his tools, catch a bass, see his friends, check out a new CB—all of them come later in the order of things. (Laura instructing the kids: "Do second things first and they lose their savor.")

He stands on the granite step scratching his elbow, which does not itch. A car goes by, fast on the curve, and honks. He sees a hand lifted, waves back. ("Saw Dan Courser out on his doorstep all by himself, looked like he just might be home to stay." "Finally had enough vacation, did he?" "Maybe he came back to clear out. Wouldn't blame him none." "Oh you wouldn't." That dumb up-and-down.) The lawn is vast, empty and unshorn. They ought to borrow the Fedders's goat to crop it, it looks like hay. Like raw scalp, there are patches of killed grass where the plow threw pebbles up on the snow last winter.

"Jesus," he says and closes the front door hard behind him. On second thought he opens it. Let them lock up empty houses in Boston.

Dan starts the car and coasts it down the hill in its old ruts. He could close his eyes: they lead to Joe Mack's. He gets out looking rushed, buys a six-pack, cold, nods to Joe, mumbles to some vaguely familiar kids who are leaning their T-shirts flat against the refrigerated cases, hands in their jeans pockets, maximizing the cool between their shoulder blades.

He gets two bottles down in two minutes, slumping in the front seat, hoping to be invisible. All the times he's come downtown just to be seen, not because he's needed anything, only to place himself in traffic and make contact. He hunches in his seat now, considering the hairy boys who yell friendly obscenities from car to car, hoist cans and thick brown bottles. Who sent the classified, one of these kids or some old crazy man, some thicknecked boozer or someone close in? Phoebe? Dougie?

He sits on his tailbone till it hurts. Then he pulls out and coasts over to the A & P, following passively where his whim goes. It doesn't matter. If he's here he must be hungry, or he must want to provide some food for his family. He follows himself in like a shadow and watches where he goes. Nobody would be out at dinnertime, no danger of meeting neighbors. ("Encountered between rice and macaroni, Mr. Courser's only statement was 'No comment.'") A month of coasting; he is slowing to a shuffle.

He dawdles up one aisle, down the next, feigning interest in the boxfronts, which are as empty of meaning as the faces of buildings in the city; thousands of separate names, words, colors, washed out by his inattention as if it were a smudging rain. He is filling his basket with junk: Mallomars, potato chips, Jell-O, sweet and comfortable as a sucked thumb.

When he sees his children—hears them, rather, hanging over the ice cream freezer, sending their voices down into its echo chamber—he doesn't bother with surprise, he is probably not surprised; he flees. (Later, when he thinks back to the instant he will remember the man who, climbing onto the catwalk of the bridge to jump, halts in terror when the policeman shouts "Stop or I'll shoot!" Something like that.) From the back he sees Hallie in baggy shorts, standing with one sneakered foot against her knee like a small ragged flamingo. Only the backs of Jon's jean knees show, stretching, his heels off the floor as he leans all the way into the freezer and calls out flavors in a disbelieving voice: "Peach Passion! Coffee-and. What's that supposed to mean, 'coffee-and'?" When he doesn't understand something he sounds contemptuous.

Dan has no more thought of abandoning his wagon than a car he might be driving. He moves sharply down the aisle and into a crosslane, escapes, heart whipping up adrenalin, asking no questions. Nor is he surprised—it is like the closing of a trap—when he turns one more corner and comes right up, fast, against a large shadowy hulk at the same height as his wagon that clarifies, focussing, into Laura, seated. She is looking calmly up at the top shelf of canned fruits. She is dazzling in her wheelchair. So much of it shines, alien in this place, it is like coming without warning on a mountain lion or a small parked car.

She must hear the abruptness of his stop as if it were a gasp because she looks up abruptly herself. A little sound comes out of her like the whimper their cat used to make whenever he jumped and landed—it seemed to fall, unbidden, from the white cat's throat, an uncontrollable cry at the effort of a long leap.

Can he get away with the casual hangdog look of a man who's stayed out for an extra beer with the boys? His lips move uncertainly towards speech and away, like a child's. There is nothing he can get away with. This is his *wife*, he thinks, overcome by the familiarity of her face, which comes from inside him, far greater than his familiarity with his own. His wife can bring him to this point and push him over with a little muscleless shove. He's always assumed it was only strangers you tried to impress, women you'd never seen from the underside. Laura's hot face is the one he has lived seeing, not his own, certainly not any anonymous beauty's, and, not his own, it is especially in his care.

He is watching her pain now, another disfigurement he has given her. She looks terrified, caught unprepared. He has not often seen her give in to terror—her pride has always been to harden to a sheen and toss the terror off—but he is making a victim of her now, two feet from the clerk who is punching prices on the canned goods, maybe listening, maybe not, twirling numbers, vaguely whistling.

Dan shrugs. It is a dishonorable thing to do but his head is jammed with static as if he's been drinking so long that all the choices look identical; he can't remember why any one matters. He raps the bar on his cart and says wistfully, "We don't have any food."

She nods so quickly he knows she was prepared to nod at anything. The forward part of her face is thickening, going red, a sudden inflammation. He does not want her to cry. Her eyes stay dry. She stares shamelessly at him instead as Hallie would stare, who cares for politeness less than for some knowledge she needs and thinks he must have.

He tries to break the stare. "Does Carol leave you like this? How the hell are you supposed to be getting what you want?"

Her voice is very steady and low. "I've learned to ask for things. No one seems to mind." The "no one" accuses him. He looks sideways at the clerk who is on his knees ignoring them.

He sees Carol coming. She is attached to her cart tensely, her knuckles white, looking vaguely from side to side like a monarch reviewing troops, seeing nothing in particular. Then they stand facing each other, all of them, thick as a little convention of bikers in the road. "The cavalry! Saved by the cavalry!" Dan shouts and blows a trumpet blast into his fist.

"You came home for a change of underwear," Laura's sister says. She goes to stand behind Laura's chair.

"No, I heard a rumor everybody was starving to death so I came to do some shopping."

Laura sits between them, hands in her lap, looking down the aisle as if genuine help might appear over the horizon. An old woman with a bluish braid and a rumpled terrycloth beach coat stoops beside her chair, holding on to the armrest, to squint down at the pineapple cans on the bottom shelf. She fiddles with her bifocals and then says to Laura in a confidential voice, "Pardon me, dear, but can you make this out? Is that a 2-7 or an 8-7?"

Laura smiles faintly and turns her head to the shelf, concentrates and says, "I'm afraid it's an 8. That's awfully high, isn't it?"

The woman raises herself slowly, as if in a dance. "I need it for a picnic," she says apologetically, "or I'd never let them get away with such a price." She shakes her head but takes the can along with her, turning it in her hands.

"She didn't even say thank you," Carol says dryly. "Look what he does to you, Laura."

Dan turns to Laura, whose foot has begun to work, clicking against its shelf in an impatient flutter. It's only that she's lost the capacity to hide her feelings, Dan thinks, almost admiring: one way to stay honest. He wants to warm her, protect her from the kind of harm he's doing. "It's a good thing you don't play poker," he says to Laura. "Aren't you going to tell me to get out of the county by sunset?"

"The two of you can have it out somewhere else, please. Somebody go get the kids and let's go home. I don't feel good." When Laura looks desperate a bluish tinge puddles under her eyes. Dan and Carol stare at her the way they would stare at Hallie in the middle of a trip when she announces she is about to be sick out the window.

"I think their father might want to go and retrieve them," Carol says stiffly and begins to wheel Laura down the aisle.

"For godsake, go get your basket, Carol, I can do that." She tosses her head as if to cast away a fly that's hounding her. "Am I supposed to lose my capacity to move just because he's here?" Which is to say, Dan thinks, retreating in search of the children, that Carol's as upset as she is: not everybody's got the kneejerks, footjerks to give herself away.

He sees them down at the end of an aisle, Jon clutching an ice cream box to his chest where it's going to freeze a little square. Hallie sees him first. She gives an unintelligible shout and leaps up, wraps her ropy legs around him, laughs and pinches his neck, perhaps accidentally. He has always expected to lose an eye to this child when she's in good spirits; an eye if he's lucky.

He turns to Jon then, who will not embrace him, possibly not in public, possibly not anywhere. Jon makes a great deal of the ice cream he's obliged to carry, like a torch in a relay race. They come with him quietly, as if caught, as if chastened. Hallie holds his hand, though. He has to restrain himself from squeezing her fingers too hard.

Carol is checking out their basketful. Laura has wheeled herself around and is stopped near the seeing-eye door, looking into its invisible field. The door makes its awful raygun noise every time anyone goes out. ("Zap, you're sterile!" they used to say; that, and more forbidding variations.) Most of the shoppers smile respectfully and a little proudly at Laura as they go, as if her presence somehow reflects well on them or their town, its tolerance, its ease of movement; something that softens their features the way puppies and children do, both up to the age of obstreperousness.

Dan has to buy his basketful for the claim it makes for him on the household.

They wheel their carts out one behind the other and Dan moves on towards his own car. "Kids!"

Jon hesitates, takes Hallie's arm, which she pulls away and shakes as if he's purpled the flesh. "What?"

He makes his father ask.

"No thanks, we'll go with Mom and Aunt Carol." He turns with such perfect assurance that Dan, bloodied, respects him for it. It is beginning to occur to him that he admires everyone's behavior but his own.

He unloads his packages into the trunk and tries to get a look at the transfer Carol can manage for Laura from wheelchair to front seat. He misses it behind so many inter-vening cars; almost misses them altogether as they go by because they are riding in a shiny red van he has never seen before. He catches a flash of Laura sitting up high right in the middle, in her chair, like an Indian queen on an elephant. Her parents again, her dear damned parents; he will have to go to his knees to thank them. His children are shadows against the far windows; they must feel huge and special, maybe even lucky. The van moves circumspectly up to the end of its aisle and turns out onto the highway.

He doesn't have to go home, following like one of Bo-Peep's children. He has seen her, seen them, and has been satisfied that they're all right; he could become one of those sweet shadowy memories now, think what he'd save himself and them. They could declare themselves Abandoned, or Destitute, or whatever it's officially called, and it would qualify them for a hell of a lot more money than he can make working three jobs at a time. He'd send gifts at birthdays, Christmas, an occasional cryptic word or two of encouragement, medical and legal inquiry. They would survive his other life better than he would.

Which is why he goes home, even to be punished. (He passes his brother's gas station, which is still open, its maws wide, car-tails visible in both of them.) The Quadriplegic's Lament, he thinks, what a contagion: Having come to the end of nothing, you will prefer pain. When the pain stops, you will know you're in trouble.

. . . .

Silently he unpacks his bags, puts away the groceries, some of them exact duplications of what Laura and Carol have bought. No money in the bank but two large economy-size boxes of spaghetti, two crunchy peanut butters, eggs upon eggs.

He doesn't want to talk, all he wants is to throw some baskets with Jon, better than talk or touching. But Jon is keeping his distance. Every room in the magical house has two doors, in the old style; as Dan enters at one end, Jon leaves at the other.

Hallie, who's staying at his heels, desperate to forgive, takes him outside to show him what they've planted: two short rows of beans, whose bright green flags are beginning to poke their way out of the mounds. He doesn't have the heart to tell her it's too early for beans, they can still be nipped by the late frosts that always pick on this hill. Sweet peas unfurl confidently against the fence. There are many blank spots where tomatoes and peppers will go. They have done it themselves (and the pansies too) and she exacts the thanks from him that children a hundred years ago might not quite have gathered from their father for harrowing and seeding a five-acre plot.

The big unplanted garden space on the other side of the split-rail fence is mottled with healthy tufts of grass and a thousand dandelions gone to fluff like pockets of fog hanging on the soil. Fallow is the word. "You know, Fallow Acres," his neighbor's voice says. "Past the blinker, up to Mill Road? Fallow Acres, the Courser place."

"Look at my sunflowers starting, Daddy!" Hallie takes him by the hand and makes him kneel in the pitted dirt. With or without their father, the children in his garden are blossoming.

. . . .

Carol, on the other hand, walks through dinner with her lips clenched, like a servant bearing a lifetime of old grudges. She puts down a warmed-over casserole in the middle of the table as though, in spite of potholders, it is too hot to handle. Clanking onto the wrought-iron trivet it sounds angrily dropped.

Dan lifts the lid with his bare fingers, eager to be ingratiating. He can't tell precisely what it is, only that it is very soft and slithery and surely something the kids won't stand for. He drops the lid back down. "Lor, can you eat this?"

"Oh—" she says, shrugging it off. She is volunteering nothing for him. "Not quite. It doesn't stay on my fork as well as some things."

Adjustments can be made, damn it, he thinks. I raised the frigging table three-quarters of an inch so she can get in here without skinning her knees. "Well, why the hell—" he begins and turns to berate Carol and take his point.

Her back is to the table as she gathers juice pitcher and glasses. But when she turns to him it is with the despairing face of an overworked housewife, neither sullen nor defensive as he might have expected. Defeated. *She can't look beaten yet*, he finds himself protesting, *we haven't even started*.

It is taking her a long time to join them at the table. Bizarrely, she reminds him of his mother who performed so many bits of urgent business relating to dinner—a ceremony of care, it was, only the ritual important, never what was done —that when he was a child he assumed she didn't like to eat. Carol hums, but conspicuously, retracing her steps, between refrigerator, stove and table. Either she is methodical or she is inefficient. One more dropped lid and he'll know which.

(She doesn't want to sit with him, that much he knows. But is it worth missing dinner?)

"Is your Aunt Carol always this busy at mealtime?" he asks the children, whose elbows are on the table again, obliterating years of training. They nod and begin to elaborate when Laura pursues the question directly, putting Dan in his place, like a Shurrock, for speaking of her sister as if she were in another room. "Yes, come on, Carol, sit down and eat before it all gets cold."

Obediently her sister sits but she looks at none of them. There is a transparency to her skin. Dan puts some of the still unidentified stew on her plate, watching her as he shakes it off the spoon. He can't decide whether it is the kind of haunting pallor that certain kinds of actresses cultivate in highflown movies or if it's simply unhealthy, a pill-taker's color, one of the least secret signs of inner ill-being.

Do Hallie and Jon notice that no one is speaking to Dan? They cover the adult silence with their news. Their lives appear to have resumed in his absence, though he can't tell how fully or with what kind of strain. They have another listener to the endless blow-by-blows of game or trip or argument; even Jon warms to him when he pays attention. He is curious to see if they intend, ever, to stop informing him long enough to wonder where he's been.

"And when I told her I'd never do *that*, I don't care what she was going to give me, even all her Barbies and all their clothes and even the camper," Hallie goes raging on, her eyes large with passionate conviction, her voice clenching and unclenching for emphasis. It looks as if Carol has covered both her ears behind the long dark curtains of her hair.

. . . .

"Carol, take a break," Dan says, gathering dishes and running water into the sink. He squeezes suds on them and gives them a flamboyant swirl. "I've learned to get off my butt after dinner like any woman. My friends think it's disgusting." He plows through the dishes vigorously; rim rings against rim and the suds climb up his wrists, rainbow on rainbow. "Has John been around much lately?"

Laura says quietly, "No, he doesn't seem to be coming anymore." She stops short of the reason. Dan sees her teetering on the rim of a deep hole.

He shakes rinse water from fork, knife, fork, spoon, giving himself time to locate the strangeness in the atmosphere. The house is charged, but not only with resistance, not with antagonism, which he expected would light the rooms with friction sparks like the flaps that used to hang down under his old Vega, striking diamond blows off the blacktop. Instead— he'll never get this straight without talking about it—even between the sisters the air seems waterlogged, heavy with some sadness he doesn't recognize from the time before he left. *Sadness* was never what lay on top, however deep it may have gone. Anger, irritation, confusion, frustration, exhaustion —all those minute-to-minute urgencies flew around like motes in the air, constant and debilitating, but—he swirls the dishrag around the sink, which seems not to have been cleaned for weeks, even he takes notice of the fatty scum that rises up the sides. But all those were *rising* emotions somehow, they set up a sort of bubbling ferment in his chest. Never this lethargy, this deadened quiet that surrounds the circle of the children's oblivious fire. It is not as if something is about to happen; on the contrary. There is a dark nimbus around them all; muffled; stoppered; defeated. He feels as if his coming has brought them the bad news they have been waiting for.

"We stayed at Uncle John's when Mommy was in the hospital though," Hallie says suddenly, an afterthought like a contradiction. "We got to ride Skeezix a lot but he threw me one time and I know he did it on purpose so I'm not riding him ever again."

Dan stops rippling the dishwater. "You stayed there when Mommy was in the hospital."

"And Aunt Donna let us take their good fishing rods down to the brook. But Hallie bent hers and—"

"I didn't bend it either, it got—"

"Your mother and I are going for a little walk," Dan says, shaking the water off his hands. He bangs his fingertips against the metal sink accidentally; they make a loud dull angry sound like something falling.

"What was that?" Carol asks, looking around.

"Nothing." His fingers are in pain. It bounces bright lights, dark blood-red, sharp prongs, all the way up to his wrist. So many accidents still remain to befall them all. "Go play your cello or something. We'll be right back."

But when he gets to the door Laura is sitting still as a toadstool in the middle of the kitchen.

"I don't think I want to go with you," she says. Her hands, heavy in her lap, seem made for such simple pronouncements. "I'm sorry. I don't know what you want to say but I don't really think I want to hear it."

He searches in vain for a gesture; at worst, a blind to hide in. Carol is watching, rapt, from the table, and the children at the edge of his sight.

"This is your house, Aunt Jemmie's, I suppose you have a right to be here no matter how I happen to feel. You even would be entitled to put us out, I guess. And they would give you the children if you wanted them. I wouldn't even fight you. But—" She sounds more resigned than angry.

As she talks, in that dead unimplicated voice, he sees white sheets of paper rise on edge and blow away, take confused flight above the rigid black fences of the Public Gardens. "Please, Dan." They swirl once and are gone. She lifts her hand, makes a broken gesture towards the door. It is a very efficient movement, as effective as anything whole. ("When you dance you always lead with your wrist," she tells Hallie, "always," and wags her daughter's hand until the little wrist juts sharply up. She moves one of Hallie's knees, arranges her calf ungently—no, unsentimentally, which is different from roughly, meaning "business," meaning "standards," a chance at perfection.)

"So—what? You're dismissing me? What are you telling me in that *voice*?"

"I suppose I'm dismissing you, yes. I think you dismissed yourself."

Hallie is beginning to cry in her corner, softly, all sucked-in air, not for show.

"Jesus, hasn't she already had to hear one of these scenes once before?" He turns to Carol as if to pin the blame a second time. But he will not go to Hallie. "This is getting boring."

"I'm not doing this for your amusement. Dan, you're only making it harder for them." Laura sneaks a quick look at the children.

"Soap opera! Fucking soap opera! I've heard that exact line before, *As the World Turns*, CBS, twelve o'clock Eastern Standard Time. Well, you know something? Maybe I've got no class but you know something? I'm not yours to dismiss." He crosses his arms and stands with his feet apart, not to be dislodged; stands like a cigar store Indian; knows how absurd he looks but stands nonetheless, his throat closed on a live coal. If there were something else to do he would do it.

Jon stifles a giggle.

Dan takes the back of Laura's chair, then, and tries to push it. The brake is on—as she has said, she isn't going anywhere. He kicks the brake violently and wheels her to the doorway, picks her up with the indifferent precision of a steam shovel while she shouts not to, calls out to Jon to collapse the goddamn chair and get it out of there; when they are reassembled on the gravel driveway he pushes off with her so hard she bucks forward, and though he tries at the last second to tip her backward, she jackknifes in the middle, folding towards her knees without a cry of protest. The little warning cry comes from behind his back where Jon and Hallie stand huddling, caught between flight and collapse beside their mother.

She lands in a tangle so implausible that he leaps forward thinking she has finally come apart, her dishevelled body shattered on the flagstones into a dozen jagged pieces. The illogic of her limbs is almost beautiful: Laura the dancer looks like she can do anything.

He stands still and looks at what he's done. That slow irrevocable tinkling down of something valuable breaking— his mother, his brother uncovering the mess of shards, his teacher finding the missing object stuffed in his desk, destroyed. Car in the ditch, dog smashed on the center line. Shreds of Laura's bathing suit bobbing in the bloodied water, small patches of green and orange and blue. Long reddish hair in thick clusters streaming on the water's surface. What has he learned since that day?

He picks her up, moving loosely, indifferently, and sits her back where her head lolls dizzily. He sets her hands on the arms of the chair, arranges them to look as if they are clutching, settles her shoulders. He tilts her head for her, as if he is about to take her picture. When her eyes stop rolling and begin to focus, Laura raises them to look at her husband.

He is back in the car. He is leaving again. This time he feels beaten off with a stick, though the stick is his own and he the one who swung it so carelessly. He is tired of his own company, boring, untrustworthy, depleted. For the first time since he was a teenager he has a raw look, the skin under his hairline is pimpling vaguely, he feels lustreless and flabby; the shape of his body is dull, slouchy, defeated. If he goes away again he is going to flicker on and off like an untuned motor in bleak weather.

Some nights Carol has simply left me sitting. She is so crippled she can't touch me, her concern is withered more than my least vivid limb. When she saw him home I could see her breathe again—escape! Graceful withdrawal! She could deliver me more or less alive and disappear. Tonight after he came and went, all she did was play her music for a while with that gauzy look across her face, doing her moon maiden. Subtle comment on the man I married. When Hallie started to sing she gave her a look, not gauzy at all. The real movie of my life or anybody's would have no cello obbligato (Carol thinks she's giving me background music) but only a perfected silence. No beautiful sound. Gaping hunks of ultradarkness, almost a slippery black like coal, like forbidden caves between one day and the next. I hear my breathing if I try but if I hold my breath in the middle of the night I feel like a girl they buried alive: feel like her in the coffin, awake,

*wide-eyed before she cries out, and feel like the mourners
aboveground too, listening to nothing, suspecting nothing.
They are grieving simply, already making peace. They
leave their flowers above my shocked head and they go.
Before they disappear I have to decide whether to shout
or not.*

He is at his brother's house. The little white Cape has a
barren yard, too few trees. The same punishing hand that has
kept the gas station so pure and plain, cleaner than any cus-
tomer needs it, has managed to clear the yard of foliage, as
if to let in the sun without interference to dry out a bog. Two
stiff little pine cuttings propped in stone urns flank the front
door; it always looks to Dan like an unmarked gravestone.
There are no flung carcasses of cars on this lawn, which is
entirely purged of its owner's ragged childhood.

Donna comes to the door, her forehead creased with
suspicion even before she sees who it is. She stares at him
appalled, though when she does see—has she been picturing
him dead all this time?—she draws back to let him pass as
if he were some inevitable force she dare not argue with. Her
chapped knees show out from under a hot pink Mother Hub-
bard, and a fold or two of baby fat that is returning to her
thighs.

John is still at the dinner table with one of his daughters,
bent over a plate in a posture that forbids conversation. (John
is remarkable, at work, for his unapproachability. His concentration is pure; anyone who comes to interrupt him falls in
with the ritual of the long silent wait. It is like drinking many
cups of tea before bargaining with a Persian merchant; when
he is ready he looks up from his tools, signals with a flicker
of his eyes that he may be addressed.)

His brother stands in the doorway without introduction. If John looks at him as if he's a ghost he'll assume they both know something he doesn't know. But finally John lifts his head the way a horse would, to go at something between his front teeth, sees him and goes on chewing. He is taking his time. His daughter, June, long-jawed and sparse like her father, melts out of the room as if such rules were agreed upon here. Dan silently takes her seat. It is warm, even though the girl was sitting on her knees.

John nods once, silently: acknowledgment? permission to be here? A combination of fear and amusement sits perilously on Dan's stomach, like beer on scotch. He listens to John's morose chewing.

"Coffee?" John is done working his teeth.

"Mm-pmp." Why do the others stay clear of the kitchen? Surely Donna in her tent of an apron was in here doing something before he came. (Laura-in-the-middle-of-things, he thinks. Laura taking on his friends, making them itch all over. Donna saves all her charm and twitchy energy for other women; John has surely intimidated her in the name of all men.)

John leans over to pour his own coffee, trying to keep the back of his pants on the chair. He reaches a long way to do it, as if it's a challenge not to get up. He sits back heavily and has a good look at Dan. The insolence of his smile wouldn't be safe outside his own house.

"Okay," Dan says, shaking him off. "Okay, you see me. Now can I ask you a couple of questions? Would you help me out?" He is careful to keep his voice casual; when John smells need he raises the ante.

His brother sucks at the cup, which is tiny, wreathed in blue forget-me-nots. (He lives among Donna's flowers like Ferdinand the Bull: they are underfoot. on the chairs, in the wallpaper. He sleeps, Dan thinks, in a fucking garden and has that parched woman on daisies, on roses.)

"The kids said they stayed here while Laura was in the hospital?" He tries to sound matter-of-fact. Common knowledge.

"They leave something over here?"

He shakes his head. The vise it is in shakes too.

"No, but I don't have the exact details of that, Buz. I want to know what happened, what she was in for." His hands, under the table, are gripping his thighs, though he would be surprised to know it.

John looks interested. He brightens, which makes his face unlengthen, his cheeks inflate. Something pulls him up to the surface of the conversation. John and Carol are a perfect match, ripening on his bad luck. They have everybody's best interests at heart but his; one of these days he's going to be scalped by somebody's good intentions flying towards him like a boomerang, taking off the top of his head and bringing it back to Laura for a bounty. "Why don't you ask her yourself?"

"Boy, you got to be brilliant to think of that. I guess I'm just not smart enough." Dan stretches his arms in front of him between saucers and soup bowls. He studies his nails, getting what pleasure he can out of his words because he knows they are the worst he could say to John, and he will regret them.

"She won't talk to you? You ever had a sense of right and wrong you wouldn't blame her for that."

"Right and wrong! Who the hell says I blame her?"

John twists his whole long body from side to side, uncomfortable. "You're such a frigging conceited asshole, I don't know how you could lay down with yourself at night, you know that?" He takes a contented sip of coffee, swallows it hard, licks his lips.

Dan looks at the ceiling. He feels as if his skin is being picked up, pinched, inspected in handfuls and dropped inch by inch. John's working over his chest now, seizing him hair by hair, looking for what? Crabs? Fleas? Letting him go, kneading, shaking his head.

"Don't play with me, big brother."

John studies him with narrowed eyes—adding it up, always totalling the red and the black. He will only give a little if he's winning.

"Okay. First," John says bleakly, "first your mother-in-law got herself a what-do-you-call-it—a pinched nerve. From dragging your wife around. Dragging her and dropping her, you're lucky she's in one piece. She got it in her back and, I want to tell you, I could hear her way the hell over here."

Dan raises his arms to gesture and drops them again. Time to learn when to defend himself and when defense is an injury.

"So there are two of them, right, lying there side by side? Two stretcher cases. And that sister, pphh, she's a real nitwit on this stuff. Personally I don't know what she's good for but not what they needed. I think she spent a lot of time on the bottle or sleeping or something."

"You sleep a lot when you're getting up every couple of hours. You get worn down. What do you do for a pinched nerve?"

"You don't do nothing. All you can do, you just get the hell off of your feet and you rest as long as you can keep from going nuts, I guess. I could never do it, I know that. I'd get Donna to shoot me first."

"Great. So her mother's an honorary cripple. Right." Dan nods. Better and better.

"So then—" At least John is enjoying this. He forgets to drink his coffee, he keeps one big hand over the cup as if he's hiding it. "It's almost funny but it wasn't so funny then, I'll tell you. I was hoping to god you broke your neck, Sonny, I really was, if you want to know." (But Sonny was his childhood name, taken out and used only on the sunny days, the occasional amiable wellfed unanimous days when John liked having a little brother.)

John begins to call off the list of catastrophes in a singsong voice the way an elevator operator in a department store would say "Fifth floor, linens, domestics, furniture, toys." It is calculated to make the list seem endless. "First, I think it was, she started complaining she felt strange. Dizzy sort of. Then she was blacking out and there was something wrong with that damn thing she sits on, you know, that little raft thing—"

"Air cushion."

"Air cushion. So she was sore, I saw it, boy, and that's no fun, I'll tell you, but you don't black out from that, right? So then they found something, a kidney stone, bladder stone, they couldn't tell at first till she went in—" And on goes John, almost merrily, because he is the one with the information this time, through the saga of the hospital visit, the diagnoses and misdiagnoses, clumsy guesses and midcourse corrections, the hobbled pursuit of an agony both painless and cunning.

Dan relaxes, finally, against the back of the chair, swamped by the futility of worry. Too late for that. (Cheater, he knows the end of the story—she looks healthier than he does. He is haunted by a dull memory of his month more or less in Boston: he feels like an observer, a peeping tom watching himself, a not very savory stranger, unbutton this one, disappear under, over, around that one. A month of ooze and itch, gasp and muffle, break like a wave and trickle down to sleep. What he never did was laugh, though; he was applying himself, keeping busy, grim as an inspector. And all the time Laura riding forward, battery-powered, into danger. And all the time he knew it, knew at least that she might be—wasn't that the point? A pervert's love of danger. Carelessness. Some men go hang-gliding for their kicks, or climb Mount Washington in winter. *What did he want to happen?* Ten years from now, he had thought and turned from it, he would meet one of his children grown who would say, "She died the year you left. Of longing, of course, of anger and uselessness, of withering up and blowing away like a dried flower out of season. Which was just as well because that was the year it snowed in June and we couldn't have dug the grave. The year you fathered four auxiliary children just in case. By Wellesley girls. The summer—")

"So *finally* it was okay, the drugs were good, Jesus Christ, have they got it down." John whistles admiration. "Even Marsh was surprised—you know, that sleepy-looking doctor, he knows a couple of things more than he looks like—he told me he figured they'd have to go in with the scissors. He said he couldn't have been happier if it was his own wife. So finally they sent her home. With a medal." John has finished his intricate tale of intrigue in the urinary tract. It is absolutely dark outside his kitchen window; no sky shows through the holes in his woods, no deep comforting blue. Dan has never in his life had so many words from his brother, nor heard so many attentive details in so steady a tone, almost like a kindly human voice.

"But what you did, Danny, running away—I ought to raised my shotgun to you when I saw you in here tonight. If you wanted to kill this woman dead once and for all after what else you did to her—" He is shaking his head hopelessly, a true mourner.

Something rustles at the door, probably Donna, kept out long enough. When John realizes they're being overheard he

begins to raise his voice, to call a roll of curses, even bangs
his fist on the plastic cloth one time. The coffee in his cup
sloshes out, a spoon clatters down under his chair. John's
quiet anger is more convincing, his brother thinks from a safe
distance. His fierceness is one of withdrawal. He isn't any
good at rage, which takes a certain size and excitability. Wasn't
John always the family minimizer, the whittler and parer?
He was the one who made you creep.

"What were you doing, Danny?" he asks in a canny voice
now. "Screwing around?"

Dan pulls back, caught in his brother's ancient knowledge
of his limits. Does it come from true disgust or from his
knowledge of himself? That is something he realizes he
ought to understand, but in the meantime it's depressing that
John is right: Dan's limits then are his limits now. "I tried to
get a job, anything, construction. Street sweeping, I would
have done that, but Jesus—people on line ten-deep with
fucking Ph.D.'s." He is apologizing.

"Your wife's having fits, she's fainting, she's falling out
of bed and you find yourself some nookie to hide in."

"You're so damn pious, pal, I wish you the same luck.
Did you ever have to put your finger up your wife's ass and
pull the shit out inch by inch?" He crooks his index finger
in his brother's face.

"You can get out of my house with that!" John is coming
towards him, going for his raised hand. "What does that have
to do with any goddamn thing?"

"It's true, though. It might not be why I left but it's true.
What's the matter, you don't like to hear it? Laura's—"

"Jesus," John says into his face, "you're the asshole, you
know that? You're the shit. Nobody would know you're talking about a woman with feelings. How come everybody in
Hyland understands that poor girl better than you do?"

"Don't tell me about my wife's feelings, all right? Everybody in Hyland understands her feelings because that's the easy part, but they don't all have to live with—" He stops, ashamed. "She's just a machine, Buz. Like I'm just a machine and you are and Donna, all the same underneath. No matter how beautiful anybody is—we're like the motors you fool around with all day long and then a little something extra thrown in. Which is why you love some of those cars more than some other ones, some of it's theirs and some of it's yours, how much work you've put in or what they cost you or just something about the way they feel when you turn the key. I don't know. I don't know what I'm saying. Only don't tell me what I ought to feel about my wife or not, or how I ought to spend my time, okay? You don't know anything about it. You're trying and you mean the best, thank you, but stay the hell out of it, okay?" After the words are out he tries to make some sense of them. He feels himself pulling up out of the slime of his confusion knowing something hard to say— something about the arbitrariness of what's important, and the privacy in which it's sheltered. The more important it is, the less it likes the light, that's the only part he is sure he knows.

He looks harshly at his brother now; he has to yield him something. Can he be provoked? John looks back dispirited. The moment of real anger has passed.

Dan moves a step closer to glare into John's eyes until he can strike a spark.

With a great sigh of obligation his brother pulls his thin shoulders back, takes a long breath and pounds into him. He grabs Dan's upraised hand in his own, looks at it a long second as if he is at a loss about what is expected of him. Then he jerks at it like an arm wrestler who's forgotten to keep his elbow down. Dan appears to be letting John shake the arm, shake all of him, pummel his shoulders. He stands like an indifferent object in the firefall of his brother's righteous anger, which is beginning to kindle now and catch. Like sex when it isn't urgent, it is enough to make the necessary moves; he will catch fire, now or later.

Dan's skin gives way, smooth and unguarded. John could be striking matches against his cheeks, holding them there till they die out. John's whole weight takes Dan backwards off his feet, knee in the groin, orange pain splashing up behind his eyes like paint.

From outside the room where she listens with both hands to her mouth and hopes her children have the TV turned up loud, Donna can hear the chairs flying, can even hear Dan's head crack sharp against a drawer, the hot handle of a drawer. She cannot hear the fine shower of sparks that falls all around him, more cleansing than she, lover of flowers, can imagine. It is far simpler for him than he deserves—she would not understand this either—and far too satisfying to be called pain (unless by John, who hopes he is making it unendurable).

"Fight back, you fucker, where are you?" Dan's brother shouts at him, wanting a contest now that he's into it, wanting one last reason in his life to tear Dan's chest in two.

"I'm doing the best I can."

He lays Dan back under a haze of light and dark, washes him with a good sample of the family curses; they cohere like entire multisyllabic words, accented regularly with the effort of the pounding. They are not very imaginative or frightening but their rhythm satisfies.

Every one of Dan's muscles is chastened with the effort of letting himself be a victim. (Remember John when he would let Dan tickle him and would never laugh, how his eyes bulged when he pushed it all into his chest?) He stays down for the count: having given so much pain, to give no more back. To take it, let himself be ripped open, his last protected places skinned, stomped on. His best speech and John's is in their hands. To close his eyes against pride and self-justification and let this good man John send him home ready to plead forgiveness.

He drives home slowly, the long way around. His knuckles are skinned the worst way, in flaps that smart more harshly than deep true cuts. He can barely hold the steering wheel for the damn petty pain, each finger separate. That kind of pain seems to make a high long-drawn-out sound in his head, screech of a chainsaw in a closed room.

The river runs along the highway for a while, then narrows like an hourglass; nearly disappears. There is a turn-out very few people use where the water reappears like a mountain stream rising fast out of the rocks. It is hidden by scrubby chokecherry bushes and silver birch. He pulls the car in and stops near the water. Of all those torn parts, only his hands go on aching. He wonders if his left thumb is broken—the pain in the joint is low, deep, black as a deadened nail.

There is one car parked half in the overhanging bushes, camouflaged as if it's been there for years, till the trees closed over it. He hopes the kids who came in the car got out, took to the bushes, didn't worry about truck lights and cops with long noses. If they hear him squat down on the pebbly shore it's all over for a while: the boy deflates, the girl goes dry. Don't mind me, he tells them, flashes it across the heavy mist, hopes they feel it—I'm on the side of anybody bare-assed under that quarter moon.

He's had a couple of fast ones here, spread-eagled on the sharp grass, the rutted dry dirt. Never Laura. Once—the only time he snuck out on Laura, though, just after they were married, for sheer panic's sake—some spongy-white girl who looked like a section of crumbly birthday cake where the light hit her, who thought his name was Don and never moved, never made a sound, just opened her thighs obediently, and ate him up with her huge eyes that reminded him there were dozens of ways to get swallowed, marriage maybe the least of them. Her black eyes and silence promised the most mute bottomless subjection; her silence was polite, something lady-like she must have thought he'd appreciate. Class.

When he went home that night Laura was asleep across his part of the bed and her own, like one side of an X. She slept without a nightgown, on her back, her breasts soft and reduced. When he got to her ankles, kissing her abjectly, gratefully, everywhere, making the other leg of the X, she woke knowing, and he watched how she took in the danger of his escape, the safety of his return. She'd been on the edge of losing him and had won him back without having to stir.

But she didn't like things easy any more than he did. Sometimes he thought she was waiting for him at the far end of every stupid thing he had to do, like a mother watching her toddler walk unsteadily towards her. *Ass*, he used to think, you don't have any news for this woman. When they come to give her word of you, she'll know before they've raised their hands to knock on the door.

As to the doughy girl he'd beached on the riverbank— "I thought you were a serious *person*," Laura said to him, sober, not angry. "All I want from you is some *concentration*. I always thought that's what marriage is: not rules or prom-ises to always do this and never do that, only a special con-centration. Like fine tuning. That's why some people are happy in the damnedest setups, you know—there's something unbroken between them that you can't see. How they con-sider each other the way they consider themselves. How *real* they are to each other all the time. Well, that concentration—can you break it and still have it?" She left the question open. It had seemed, over the years, to answer itself, different the first year from the fifth and the fifth year from the tenth.

He watches the bushes shake as the couple emerges into the foggy wash of light. They stumble a little, their real lives coming back to them, the hour, the highway, the consequences, the slight embarrassment of meeting his parked car under the dark brow of trees. The boy pulls the girl into the light with one hand, gently, as if, at last, out of some colossal danger. Heads down, they get into their car and back out fast.

Concentration. He is looking at the word, trying to see around it. It puts Laura in the middle but it leaves a little walking space around her, a border of his own. Negotiable. No one else needs to know what it means that a part of Laura wants to meet a part of him protected and unchanged; and the rest of the two of them can burn off, like tar flickering off the hardwood of their skis when they lay the torch to them, leaving a rich invisible shield.

All those fairy tales he read to Jon, then Hallie, till they slept—the ones he didn't grow up with—the Happy Prince, the Tin Soldier, half a dozen others, wasn't there always that heart like a fist that wouldn't burn? And the townspeople or the mayor, whoever, would gape and finger the small cool heart and always stammer that it couldn't be?

Fairy tales! he thinks. Holy Jesus, times have changed since he used to sail beer cans and condoms effortlessly out into this river, and all the nights of his life flowed downstream with them.

Enough to bundle me into bed on a night like this, it is easier for Carol to dose me with Valium than to worry about my sleep. (No sin to her, she chews pills every hour on the hour for everything from real life, which she calls "anxiety," to cracking nails, which she calls "disease.") I am a country girl, pure of heart, half the capsules freeze on my tongue, in my throat. In the hospital they thought I had an injured epiglottis. When I could say "Injured epiglottis?" they had to say "She's fine." It was the pills, only my gorge rising.

I am bobbing in my sleep, dreaming of my dress caught under a chair, I hear the door and want to yell some warning but something freezes me. He comes into the sunporch where we have the single hospital bed, comes with a strange gait, have I forgotten his walk after a month or is it changed? He stands for a while but I can't raise up to see. Then he is dropping clothes, scrape of buttons on the bare floor. What is he going to—he turns on the light beside the bed and forces my eyes open and I'm afraid of his anger and what he will take from me for turning him out. He has never hurt me in the tradition of his family except

But he is—God in heaven or God out, he has been raked and battered, he is grated on all sides, everything matted with sweat and cinnamoned-over with dried blood. He is proud of his wounds and wants me to be proud, I can see the way he engages my eye. Have I sent him off to fight for me? Has he rolled the car in a ditch for me? I don't remember asking him to do that. So pleased to be in pain and here, he sits and makes himself pant softly. A cut beside his ear is bubbling up, a slow dark trickle. I know what he is doing and so he fails to do it but always, always why do I want to put my lips into the flow? I want to lick it clean. I would say "You don't impress me, Danny. I don't need your gift of suffering, it isn't nearly enough.

Have I got shaving cuts and boxers' bruises? Can you dare?"

His eyes are shining at me, though, like Jon's when he sat up all night one time to comfort me. They are more shine than seeing, like an owl's in daylight. Well. What are the mourners aboveground to do, Laura Jane? Throw themselves into the grave? I don't want to be untouchable. I'd rather be the shape of their life. If they're the shape of mine. I'll give up some pride for that. I could live down here alone if I lost the rest of my life, if he took the children it would make me into Job, that's all, obnoxious Job who nearly strangled on his own tears. I could   yes   live without the children too. I would only be deaf blind and voiceless, bodiless the least of it. Once he said to me Would you trade a child for your old body? The cruelty of that— but let me pity him his need to know what it feels like where I am, he wants to know and can't unless I tell him. To get it back, he meant. Dance and make rhubarb pie and bake the Christmas cakes and touch me here and here?

Short tour of my body's blasted outposts. Jiggle of longing in the gut, the throat, a welling-up. (Christmas cakes, a dozen at a time. One year we grew our own citron but it didn't last till Columbus Day, let alone Christmas.) Piety is not a possibility. We were outside doing the leg bag when he asked me. I watched a part of myself, refuse of myself, feed the thirsty grass out back. ("Ours feeds it too," he said, with some perspective, "only a longer way around. You just don't need to file the specifications for your leech field with the town clerk.") Remember the pleasure of the hard welcome thwack of the toilet seat against your flank, the ecstatic giving-up, feeling the bladder unclench and shrink? I have that moment of holy gratitude to miss, those tears in the eyes sometimes.

Proves you're always only a body more or less endowed.
Imagine tears in your noble eyes for a good long pee? Not
only? Tears for other things? Then what's left I have, I
am, I still will be. There's plenty left to cry for.

"I am no sentimentalist, trust me," I told him. His
hand turning the fastener on the bag was large and brown,
always something lodged under the nails or in the whorls
of his fingerprints in spite of scrubbing: creosote, sawdust,
30-weight oil. "But I wouldn't trade a child, not any child,
to be able to dance. How could I? Or bake or even tickle
you. I wouldn't dare to trade a day of anybody's life, no
matter who—I don't think. They've got theirs and I've got
mine and I don't think I'd want to negotiate if I could."
If that answer comes back on me in my sleep I'll let you
know, I said, imagining self like a gigantic belch rolling
up and stifling generosity, stifling peace, filling my mouth
with bile.

Because I'm a literalist really. I saw first Jon, then
Hallie in small wooden coffins Dan would have made.
Their faces remote, their own—more accomplished even
than I in death, hands holding flowers. (No, Jon—give
him his baseball cards.) But anyway—pictured myself
moving like any mother above them, swaying and beating
my forehead with my fists, which were restored and ordinary and useless against this. What would I do with perfect hands if they were empty? And Dan floating farther
and farther away, we were less each other's than ever
because we would hardly be ourselves then.

Let me be their bewitched mother, everybody still
quick with noise and needs. I know it's an extreme game
to play but look what it jolts for me. You see, no grasp—
it seems like such a small thing. Now they jostle and buck.
They fit me in their life between their friends, no crueler

than any children. They come home nights, get off their
bikes, kiss damply. Dan is saying yes to me (bleeding
hopefully at the ear, trying for pain) and kisses damply
too. Carol says no—I think she is upstairs packing for her
getaway. Carol is dry, my sister makes herself dry and
angry, turns her life inside out till it cracks straight through.
She doesn't know she chooses her pain. None of it's sur-
prising: I changed, Dan changed and went away, breathed
a while in his own air, changed and came back. That's all.
Not much of the changing goes to the bottom, where we
breathe. And the rest of my life is moist, digesting ele-
ments like that good unplanted soil that strengthens for
him daily. That's what he always forgets about fields lying
fallow, I mean to remind him all the time when he mourns
his losses: how endlessly they work in their sleep, his fields,
dreaming of next year's garden.

In the pale wash of the lamp Dan sees how deeply cut
the familiar lines of her face have become, down which acid
tears have run and run, cutting their channels. Is it the light
that lacks mercy or her own marred life, how he has mis-
shapen it? (If she is no girl anymore, he is no boy.)

(The two sisters are whispering behind the lilac bushes
off Brattle Street, Laura taller, thicker than her frail pointy
sister, smoothing the hair behind Carol's ears absently as she
listens, Carol complaining, endlessly droning the long held
notes of her cello. The way Laura used to play with Hallie's
hair: that constant busy touching of concern and helplessness.
Running her hand down his back when it was turned to her
in bed—so cool, she would say, who'd ever expect you to be
so sweet and cool?)

She looks up at him, slowly circles the bloody islands of

his face. When the angle of light changes on the planes of her nose and cheek she loses fifteen years. What is he to believe of his life?

"You came back, Danny. Why did you come back?" Her voice is so tired, half awake or half asleep—whichever way she has to come he is distracting her from some warm concentration.

He sits naked on the edge of the bed. "Since when do you want to get things all said, chicken? You used to tell me to shut my mouth and drive." He smooths the hair from her eyes. It is getting long again, red again, it makes her blink to have it lifted. "You used to cover up my mouth with your hot little hand, like a goddam Ace bandage. Like this. Remember?" He picks up her wrist roughly and holds her fingers to his mouth, pressing hard. He presses till it hurts, her curved hand against his lips against his teeth. She could be touching him anywhere: he feels it to his toes.

A NOTE ON THE AUTHOR

Rosellen Brown was born in 1939. She is the author of a novel,
The Autobiography of My Mother; a collection of stories, *Street Games*;
and two books of poetry, *Some Deaths in the Delta and Other Poems*
and *Cora Fry*. She lives with her husband and two daughters
in Peterboro, New Hampshire.

A NOTE ON THE TYPE

The text of this book was set on the Linotype in Garamond No. 3,
a modern rendering of the type first cut by
Claude Garamond (1510–1561). Garamond was a pupil of
Geoffroy Troy and is believed to have based his letters on the
Venetian models, although he introduced a number of important
differences, and it is to him we owe the letter which we know as
old style. He gave to his letters a certain elegance and a feeling of
movement that won for their creator an immediate reputation and
the patronage of Francis I of France.

This book was composed by Maryland Linotype
Composition Company, Inc., Baltimore, Maryland
Printed and bound by The Haddon Craftsmen, Inc.,
Scranton, Pennsylvania